PENGUIN BOOKS

SINNERS
consumed

Somme Sketcher is an internationally bestselling author of dark and mafia romance.

She is best known for her Sinners Anonymous series and for writing the slowest of the slow burns (for which she is not sorry at all).

Also by Somme Sketcher

Sinners Anonymous
Sinners Condemned
Sinners Atone

SINNERS
consumed

SOMME SKETCHER

PENGUIN BOOKS

PENGUIN BOOKS

UK | USA | Canada | Ireland | Australia
India | New Zealand | South Africa

Penguin Books is part of the Penguin Random House group of companies
whose addresses can be found at global.penguinrandomhouse.com

Penguin Random House UK,
One Embassy Gardens, 8 Viaduct Gardens, London SW1 1 7BW

penguin.co.uk

Published in Penguin Books 2026

001

Copyright © Somme Sketcher, 2022

The moral right of the author has been asserted

Penguin Random House values and supports copyright.
Copyright fuels creativity, encourages diverse voices, promotes freedom
of expression and supports a vibrant culture. Thank you for purchasing
an authorised edition of this book and for respecting intellectual property
laws by not reproducing, scanning or distributing any part of it by any
means without permission. You are supporting authors and enabling
Penguin Random House to continue to publish books for everyone.
No part of this book may be used or reproduced in any manner for the
purpose of training artificial intelligence technologies or systems. In accordance
with Article 4(3) of the DSM Directive 2019/790, Penguin Random House
expressly reserves this work from the text and data mining exception.

Set in 10.86/14pt Fanwood
Typeset by Six Red Marbles UK, Thetford, Norfolk

Printed and bound in Great Britain by Clays Ltd, Elcograf S.p.A.

The authorised representative in the EEA is Penguin Random House Ireland,
Morrison Chambers, 32 Nassau Street, Dublin D02 YH68

A CIP catalogue record for this book is available from the British Library

ISBN: 978–1–911–74664–5

Penguin Random House is committed to a sustainable future
for our business, our readers and our planet. This book is made from
Forest Stewardship Council® certified paper.

A NOTE FROM SOMME
Somme

Dear reader,

Thank you for picking up a copy of *Sinners Consumed*! I hope you love reading it as much as I loved writing it.

I wanted to remind you that *Sinners Consumed* is book two of a duet. Penny and Rafe's story begins with *Sinners Condemned*. Also, if you haven't read *Sinners Anonymous*, then I strongly suggest you read that first, because a lot of the plot carries over from that book to this one.

Before you dive in, you should know that this book is a **dark romance**. There are several triggers, including talk of alcoholism, suicide, murder, sexual assault, and child sexual assault. Please read at your own risk.

Love,
Somme x

Penny

I stand behind the bar while Raphael sits in an armchair on the other side of it. His eyes are trained on a bland bit of wall behind my head, a poker chip spinning between his swollen fingers.

The lounge is too pristine for all this blood. Too bright, too quiet. I can practically hear the sins dripping off his body – some his, some not – and staining the carpet at his feet red.

I rest my sweaty palms on the bar and swallow.

'Want me to call someone? Your brother?' His lips tilt into a humorless smirk, and I remember the sight of Gabe's bloodied, naked body and the menacing glare he shot me through the windshield. I shiver. 'The other brother, I mean.'

He shakes his head once.

Well, then.

I shuffle from one slipper-clad foot to the other and stare at him for a few ticks of the grandfather clock on the mantle. I skim over his ruffled black hair and open collar. He popped off the stitches that held his gentlemanly persona together the moment we boarded the yacht – his collar pin and cufflinks. As they bounced over the swim platform, I managed to catch them before they disappeared into the Pacific. Now, as I glance down at the diamond dice cufflink next to my trembling hand, I wonder how they ever fooled anybody.

Is this what a breakdown looks like? I wouldn't know. Despite the fact that, by the end, my mother would stand naked in front of the record player in the hallway, crying along to Whitney Houston's most heart-wrenching ballads, or that my father would smash his head repeatedly into the bathroom mirror, their demise was slow. More of the crumble I expected, rather than a sudden *crack* I didn't see coming. When I look up from the cufflink and back to Raphael, I'm startled to find he's staring right at me. A half-lidded gaze, blackened by the type of recklessness that makes your survival instinct kick in. The type that'd make you cross the road if you saw it in the eye of a stranger, or jump back out of an Uber if it greeted you in the rearview mirror.

I turn to the liquor wall. Not because his expression scares me, but because I know it shouldn't heat the space between my thighs. I'm *sick*.

I reach for the First Aid kit and a bottle of Smuggler's Club whiskey.

'Vodka.'

My shoulders pull taut. 'Since when did you start drinking vodka?'

'Since you said you wouldn't kiss me if I drank whiskey.'

A hot tide carries dizziness to my head and warmth to my stomach. The sensation only intensifies when I turn around and find no humor in his eyes.

Stepping out from behind the bar, I cross the lounge and into his orbit, my heart beating a little faster with every step. His eyes track me, hardening when my legs come into view.

'Put some clothes on, Penelope. My men are onboard and I don't want to kill anyone else today.' He drops back in the armchair, running a busted hand through his hair with a careless sweep. 'Those fucking thighs,' he mutters at the bland bit of wall again.

Kill. So Blake's dead. Christ, I thought maybe he just gave him a little concussion, or something. What could he have done that was so bad?

Still in shock from waking up to the sound of Blake's body bouncing off the hood of Raphael's car, I don't have it in me to argue about how if a man sexualizes pajama shorts and a tank top then that's his own fucking problem. Numb everywhere but my center, I pick up the throw slung over the arm of a sofa and wrap it around myself. I have every intention of placing the liquor and First Aid kit on the coffee table and scurrying back to the safety of the bar, but Raphael's arm shoots out, wraps around the backs of my legs, and pulls me onto his thigh.

My pulse slows to a syrup-like rhythm, too sticky to beat properly. My vision dims at the heat of his body seeping through the blanket and soaking into my own. He's hard and warm and danger rolls off him like a sonic wave.

He tightens his grip on my waist, and my eyes fall down to his arm. His jacket came off not long after his cufflinks did, and now his sleeves are rolled up to reveal inked forearms covered in blood, too. The King of Diamonds stares back at me expectantly.

I turn away and grab the First Aid kit. Nonchalance isn't the easiest expression to wear, not when a heartbeat thuds against my shoulder, and hot, heavy breath tickles my throat. My feeble poker face is immediately undermined by the tremble in my fingers as I pry open the white and red box.

Blankly, I stare at the foreign objects inside. 'Hold on; I need to Google this.'

A bloody grip on my hip keeps me from jumping up. 'The clear liquid is saline solution. Soak a cotton pad in it.' He spreads a large, busted paw over the curve of my thigh, sending a fever-like chill through me. 'Then clean up my hands.'

I can barely concentrate on the task; I'm too busy blistering under his stare and pretending like his hand on my thigh doesn't affect me at all.

I pause with the cotton pad hovering over his knuckles. 'This might hurt.'

His laugh is rusty and my ears grow hot. 'I think I'll survive.'

His gaze continues to press on my cheek as I wipe down his wounds with clumsy dabs and a scrunched-up nose. When the tension grows so thick it slows my movements, I say, 'For a man who prides himself on not having busted knuckles, you sure know your way around a First Aid kit.'

This time, his laugh is softer. 'I'm from a family of thugs. Patched up more than a few bullet wounds in my time.'

He lifts his right hand to inspect my handiwork, and once he deems it satisfactory, he slides it up my leg and places it on my lower stomach. The feeling of his busted pinky finger resting on my pubic bone makes me want to rub my thighs together. My next breath comes out shaky and ragged. He moves his left hand so I can work on it.

'Well, now you're a thug too,' I mutter, soaking more cotton in saline. 'What did Blake do?'

'Pissed me off.'

I swallow. 'So you killed him.'

His palm presses harder into my stomach, and his chin comes to rest on my shoulder.

'He was eyeing something up that doesn't belong to him.'

His deep voice is bottomless, and for a brief second, I close my eyes and fall into it. *Is he talking about me?* Blake was close enough to the car to bounce off the hood and wake me up. That, plus his creepy behavior toward me in general, makes it plausible he was 'eyeing' me up, but the way Raphael says it makes my spine go rigid. Because his words come with a heavy insinuation tacked onto the end. *It belonged to me instead.*

Panic and annoyance fill me in equal parts. Just because I have a constant feral urge to rip all his clothes off with my teeth, it doesn't mean I've suddenly tossed all my beliefs about men out the window. No man has ever made me as . . . *dizzy* as Raphael Visconti does, but that doesn't mean I'm suddenly *his*.

He's an anomaly, not the exception.

I drop the cotton pad with a soggy *plop* and twist around to look at him. Christ, he's close. So close my nose grazes against his. I push the breathlessness away and harden my stare.

'I don't belong to you, either.'

A humorless smirk stretches his lips. 'I don't want you, Penelope.' Before his omission has time to sting, he brings his hand to my jaw and grips me there. 'But I'm going to take you anyway, and then I'm going to ruin you.'

I blink. 'What?'

'It's only fair,' he says, tone devoid of emotion.

An awful sense of dread creeps over the planes of my shoulders and squeezes the nape of my neck. 'Why?' I breathe.

He doesn't miss a beat. 'Because it's only a matter of time before you ruin me.'

I don't have a comeback, but it doesn't matter. I wouldn't have gotten it out by the time hot hands come down on my hips, lift me up, and carry me out of the room.

Penny

Oak-clad walls, cream carpets, and drips of blood pass in a blur. I make eye contact with the serpent poking its vicious head out from underneath the open collar of Raphael's shirt and tighten my grip on his neck.

'Where are we going?' Although, my heart already knows.

'My bedroom.'

'Why?' I whisper.

He shifts his forearms under my ass. 'So I can fuck you, Penelope. Why else?'

I knew the answer to that question, too, but it doesn't stop the shock electrifying my skin. It's the brazen way his silky voice wraps around the sentence. Flippantly, factually, like it's his God-given right to fuck me. Like he didn't hear me when I told him I'm not *his*. Makes sense, I guess. God gave him everything else.

My pulse strums so violently in my clit the rest of my body feels weak. Still, I know I should put up some sort of protest. I smack my forehead against his chest and make a half-assed attempt to wriggle out of his grip.

'Well, I don't want to fuck *you*, asshole.'

His shoulder connects with a door and we burst through it. One hand slides between my thighs and cups me over my pajama shorts. It's a rough, audacious hold that makes my eyes roll to the back of my head. His now-damp hand comes back to my hip.

'Uh-huh,' is all he says. I catch the serpent's smirk before Raphael tosses me on the bed.

I bounce twice, then scramble up to the headboard and press my back to it like it's a life raft. Like it might save me from the six-foot-four monster with the reckless stare, looming at the foot of the bed.

We lock eyes and his half-lidded eyes only pull me deeper into dangerous waters. Nerves crawl through my veins like spiders, because I'm not entirely convinced he's bluffing. But then he pops the top three buttons of his shirt, and, well, suddenly I don't give a fuck if he's bluffing or not.

My breathing shallows and I watch him watching me, his eyes roaming over my body like he's considering where to start. I lost the blanket somewhere between the lounge and the galley, and now I'm cursing myself for wearing my shortest shorts to sleep in Raphael's car.

My focus drops to the bulge straining below his belt. I cross my legs in self-preservation.

'Thought you took girls on dates before fucking them?'

His eyes rake over my tits. 'Do I?' he asks dryly.

'That's what they say.'

A demonic smirk tilts his lips. 'And what else do they say?'

I swallow. 'That you only fuck from behind.'

His gaze lifts to mine, flashing black.

'How very gentlemanly of me.'

In one swift motion, he sheds his shirt, balls it in a bloodied fist, and tosses it on the floor.

Jesus, Mary, and Joseph. All other characters in the Bible too. Backlit by the early morning sun streaming through the window, he's a mountain of muscle and sin, and no amount of ink staining his body can conceal his brawn or definition. Rubbing a bloodied paw down his abs, he takes a lazy step toward the bed, a move that makes my mouth water in anticipation and my toes curl in fear.

He looks up at me warily. Spreads his arms like we've found ourselves in an unfortunate situation, and the consequences will be less painful if we just accept our fate.

'Guess you were right.'

The sunbeam cutting across the playing cards and scriptures on his chest traps the meaning of his words: *I'm no gentleman.*

I shouldn't be so stupefied. I knew it from the beginning. From the moment I sauntered up to him at the bar and his gaze heated the flesh through the slit in my stolen dress. But I guess being faced with the reality is scarier than the fantasy.

And Raphael Visconti in all of his sinful glory, is scary as fuck.

Clink, thawp. His belt slides from its loops with a flex of a bicep. It sounds like the crack of a whip and it sobers me immediately. On instinct, my eyes dart to the door, and I wonder if I'd make it past the monster if I ran fast enough. Deciding there's not a chance in hell, I stifle a groan and stare at the sheet by my thigh instead. Run a trembling hand over the cream Egyptian cotton and make a shitty joke, as if it'll poke a hole in my unease.

'I knew you ironed your sheets.'

An animalistic grunt spills from the bottom of the bed. I look up just in time to catch ink dipping under black boxers before a strong hand grips my ankle and yanks me flat. The ceiling disappears as quickly as it arrived, obstructed by shoulders wider than a soccer field and eyes just as green.

Sweet, holy hell. Despite only being five-foot-two with a

straight spine, I've never felt small before. Guess most girls whose thighs chafe in summer have the same issue, but when Raphael's hot, heavy body comes down on top of mine, pinning me to the bed with steel muscle and ill-intent, I feel like I've been swallowed by an eclipse.

Despite the delirium-inducing warmth, I shiver when he grabs my bun, tugs my head back, and nestles his face into my throat. 'Do me a favor, Penelope,' he growls against my racing pulse. 'Unless you're moaning my name or sucking my dick, keep your fucking mouth shut.' Another tug on my bun, another crackle in my clit. 'I'm so sick of the shit that comes out of it.'

I know I'm meant to be furious, but fuck, it's hard to be angry when you're melting under meat and muscle. Hard to *think*. His torso skims down my body, his hands following suit, until he's nestled between my thighs. Thick, swollen fingers curl over the waistband of my shorts, and my heart gives up beating altogether.

Fuck. Is he going to finish what he started in his office? I don't know if I'll be able to handle it. I haven't been able to handle the mere idea of it. I've used the shower head on my clit four times thinking about it, and haven't made it past the third imaginary lick before –

Oh, god. He rips my shorts down my legs, and with his absent-minded toss, they disappear into the shadows behind him. He glances quickly at the strip of lace covering my pussy, then buries his face into it.

My gasp melts into a shudder at the warm, wet pressure. Some mine, some his. A deep rush of pleasure spreads out from my center and through my limbs like a wildfire, hot and uncontrollable.

I know I won't survive it.

When I feel his tongue push the fabric of my thong into my entrance, I clamp my teeth over my bottom lip to stop myself from moaning. I might not be in the right state of mind, but my desire to not give this man the satisfaction of breaking me is instinctual.

I squeeze my eyes shut and try to think of anything but what's going on between my legs, but it becomes impossible when he yanks my thong off, too. My lids pop open just in time to see him fist my panties and toss it in the direction of his dresser. They fly through the room and land on a lamp.

He glances up at me. 'Mine now.'

'You fucking my panties, or something?'

A hard flick on my clit makes stars flash in front of my eyes.

'Or something.'

Christ. The thought of him jacking off into my panties has my head spinning. It's so crude, so *ungentlemanly,* and it's obscene how flattered I am. With a rough tug, he pulls my legs apart, clamps my knees to the bed, and sits up just enough to study what's in between them.

Blood thrums in my ears. A light breeze cools the slickness coating my pussy and inner thighs, making me shiver. Raphael gives a small shake of his head, then brushes a surprisingly gentle thumb over the tuft of hair down there.

'They tailor made you to my liking, Queenie,' he murmurs. Then his tone sours. 'Of course they fucking did.'

Queenie? I'd thought I imagined him calling me that in the car. Why is he calling me Queenie? But then he drops to his elbows, slides his shoulders under my knees, and licks from entrance to clit. Immediately, I file the thought into a box labeled *Questions for when Raphael Visconti doesn't have his face buried in my pussy* and drop my head against the pillow.

The next hot, wet stroke of his tongue comes slower, punctuated by an angry suck on my clit. I force myself to slow my breathing and relax my thighs, because I know not only will I not survive this, I won't make it past the next five seconds at this rate.

My blood turns to steam and rises, creating a haze over

the bed, growing thicker with every crazed lick and hard suck and guttural groan. Every nerve in my body has slid south and come alive. Jesus, I can't come already. Partly because I don't want to give him the satisfaction of knowing how hot he makes me – although it's pretty obvious by the sloppy sounds coming from my entrance every time his tongue dips into it – and partly because I don't want him to know how pathetically inexperienced I am.

I've only ever had sex with two men; neither went down on me. Guess there's not much room for it in the back of a souped-up Honda. They didn't care about getting me off, anyway.

Despite Raphael's enthusiasm, I'm pretty sure he doesn't care about my pleasure either. His hands grip me so tightly his busted knuckles disappear into my flesh. He holds me where he needs me, tilting my hips upward to take longer, angrier laps from me.

Right now, I couldn't care less about his motive. Each lick brings a fresh wave of delirium, bigger and scarier than the last.

'Oh, *fuck*,' I moan when he swirls his tongue around my clit for a sudden change of pace. He groans in approval and buries his face deeper into me.

The pressure builds, driving me mad, until I'm so close to coming the ceiling breathes above me. I release the bed sheets and dig my fingers into his thick hair, pulling his head back.

Our eyes clash; mine filled with desperation, his blackened with irritation.

'I think I'm gonna –'

'Don't you dare.'

After a final nip on my clit, he throws me on my hands and knees and closes the gap behind me.

'These. Fucking. Thighs, Penelope,' he hisses. His hands are rough and selfish as they skim up the backs of my legs and palm my ass. 'Had to change the uniform because of these thighs.'

Despite my skin humming in anticipation, I frown. 'What's wrong with these thighs?'

He slaps my ass, hard. My head drops to the bed, allowing the pillow to absorb the brunt of my moan.

'They piss me off.'

I don't have a clue what he's going on about, but I don't care. Not when he grips my ass and sinks his teeth into a cheek. White-hot pain carves a frantic path to my pussy, where it settles into a satisfying throb.

'*Ow!*'

'Shut up.'

'Jesus,' I growl into the pillow. 'Thought you were charming.'

A dark chuckle cools my pussy lips. 'Not in the bedroom, Queenie.'

'Yeah, no shit. Why does anyone fuck you when you speak to them like – *oh, god.*'

He slices through my sarcasm by sliding two fingers inside of me. As maddening pressure grows and blooms with every unwilling rock of my hips, a strangled sound rises up my throat and fills the room.

Behind me, Raphael makes a noise of satisfaction. 'You're so tight, baby. You're so . . .' His free hand spanks my ass again, loaded with his frustration. '*Cazzo. Sei perfetta.*'

A shaky sigh escapes me, the neurons in my brain firing with what I learned in *Italian for Dummies*.

'More,' I mutter into the pillow, not entirely sure I want him to hear me. He responds by pressing his heavy chest to my back, bracing himself with a hand by my head. I turn to look at it. A busted, bloodied paw resting on luxury cotton, it ended a life less than an hour ago. For *me*.

I squeeze my eyes shut. The thought shouldn't bring me closer to the edge.

Raphael pushes his fingers deeper inside me and holds

them there. His lips come to the shell of my ear with a loaded question.

'How many other fingers have been in this pussy, Penelope?'

The violence in his tone tells me any number greater than zero will be too many, but I want to avoid the subject of being inexperienced, so I turn to flippancy.

'Dunno. That'd be a lot of fingers to add up.'

That earns me a hard thrust into my pussy and a bite on my ass. My lids pop open, just in time to see the hand by my head curl around the bed sheet.

'I just killed a man for looking at you. Think I won't kill a few more for having their fingers inside of you?'

Breathlessness sweeps through me and heightens my pleasure. 'I'm just saying; that's a lot of math at a time like this.'

He abruptly pulls his fingers away. A mix of hollowness and desperation replaces them, but it only lasts a few moments, then I hear the *snap* of an elastic waistband and he pushes his length into me with one hard thrust.

My walls burn from the girth and the shock, tearing a cry from my throat. Raphael's head follows mine to the pillow, coming to rest by my cheek. 'How many dicks then, smart-ass?'

I let out a strangled sob in response and twist my head away from him. Behind me, I feel his stomach tense against my ass. He pauses, then pulls out slowly, almost the whole way, before entering me again with more caution.

When a light kiss touches the space between my shoulder blades, my spine goes rigid and something warm and unsavory fills the space inside my rib cage. The move is at odds with rough hands and the burning down south. He's trying to be nice, to allow me to adjust to him.

I don't fucking like it.

But after a few more lazy thrusts, my breathing slows, the fire simmering to a much more pleasurable heat. I adjust my weight to accommodate more of him, and with every slow slide and dark breath that skitters up my back, the ache in my core turns into a desperate pulse.

More, I want to scream. *Fuck me like you entered me. Fuck me like you would all the other girls.*

But I don't have the humility to ask for it. Instead, I press my forehead into the pillow and arch my back, subtly trying to get him deeper.

A hand runs through my hair and pulls out my bun. Strands of red fall around my shoulders, then disappear from view as Raphael scoops them up into his fist and holds them at the base of my neck.

'How many dicks, Penelope?' he asks again, a softer edge to his tone this time.

Oh, so he's serious about it. I'm set on telling him a lie. I want to piss him off. Want him to fuck me harder.

I tense my shoulders and brace for impact.

'Too many to count.'

A feral hiss coasts over my back as Raphael pushes inside of me with a violent, fire-starting stroke. My head bumps against the headboard, and when he thrusts into me again, his hand comes down on top of my crown.

I realize it's to cushion the next blow. The move is too tender, too *gentlemanly,* and a spark of irritation flickers in my core.

I twist out of his grasp and look back at him. We lock eyes and my next breath stutters.

Fuck. He looks like a king. Every inked muscle contracting as he fucks me. I get it now, why he only fucks women from behind. He knows they wouldn't survive watching him impale them, and if they did, there's no doubt they'd want to get fucked again.

Other girls. In a moment of madness, I'd thought I wanted him to fuck me like he fucked them, but now, the idea fills me with bitterness.

As our eye contact deepens, he slows his thrusts and his gaze heats.

Annoyed my overworking brain decided to join the party, I rest on my forearms and slam my ass down the length of his dick.

'How many women have you fucked, *Raphael?*' I snap back.

His jaw tightens and he throws his head back, hissing something dark in Italian at the ceiling. He releases my hair and runs his hand down his throat. When his eyes fall back down, he glares at my ass like a maniac.

'Do that again.'

The sudden power reversal tightens my nipples. Through half-lidded eyes, I watch him watching me, as I slide all the way up to the tip of his dick and hold myself there. His gaze lifts to mine in confusion.

'Say please.'

Ba-dum. Ba-dum. Two heartbeats pass, threatening to crack open my chest. For the stupidest of moments, I think he might actually say it.

It only takes another moment to realize I'm more stupid than I thought.

His hands grip my hips so tightly they threaten to bruise my skin. He plows himself into me without restraint or mercy, sending my eyes to the back of my head.

'Please?' I hear him growl. 'You want me to *beg* ?'

Heat swells between my thighs with every angry thrust. Fuck, I'm so intoxicated by fullness and *man* I fear I might overdose on it. I bury my head into the pillow and bite down on the fabric for all of three seconds, until another hiss touches my ears and fingers weave into my hair.

Raphael tugs my hair so hard I'm pulled into an upright position in his lap. My back lands against his hard chest, my thighs flush with his.

'Do I look like a man who begs, Penelope?' he snarls, yanking down the straps of my vest top and bra. He folds down the cups and then, with a frustrated grunt, unhooks it at the back and hurls it out of view.

Briefly, I'm taken back to a rain-soaked car, *Driving Home for Christmas* crackling on the radio. In what parallel universe did Raphael Visconti give me a black Amex in exchange for taking my bra off?

As soon as the cool air touches my bare breasts, he warms them in his busted hands, molding them to his liking. My nipples ache with the need for attention, and I'm not disappointed when he squeezes them between his thumb and forefinger.

'Fuck,' I moan, throwing my head back against his collarbone. I grind against his cock, relaxing myself until he's so deep inside me my ass is flush with his base.

He wraps an inked forearm around my waist, pinning my body to his. His other hand gives my breast a final squeeze before sliding down to my clit.

The second he presses two fingers against it, I know it's game over. He strokes up and down, stoking the flames in my lower core until they threaten to set me ablaze.

I rock against his cock and push against his fingers, desperate to chase the high. 'Don't stop,' I breathe, rolling my head to the side when Raphael's teeth carve an electric path up my throat. 'I'm gonna –'

My eyes pop open as his fingers leave my clit.

'What are you – ?'

'Say *please*,' he mocks.

I slow the roll of my hips, absorbing his words. *You have got to be shitting me.*

I'm so high, so *feverish*, that, although I'm too stubborn to say please, I'm also too desperate to argue. Instead, I bring my own hand between my thighs.

Raphael catches my wrists in one hand and roughly pulls them above my head. A dark chuckle vibrates my back. 'Nice try.'

He brushes his knuckles against my throbbing clit, building a slow-moving tremor again. 'Say please, Penelope.'

I wrestle against his grip, but it's immovable. 'Fuck off.'

'I don't know what language that is, but it's not how you say please in English.'

My breaths quicken as the pressure builds again, and for a maddening moment, I think he's forgotten his stupid game. But when my nails dig into his thigh and I let out a cry, he withdraws the pressure.

'No,' I whimper.

'Say it.'

'No –'

When he rubs me again, I shake my head in panic, knowing I can't deal with what's coming.

'Don't stop.'

'What's the word, Penelope?'

'I can't –'

'Just fucking say it.'

'*Please.*'

It escapes my lips in a desperate, breathy whimper, and even as Raphael's fingers rub me harder and faster, I know the sound of it will haunt me later.

Right now, though, I couldn't give a flying fuck. Delirium explodes through my veins, eating up all the oxygen in my blood. The fire rages hot then cools to a lethargic warmth, filled with relief.

My head falls heavy against Raphael's chest, and his strokes against my pussy grow soft and gentle. His breathing slows.

'Good girl,' he whispers, planting a tender kiss on my neck.

Good girl. I don't hate that he calls me that; I hate how it blooms in my chest like a flower. Then its petals wilt, rotting my insides, and I squirm to get it out of me.

Painfully aware of his rock-hard cock still pulsating inside of me, I know I need to fuck the feeling away. I need to bring the man to an orgasm, if only to level the playing field and make him come as undone as I just did.

He lets me push his arm off my waist and drop forward on the pillow. His thighs flex against mine, and I twist to look at him.

He regards me with dark, suspicious eyes. When I slide up his dick again, he turns his attention to my ass and takes a slow, deep breath. I've learned my lesson – I wouldn't get a *please* from this man even if he was trying to stop me lighting the world on fire – but the way he grinds his teeth as he watches his length disappear inside me is almost worth it.

He lets out a noise of satisfaction. Gives a small shake of his head.

'You're perfect. You know that?'

My heart churns. Right now, I need steel, not silk. I move to look away, but he grips my jaw to keep me there. With his other hand, he grabs the top gathered on my waist and uses it like a handle to push himself deeper inside me.

'You want to know how many women I fucked,' he grinds out.

'No,' I whisper. Truthfully, I'd rather pour hot wax in my ears than hear the answer.

He laughs darkly. 'Good, because I have a better number. How many times I've fucked my fist thinking about you.'

A languid fascination drifts through my core. My tender clit starts thumping again. Christ. A man like Raphael doesn't get himself off, not with a fist nor with my panties. It's so primal. So *uncontrolled.*

I burn with the need to know more.

'How many times?'

He rakes his teeth over his bottom lip, eyes glinting. 'Too many to count.'

Well, I guess I deserved that answer. I arch my back deeper, my nipples grazing against the bedding and igniting a fresh heat within me. 'What do you think about?' I whisper.

He pulls from my jaw and rakes both hands down the side of my body, tracking his movements. 'This isn't far off, Queenie.'

I half moan, half laugh. 'Dreams really do come true, hey?'

He glares at me, but amusement softens his irises. 'You talk a lot less shit when I fuck you in my dreams.'

Before I can think of a witty response, he winds his hand into my hair and pushes my face down into the pillow. Clearly, he's done entertaining me. A strangled moan escapes my lips with every thrust, and when he picks up ferocity and pace, punctuating each stroke with callous Italian, molten heat spreads throughout me.

'Fuck, Penny,' is the last muttered oath that slides from his lips before the wall of his stomach tightens against my ass and a different type of warmth fills me.

As I melt into the bedding, body slack, Raphael's weight comes down on top of me. He's heavy and all-consuming, and I find that I don't mind one bit.

My lids flutter shut for the briefest of moments. I listen to his heartbeat thump slightly out-of-sync with mine. Feel his breath cool the sweat on my nape. When his touch softens on my hip and he slips out of me, he plants a hot kiss on my neck.

'You were amazing.' The bed dips, and the *snap* of elastic as he pulls up his boxers echoes in my ear. 'Unfortunately,' he adds bitterly.

Clutching the sheets to my chest, I twist around, watching his inked back as he saunters toward the bathroom.

He slows to a stop and palms the back of his neck, before turning to pin me with a dark expression. 'Condom,' is all he says.

My blood runs cold; a stark contrast to the hot juice running down my inner thigh. *How could I be so stupid?* Embarrassingly enough, the thought of using protection didn't even cross my mind. Not when Raphael declared he was going to fuck me, nor when he followed through with venom.

I let out a shaky breath. 'I'm on the pill.'

His eyes narrow, annoyance pulling his jaw taut. The word *why* dances somewhere between the door and the bed. Of course, I don't tell him I've been on it since I was thirteen to regulate my periods.

He runs a busted hand down his throat, settling his gaze on the headboard behind me. 'You clean?' he asks tightly.

I stare at him in disbelief. 'Are you?' I snap back.

His eyes fall down to me in bitter amusement. 'Yes, Penelope. I'm not usually stupid enough to fuck a broad without a condom.'

And then the bathroom door slams shut behind him.

Penny

The sound of water splashing on tiles brings my attention to the bathroom door. The longer I stare at it, the harder unease presses down on my chest.

Raphael called me a *broad* and now he's washing me off his body. But now that I've let him inside me, I have this awful feeling I won't be able to do the same.

I sit up straighter, trying to ignore the fresh trickle of cum pooling between my thighs. I didn't realize Raphael was living on the yacht, but jeez, why wouldn't you? I study the bedroom – cabin – for the first time. Black curtains, cream walls. Soft fabrics on hard furnishings. It's definitively him, and everything that isn't belongs to me. The panties swinging off the lamp. The shorts crumpled on the window seat. My stuff looks as out of place in this room as I feel.

The air is so awkward it stiffens my limbs. I lie back and succumb to it, staring at the ceiling. After what feels like hours, but is probably only minutes, I realize the shower is still running. That awkwardness heats into embarrassment.

Is he waiting for me to leave? Jesus. Aside from not taking me on a date and fucking me without a condom, he's treated me like every other woman. He fucked me from behind, and he fucked me rough. Maybe he expects me to be gone before he gets out?

Sick at the idea of him coming out of the shower and being annoyed I'm still lazing in his bed, I jump out of it. I scramble around for my bra and shorts, put them on, then yank my vest top over my breasts.

Now what?

I wish I knew what the regular one-night-stand etiquette was. It might give me some insight into what to do after a one-morning-stand. I could have probably figured it out with a bit of common sense, if, you know, I wasn't stranded on a mega yacht in the middle of the Pacific.

Oh – one I also happen to work on.

If my head wasn't already spinning, I'd smack it against the wall for my sins. I'm such an idiot. The second I leave this room, I run the risk of bumping into a coworker.

Taking a deep breath, I squeeze my eyes shut and mentally place two scenarios side-by-side. The first, is Anna's shocked face when she sees me in my pajama shorts creeping out of Raphael's room. The second, is Raphael stepping out the bathroom in a low-slung towel. He's looking at his phone and slows in surprise when he realizes I'm still in his bed. *Oh,* he says, running a hand over his neck. *I thought you'd have left by now.*

Absolutely not.

I rip open the door and scurry down the hall. I find one slipper at the end of it; the other in the crew mess. I ignore the Chief Officer and First Engineer having breakfast and dart up the stairs, where the blanket is slung over the railing. Other members of the ghost crew step aside to let me pass, biting their lips and glancing at their watches, but I keep my chin tilted high and my mind on the swim platform.

Next mission: hitch a ride back to the Coast.

Shivering by an open door, I press my nose against the window and squint out to the Pacific. It's bright and blue and not a single vessel bobs over its turbulent waves.

Come on. I touch the pendant around my neck, as if to remind it that *lucky* girls would suddenly chance upon a shuttle leaving for the port any second.

Nothing.

My sigh mists up the glass. I need to find someone and beg them to take me over. The bosun and his deckhands are usually hovering around the platform, cleaning jet skis in the garage or washing down the decks.

Wrapping the blanket tighter around myself and bracing my bones for the cold, I step outside to see if I can spot any signs of life. I'll probably die of hypothermia, but it's favorable to dying of embarrassment.

'You gonna swim home?'

The harsh wind carries a cashmere-coated question to my back. My shoulders snap into a tight line. I turn to see Raphael leaning against the frame of the French doors, humor dancing in his eyes.

Christ, he looks handsome. Fresh suit, fresh shave. The only sign he'd beaten someone to death a few hours ago are his busted knuckles gripping a kitchen towel.

I swallow the rock in my throat. 'If I have to.'

'Mm. Long way to swim on an empty stomach.'

His phone buzzes. He pulls it out of his pocket and turns his attention to the screen. 'Get inside, Penelope,' he says, without looking up. 'I'm not done with you yet.'

I stare at the side of his face for a few beats, then out to the ocean.

As I reluctantly cross back into the warmth of the sky lounge, Raphael cracks my ass with the towel like a whip.

***

I'm starting to think I fell asleep on my couch while reading *Lucid Dreaming for Dummies,* or something. Maybe I didn't really get into Raphael's car last night, he didn't really kill Blake, and I'm not really sitting in the crew mess with his cum drying on the inside of my thigh.

Because, surely, Raphael Visconti making me breakfast can't be real.

My glare cuts through the room and into the kitchen where he stands over the stove, poking eggs with a spatula. His cell is tucked between his ear and shoulder, and he barks ragged Italian into its mouthpiece.

The harsh spotlights highlight all of the man's contrasts. The sharp suit that's at odds with his busted knuckles; his callous foreign monologue that conflicts with the sophisticated roll of his wrist as he swirls the contents of his vodka glass. The sight is a source of tension, and I sit here with a straight spine and curled fists, bracing in case it combusts in my face.

He abruptly hangs up and tosses the cell on the counter. It starts buzzing immediately, but he ignores it in favor of dishing up breakfast. As he strolls toward me with a loaded plate in hand, he snatches the phone back up and continues his slew of Italian.

The plate clatters between my fists, and he heads back to the kitchen.

My gaze flicks down at it and my throat tightens. Scrambled eggs, salmon, and sourdough toast – my favorite. Does he make breakfast for every woman he fucks, or just the ones he kills men for?

For a while, I find comfort in autopilot. Fork to eggs, fork to mouth. Chew, swallow, repeat. But when a dark shadow shifts over my toast, I realize it's impossible to be mechanical when Raphael is standing so close.

My fork stills mid-air and I swallow, then force my eyes to climb the sharp front crease of his trousers and meet his blistering stare. It doesn't waiver, even when he rests his palms on the table and dips to steal the egg off my fork.

Christ. A rough shiver vibrates through me, still rattling my insides long after Raphael has sauntered back into the kitchen.

I let my fork clatter to the plate, my stomach too full of unease for any more food. Him swiping my breakfast gave me the same gut-wrenching feeling as his kiss between my shoulder blades did, or his hand against my crown, cushioning the blow of the headboard.

Gentle. Thoughtful. *Intimate.* All my reservations about being here rise to the surface, and suddenly, I need air that doesn't taste like a . . . boyfriend.

I scrape my chair back, earning me a sideways glare from the kitchen. I ignore it, take my plate to the sink, and start running the hot water to wash it up.

Raphael comes up behind me and cages me in. Burning up at all the points where his suit touches my skin, I try to slow my breathing and focus on the suds fizzing in the basin.

His Italian so close to my ear makes me feverish. When he pauses to let whoever is on the line speak, he slides his arms through mine and takes the plate from me. I can only grip the edge of the counter and watch his large, damaged hands as they swipe the dish sponge over the plate until it's sparkling.

So, even on his darkest days, this man is domesticated. This isn't helping with my unease in the slightest.

The moment he gives me an inch of breathing room, I mutter a *thank you,* then bolt like a racehorse toward the door. His hand catches me just above his watch on my wrist, and he tugs me around.

With a cold glance at my shorts, he switches to English.

'Where do you think you're going?'

Anywhere you aren't. 'Upstairs.'

He frowns and motions for me to wait, then he disappears down the stairs. Minutes later, comes back with a Stanford hoodie on a hanger. He holds it up beside me, looks down at the hemline and gives a curt nod of approval, as if he deems it long enough.

'Put this on first.'

I don't argue but I wish I did. Because the moment the collar brushes over my nose and assaults me with his warm oak and mint scent, an awful realization fissures my heart.

One-morning-stands hurt.

***

There's a small living room at the back of the yacht. It sits three floors above the swim platform, and its large bay window frames the storm rolling over the Pacific.

I snatch up a cushion from the sofa, crawl onto the window seat and press my burning face against the cold glass.

It took ten minutes to find a suitable room to hide in. My only requirement was a door that locked from the inside. Now, Raphael's men can't glare at me, and the yacht cleaners can't side-eye me over their vacuums. I knew I'd found the perfect place when I found no cameras tacked to the ceiling, and a finger-sweep over the coffee table turned up a layer of dust.

The obnoxious tick of a grandfather clock tells me it's been over an hour since I last moved. I fear if I do, I'll start climbing the walls. My body buzzes with a million questions, none of which I have answers to.

Why didn't Raphael shove me onto the first shuttle heading back to shore?

Why did he make me breakfast?

Between all the suits, when the fuck does the man wear his college hoodie?

I peel my face off the glass and nestle my nose in the collar. Christ, I should really stop doing that, because his scent soaks into my skin and heats it every time. He smells so *good*.

In a sudden rush of female solidarity, I hope he doesn't treat all his one-night-stands like this, not if he seriously doesn't plan on seeing them again. Because being booted out while he's in the shower would have been favorable to wearing his warm clothes and tasting his delicious eggs.

Sighing, I lift my head and glare out to the Coast. The sight of an incoming shuttle makes my throat tighten.

Is the staff heading here for work already? The thought of Laurie catching me strolling around the yacht on my day off wearing Raphael's hoodie as a dress makes my blood itch. Sure, the look on Anna and Claudia's faces would be priceless, but still, I know what I'd look like to them: just another girl who dropped her panties and let Raphael Visconti fuck her from behind.

Pathetic, really. At least the other two guys I succumbed to wooed me with sweet words, even if they turned out to be fake as fuck. Raphael hadn't even unleashed his signature charm on me; he just killed a man and carried me to his bedroom.

Squinting under the sun, I press my face to the glass and realize I recognize the lone figure in the Carhartt beanie seated at the back of the boat.

Matt. What the hell is he doing here?

Heart racing, I fly out the room and take the back stairs two at a time, until I'm shivering on the swim platform to greet him.

As the boat bumps against the fender, he cups a hand to his brow and looks up at me.

'What the fuck, Pen?' is all he says.

He stares at the Stanford logo on my chest as Griffin strolls out of the lounge behind me, kicks his legs apart, and roughly pats him down. He gives a nod of approval to the suit driving the boat, then pins me with a blistering glare.

'You're trouble kid,' he grunts, before slamming the lounge door so hard the glass rattles.

Yeah, whatever. I'm too taken aback by Matt's sudden arrival to care about my reputation among Raphael's men.

Icy wind whipping around us, we stare at each other for a few beats. I open my mouth to cut through the silence, but Matt glances at the camera masquerading as a heat lamp above our heads, and pulls me toward him by the hips.

'Blink twice if you've been kidnapped.'

I pause, then blink twice.

His eyes grow wide, then he shoves me away and runs a shaky hand through his hair. 'Fuck. Seriously?'

'Nah. Just wanted to see what you'd do if I'd said yes.'

He considers this. 'Jack shit,' he admits. 'I'm not exactly going to beat up Raphael Visconti, am I?' He nods out to the raging Pacific. 'I'd be sleeping with the fishes by lunch.'

My laugh softens the tight line of his shoulders. He runs a look of disbelief down my body and shakes his head. 'Tell me – why did I wake up to a man with biceps the width of my head hammering down my front door?'

'What?'

He gives the suitcase at his feet a little kick. *My* suitcase. I hadn't even noticed he was holding it. 'Yeah, he kicked down the door to your apartment and told me to collect all your stuff.' He rolls his eyes. 'If he'd asked, I'd have told him I had your spare key.'

My heart sinks a few inches in my chest. Why would I need my stuff? And although I was joking, maybe I *have* been kidnapped. Otherwise, why the fuck couldn't I go and get it myself?

'Oh dear,' I mutter.

'Oh dear indeed, Pen.' Matt glances behind me, curiosity warming them. 'Can we go inside? Your lips are turning blue.'

I know he cares more about getting an *MTV Cribs*-style tour than my health, but I lead him through the yacht regardless. His slew of *holy shit*'s and *fucking hell*'s echo off the mahogany walls, and by the time we enter the lounge, he's buzzing with excitement.

'Imagine being so rich you live on a yacht,' he exclaims, yanking off his beanie and flopping down on a sofa. 'Do you know how much it costs to run a boat this size?'

'No. Do you?'

He looks at me seriously. 'A fuck-ton of cash.'

Smiling, I flick on the barista machine behind the bar. 'You're just a walking, talking calculator, aren't you Matty? Coffee?'

'On Raphael Visconti's yacht? Obviously.'

I make us both flat whites and join him on the sofa. He eyes me over the steam rising from his cup. 'Come on, then. What's the deal?'

I hitch a shoulder. *To hell if I know.* 'I think . . . well, I don't know. I think we're fucking.'

I use present, not past tense, because the suitcase sitting in the corner of the room suggests I'm going to be hanging around for a little while.

Matt blinks. 'You're fucking Raphael Visconti.'

'Can you stop saying his full name like that? Sounds like you want to fuck him too.'

He ignores me. 'You're fucking Raphael Visconti on his mega yacht.'

'Are you telling me or asking me?'

He looks at me like I'm an idiot. 'I'm reiterating the fact in the hope you'll stop looking like you're about to cry and realize how lucky you are.' He shakes his head, a bitter edge to his expression. 'Bet his dick is *huge*.'

Lucky. My necklace grows denser. I don't feel lucky. Raphael's hot body flushed against mine only raised more questions than answers, and now there's a constant stream of unease running through my veins.

My fingers curl around my coffee cup so tightly it scalds my skin. I have the sudden urge to grip Matt by the collar of his puffer jacket and beg him to help me.

Instead, I claw together some decorum and glare at the space above his head. 'I don't know what this is,' I mutter.

'You're friends with benefits.'

'We're *not* friends.'

'Enemies with benefits, then. Jeez, Pen. Have you never had a fuck buddy before?'

My gaze slides down to his shit-eating smirk. Something about my expression wipes it right off.

He nods. Sets down his coffee cup and switches into teacher-mode 'All right, I've got you. Believe it or not, I've had a few fuck buddies in my time, and here are the top three things you need to know.' He pops out a finger. 'First of all, you've gotta be sure about what you want. Do you want to stay on this mega yacht and fuck the billionaire Raphael Visconti, yes or no?'

I don't bother telling him his question is skewed for a biased answer. Instead, I glance at the blinking camera above the bar and nod tightly.

He grins. 'Yeah, no shit. Okay, then second of all, you need to make sure you both understand it's not serious.'

'What do you mean?'

'For about a year, I was sleeping with this girl three times a week. Then one night, I realized her toothbrush was in my bathroom – and *not* her spare.' He stares at me pointedly and rolls his eyes when he's met with my blank expression. 'Turns out I was her boyfriend and I didn't even know it. My point is, *communicate*. You've got to be clear with your intentions from the beginning.' He smirks. 'Give him your bitter monologue about love being a trap – he'll get the hint pretty quickly.'

My laugh comes out easy. Suddenly, I realize the unease in my system doesn't feel as venomous as it did before. 'And the third?'

The grin melts from his face. He leans over and grips my arm. 'The third, is to always remember that being friends with benefits can't last forever. I'm sure the same is true for enemies with benefits, too. Don't stay too long, all right?'

My throat clots. 'What happens if I stay too long?'

A sad smile tilts his lips. 'You'll get trapped.'

It's those three words that are still haunting the inside of my skull ten minutes later, when we're standing on the warm side of the French doors, watching Raphael's men load up the small craft.

Matt sighs. 'Odds on me getting thrown overboard before we get back to Devil's Dip?'

Griffin looks up and glares at me through the glass. I sigh too. 'Pretty high, I'm afraid.'

'If I die, tell Anna I loved her.'

'You don't love her, idiot.'

He grins. 'I know, but it sounds kind of romantic, doesn't it? Anyway –' He turns and grabs my wrists. 'Repeat my three tips back to me.'

I bite back a smile. 'Be sure of what I want, make sure he's on the same page, and . . .' My smile dims a few watts. 'Don't fall in love.'

He looks down at me like a proud father. 'You're not as stupid as you look.' Before I can fight his insult with a better one, he pulls me in for a hug, his chin coming down on my head. 'And most importantly, relax and enjoy yourself. Suck some dick, get your pussy eaten –'

'Matt!'

His laugh vibrates against my cheek. 'In all seriousness, don't take it too seriously, all right? Men fuck without feelings all the time. Women can too.'

I pull back, flushed from his vulgarity. 'You're a pioneer for the feminist movement, Matty.'

He winks. 'Yeah, yeah. I'm a pioneer for whatever will get me laid.' Griffin raps an angry knuckle on the door, making him flinch. 'Fuck me,' he grunts, tugging on a beanie. 'Way to ruin a moment.'

'You're increasing your chances of getting chucked overboard by the second.'

'Yeah, I better get going,' he says, zipping up his jacket. 'Listen, I've put some snacks in your suitcase. Those peanut butter ones you don't think I realize you've been stealing from my cupboard.'

I frown. 'That's oddly nice of you.'

He chucks me under the chin. 'Yeah, well when I packed them, it was six a.m. and I thought you'd been kidnapped.'

I laugh. 'Well you can't take them back now.'

'I suppose not. Oh – one more thing. Be home for Christmas, all right? I banked on you also being a loser with no family. Got a turkey in the freezer and I've already bought us those silly Santa hats.'

The pit of my stomach warms. 'Wouldn't miss it for the world.'

Matt blows me a kiss from the shuttle, just before he shrinks to a small dot on the horizon.

With my fingertips on the window, I watch until he disappears entirely, partly because I'm worried he truly will get tossed overboard, and partly because I miss him already. He's shaping up to be a good friend, although I'd rather claw my eyes out than tell him so.

Once there's nothing on the Pacific but sea foam, I turn around, press my shoulders against the glass, and take a deep breath. Matt's three tips have lit a fire inside me; kidnapped or not, I'm going to hunt down Raphael and lay down the law.

Penny

A new cool-headedness chases me through the yacht. It pushes me through closed doors and down empty corridors, but promptly disappears when I burst into the library and see Raphael in the middle of it.

With a hammer in his hand and a nail tucked into the crook of his mouth, he doesn't look up from the pile of wood at his feet. My pulse slows with my movements, and suddenly, I'm not really feeling the whole sassy independent-woman thing anymore.

I drop my clammy hands to my sides and curl them into fists, then watch as he tugs the nail out of his mouth and drives it into a wooden board with the loose *crack* of the hammer.

He doesn't look up. 'Did you get your clothes?'

'Y-yeah.'

His gaze skims up from the floor to my thighs and darkens. 'You going to put them on?'

I don't reply. Instead, I watch him, stupefied, as he hammers another nail into wood and splinters it. 'Fucking IKEA,' he mutters under his breath, giving the plank a kick with his shiny leather wingtip. 'You people have whole houses filled with this shit, you know?'

No, I don't know. I don't know who *you people* are, what he's building, or what the fuck is going on. The tension swells in my chest and bubbles up my throat, before slipping past my lips in a much less sophisticated way than I had planned.

'What is this?' I blurt out.

He raises a brow. 'A bookshelf.'

His answer catches me off guard. *A bookshelf? From IKEA? Aren't those built with those little wrenches?* Okay, maybe he really has lost the plot.

I shake off the thought and scramble to get back on track. 'No, *us*.'

His hammer pauses mid-air, eyes tracking my hand as it darts back and forth. *Me and him, him and me.* His expression conveys I'm ridiculous for lumping us together in this way.

The next *crack* tenses my spine, and he slips another nail into his mouth to conceal his smirk.

'You're staying here for a while.'

'Yeah, but *why* ?'

He picks up a pamphlet from his desk and holds it up by the window. 'You don't happen to read Swedish, do you?'

I grit my teeth. 'Tell me *why*, Raph –'

'Because I said so,' he growls back.

The sudden venom in his tone sweeps away my next breath. I suck in a lungful of air to steady myself, and roll my shoulders back, refusing to crumble.

'It doesn't make sense,' I say slowly. 'You hate me.'

There's a bitter edge to his laugh. 'That's what you think, huh?'

My cheeks warm. 'You think I'm unlucky, at least. Why would you want to be stuck on a boat with someone who's bad for you?'

He glances up at me, indifference masking the chiseled planes of his face again. 'You eat burgers.'

I frown. 'What's my diet have to do with anything?'

Crack. 'You eat burgers, although you know they're bad for you. It's the same thing, Queenie. You're bad for me –' his stare carves a hot path down the front of my hoodie-clad chest, lands on the hemline, then he licks his lips '– but I still want to eat you.'

Jesus Christ. There's something about the way his silky voice sharpens on the word *eat* that sends an electric thrill through my lower core.

I dig my heels into the plush carpet and try to focus on Matt's three tips, but they're starting to grow hazy behind my eyelids. *What order were they in again?*

Another crack of the hammer splinters the corner of the wood again. He frowns, looking down at the tool in his hand, like there's something wrong with it rather than the ridiculous amount of force he's putting behind each blow.

I open my mouth to protest, but nothing aside from hot air comes out of it. This was not how I thought this conversation was going to go. I thought I'd sail in here, lay down my terms and conditions to this arrangement, and then after a little negotiation, maybe, just maybe, I'd get fucked again over a soft surface and under cleared air.

Now, I'm not so sure it'd even be ethical to have sex with him at all, because he's clearly lost his mind. I'm about to tell him so when his cell buzzes against the desk, cutting me off.

'Yeah?' He glances at his watch. 'Fine. Have the jet ready to go in an hour.'

A sour taste rises to my tongue, and suddenly, I realize I could have got this all wrong. *He's leaving?*

He hangs up and glances over at me, irritation flecking his green eyes. 'Problem?'

I stare at him. He really plans on leaving me on this boat while he flits off on a jet? Maybe I should have double-checked with Matt what enemies-with-benefits actually means, because my vision of steamed-up portholes and violent orgasms has just gone *poof*.

Self-preservation forms a wall around my heart. 'What if I don't want to stay here and fuck you?' I snap. 'Did you think about that? I have a life, you know, and guess what? It doesn't revolve around you and your personal problems.'

He tears his eyes from his IKEA project to me. After a few tense seconds, he spits the nail out of his mouth and leans back against the desk.

It's the first time since I stomped into this room that he's given me all of his attention. I'd forgotten how heavy it feels, how uneasy it always makes me.

'So tell me that, then.'

'What?'

He tightens his cufflinks. 'You're a grown woman, Penelope, and I'm a reasonable man.' *Yeah, tell that to Blake's lifeless body.* 'So, drop the hypotheticals and tell me what you want.'

Under the heat of his stare, I try not to shrivel. Instead, I steel my jaw and match his indifference.

'I don't want to stay on this boat and be your fuck toy, Raphael.'

He nods once, jaw taut. 'Okay, now tell me that again, but closer this time.'

I frown. 'Huh?'

Without breaking eye contact, he unbuckles his belt. The *thawp* of leather passing through loops makes me stiffer than the loudest *crack* of a hammer ever could.

'Come over here and tell me you don't want to fuck me,' he says quietly.

Ice freezes my veins. When I glance to the door over Raphael's broad shoulders, he laughs darkly.

'Silly girl,' he rasps, gaze flashing with molten amusement. 'Your eyes always give you away.'

A staggered heartbeat. A strangled moan. Then I kick the half-built bookshelf into his path and make a run for it.

Rafe

If I'm being honest, I always knew that if I fucked Penelope, I'd break my rule and fuck her more than once. Knew it long before I found out how tightly her cunt grips my cock.

Ah, well. That rule wasn't the first thing I broke today; won't be the last, either.

Dark humor fills me as Penelope slams the door behind herself, making the portholes quiver in her wake. I'm sure she's expecting me to chase her, but where's the fun in that? Instead, I down the rest of my vodka, shrug off my jacket and drape it neatly over the backrest of an armchair, tap out a text to delay my flight, then switch over to my security camera app.

That amusement melts into a tight laugh. *Silly girl*. She flew out of the library and took a left into my private quarters. Each room connects with the next, following the semi-circle shape of the bow. All I have to do is stroll out of this room and take a right, and we'll bump into each other in the living room or my cabin.

Either will do absolutely fine.

As I slip out of the library and into the meeting room behind it, a reckless thrill racks through me so violently, I can taste it at the back of my throat. In the spirit of being honest, I must admit I *love* playing games with this girl.

Especially when the loser gets spanked.

The meeting room melts into my study, and as I draw nearer to the connecting door, incoming footsteps and ragged breaths seep out from the gap underneath it.

For pure theatrics, I crack the belt in my hand, and no sooner than the *thawp* pollutes the air does a muffled squeal soak through the door and touch my groin.

Penelope crashes into my chest the moment I yank the door open.

'Going somewhere?'

As always, her eyes answer for her, darting into the study behind me. Suddenly, I understand why she cheats at card games. It's not because she fancies herself as a swindler, but because she'd never win fair-and-square with a poker face that bad.

I'm half-tempted to fuck an impassive disposition into her before allowing her off the boat.

When her tense stance suggests she's going to make a break for it, I crack my belt again, *hard*. The noise flashes in her eyes like a warning sign well-received. She comes to a sudden stop, her gaze sliding south to the leather in my hand.

'What's that for?'

'Come here and I'll show you.'

But of course, disobedience drips from Penelope's pores and she does the exact opposite. I chase her staggered retreat to the armrest of the sofa, reaching out and grabbing her by the scruff of my hoodie before she can break her back falling over it.

'What a coincidence – this is exactly where I wanted you.'

She lets out a strangled noise that dulls when I flip her onto her front, bend her over the armrest, and push her face into the seat cushion. Preempting her struggle, I pin her thighs to the side of the sofa with my own.

Her hands scrunch into fists by her head. 'I don't want to alarm you, but I think you're having a breakdown.'

I bite back the humor rising up my throat. I'm not having a breakdown; I'm having a *break*. Taking a hiatus from pretending everything is fine-and-fucking dandy. How much longer could I have looked out my window to the raging fire outside and convinced myself it's a beautiful summer's day? Fuck it. I'll open the front door and let the flames lick my skin. Let the smoke blacken my insides.

My world is on fire, and I want to punish the girl who lit the match.

My touch is rough and self-serving as I run flat palms over the backs of her thighs. Fuck, I love everything about these thighs. The way my fingertips disappear into her flesh when I squeeze them. How they taste when I can't resist sinking my teeth into them.

I grab her shorts and yank them down, exhaling at the view. *What's in between them.*

Her pink pussy lips spill out from between quivering legs, bordered by soft, auburn hair. The sight pulls my muscles taught, and I can't resist the temptation to brush my knuckle over them. I wish I hadn't, because when Penelope rises on tiptoes for more, her bare ass grazes my cock through my slacks and sends a river of sizzling *need* through my veins.

Clenching my jaw, I flatten my palm on the small of her back to stop her wriggling. Take a step back and glare at the ceiling long enough to let the impulse pass.

Belt. Right. Gripping the buckle in my fist, I run the length over the back of her thigh. A dark excitement slides south and pulsates in my groin at her muscles tensing under mine.

The leather reaches the curve of her ass and I hold it there. 'What was it you wanted to tell me again?'

Her labored breathing stops. 'Nothing important.'

'Answer me, Penelope.'

Her fingernails dig into the cushion. She sighs. 'I don't want to stay on this boat with you.'

Her shoulders stiffen in anticipation, but when the blow doesn't come, she glances back at me through a curtain of hair, her violent eyes tinged with caution.

I meet it with a perfect smile. 'Lucky.'

She frowns. 'What?'

'That's your safe word, Penelope. I have a feeling you're going to need it.'

My belt comes down on her ass, halting her protest. It was the lightest, most restrained spank I could muster, but still, the *crack* is satisfying and her cry is electric. It soaks into my skin and charges all the atoms underneath it.

'Can't hear you,' I grind out. 'Try again.'

'I'm *not* staying –'

I spank her again, this time a little harder. A pink blush blooms against her pale cheek, and I skim my thumb over its soft heat in morbid fascination. 'Maybe say it louder?'

'Maybe get a fucking hearing aid?' she hisses breathlessly into the pillow.

When she braces again, I wipe away my smirk with the back of my hand. Either this girl has a medical condition that makes her physically unable to keep her mouth shut, or she actually enjoys the brunt of my belt.

My gaze travels over the curve of her back and drinks her in.

I'd laugh in disbelief, had the little brat not ruined my life. Because now, as the harsh winter sun streams through the portholes, dancing over her skin and highlighting the red in her hair, it's obvious she'll be my downfall. Just fucking *look* at her. In my hoodie, of all things. It swamps her frame and I'd tear it off to get a better look at what's underneath, if I didn't feel such a masochistic pleasure from her wearing it.

Begrudgingly, I get it now: why men like seeing women in their shit. Wearing my clothes, my watch, it feels like she's *mine*. Until I'm done breaking her, at least.

Spurred on by her insolence and the odd tightness in my throat, I brace my other hand on the small of her back and whip her ass again. The impact is hard enough to lurch her body half a foot forward. Every curse word under the sun spills from her lips, followed by a breathy moan. The lust-coated sound tugs on my cock like a siren call, sending a dull, restless ache to my balls.

Fuck. She's enjoying this. Massaging her red cheek with my palm, I slide my other hand between her thighs and graze my fingertips over her pussy lips for confirmation. She's so wet, so *hot*, my vision dims for a moment. All I can hear over the roaring in my ears are Penelope's strangled little sighs.

So, Penelope likes it rough – as if I needed any more evidence Fate has tailor-made my doom card to my exact liking. But because the girl has a talent for turning me into a mad man, a sudden, vicious thought heats my chest. *How does she know she likes it rough?* Who else has broken their belt over her ass and brought her to that conclusion?

Blinded by a spark of rage, I grip the belt at my side and plunge two fingers inside her. She clenches around me so tightly, that I swear I see stars on the backs of my eyelids.

'Whose pussy is this, Penelope?'

It's a ridiculous question, one that's never come out my mouth in my fucking life. I couldn't care less who a girl fucks after I've emptied my balls inside her. Hell, as long as I'm not getting my cousins' sloppy seconds, they can do whatever they want. But the thought of another man laying claim on this girl, *my* Queen of Hearts, even long after I'm done with her, has turned me into a rabid dog, barking out shit I don't mean.

'Answer the fucking question,' I snap, scissoring my fingers inside of her.

She goes rigid. Curls her hands under the pillow and buries her face into the top of it. It's barely a whisper, but I hear it through a megaphone.

'Mine.'

A growl rises up my throat, and I catch her garbled, 'But we can share!' as my belt whistles through the air and breaks over her ass.

I let my belt go slack in disbelief. If the sight of her squirming against the arm rest for friction didn't send a heady fire along the length of my dick, I'd be impressed at her pig-headedness.

'Share? You think I only want your pussy on Wednesday and Saturdays, or something?'

'You'll get what you're given,' she mumbles. But I know she regrets her choice of words, because she squeals an apology when my hand curls around the hemline of her hoodie to keep her in place and throw my back into the next blow. It's fueled by hot jealousy and obsession and the moment the *crack* pierces the air, I taste regret. It was way too hard.

Fuck. I glance up to assess her reaction, but she gives me nothing except curled fists and heavy breaths.

'Penelope.'

She turns her face toward the backrest and my fucking throat tightens.

'*Cazzo,*' I mutter, letting my belt slide from my hand. I follow it to the floor, sinking to my knees and planting a gentle kiss against the fresh welt on her ass. It's not lost on me that the fortune teller said the Queen of Hearts would bring me to my knees. Turns out, she meant it literally. 'Talk to me.'

'I'm fine,' she bites out in a tone that suggests she's anything but. 'Don't stop.'

With the heat of her cunt warming my face, I can't resist nestling between her thighs and licking her from clit to ass. Her muscles soften against my ears, letting me in.

'Whose pussy, Penelope?' I ask again, gentler this time. I punctuate the question with a swirl of my tongue around her entrance. The tremor that vibrates through her makes me repeat the move.

'Mine.'

'Yours?'

'Yes.'

I pause. 'And will that still be your answer when I spank you so hard you cry?'

Her thighs tighten around my jaw. Christ, in this world, it's a blessing to die from old age and not a bullet, but I'd happily take being crushed to death by Penelope's thighs as an alternative option. Like that Bond Girl in *GoldenEye*.

She inhales a shaky breath and inches herself down on my flat tongue. 'Yes.'

Irritation heats my belly. I skim my teeth along her folds, before sucking on her clit. It leaves my mouth with a wet *pop*.

'And when I make you cry, will you use your safe word?'

Her turn to pause. 'No.'

Rising to my feet, I push her ass away with an angry shove, but catch her just before she falls over the edge of the arm rest.

'You're a stubborn little bitch, you know that?'

She twists her head, lifting her eyes to mine. Fuck, they are as blue as the ocean and look like they are just as wet. 'Yes,' she says quietly.

I huff out a dry laugh, but it's devoid of all humor and catches in my throat. Stubborn is an understatement. This girl wouldn't give me what I wanted if I dragged her out to the middle of Devil's Dip, stripped her naked, and flogged her.

Raking my fingers through my hair, I turn my attention to the quilted wallpaper, needing a respite from Penelope's doe-eyed expression. This is one of the many reasons I only fuck girls from behind. Thing is, I learned this morning that when

Penelope withholds her focus from me for too long, I have a sick habit of forcing her to look at me anyway.

Shaking my head, I let my eyes fall back to her ass. Red and ruined. The violent throb in my cock is at odds with the unease in my stomach. Ironic, really. I dragged her onto this yacht with bloodied hands, with every intention to ruin her before she did me. And yet, one stray tear has got me in a chokehold, wondering if shit like chocolate and hot water bottles will stop another from falling.

This must be what *rock-bottom* means.

I push away all simp-like thoughts about candy and aftercare and slide my hands under her hoodie, gripping Penelope on the dip of her hip.

Fuck it; I'll give her the best orgasm of her life.

I stoop to kiss her ass again, muttering something embarrassing in Italian, but just as I'm about to sink back between her cheeks, a hand grabs my forearm and stops me.

My gaze slides up to Penelope's. It hardens the longer I'm trapped in it.

'Don't be nice.'

My jaw tightens. 'Why?'

'I don't like it.'

We stare at each other for a few tense seconds, her words and their meaning soaking into my skin like acid rain. So, not only does she like it rough, she *only* likes it rough. Stormy thoughts of other men and their belts zap through me, dissolving all guilt.

My eyes never leave hers as I snatch the belt off the floor. I wrap it around my busted fists and pull it taut. Penelope exhales and drops her head to the cushion, but I pull her up by the hood of my sweater.

'What are you – ?'

I cut her off by sliding the strap of the belt into her mouth. I fist both the buckle and loop in one palm and yank her up onto her hands, like she's on reins.

As my lips graze the shell of her ear, my tone lowers to a warning. 'If it gets too much and you don't use your safe word, I'll tie you to my bed and torture you with nice things. Got it?'

Her gaze slides sideways, laced with suspicion. 'Like what?' she gargles.

I pause. Fuck knows – I've never done those type of nice things for a woman in my life. But now I'm leaning over her, my erection is pressing against her bare ass, and the warm, wet heat of it is burning through my slacks. I can't focus on hypothetical torture at a time like this.

'You know, romantic shit,' I grunt out.

I catch her look of alarm before adjusting the slack on the belt so I can get behind her without snapping her jaw.

My cock aches to be released, springing to attention the second I yank down my zipper. When I sink my head into her folds, white delirium trickles through me like venom, electrifying my nerves and poisoning my brain with feverish thoughts. Like, how the fuck will I last longer than a few minutes now that I've got Penelope gagging on my belt?

Christ, she's tight. Fighting every sadistic whisper in my brain, I slow my pace and let her body guide me inside her. Drawing back when her spine straightens under my palm, I then give more of myself when she pulls taut against my belt, trying to drop to her elbows and lift her ass up for a deeper angle.

The sound of frustration pulls my eyes up to meet hers. She's straining against leather to look at me, conveying her annoyance with my leisurely pace.

I smile.

She scowls.

Then I drive into her, *hard.*

Her head falls forward, and the sight of her clamping down on my belt to stifle her moan is so hot I can barely stand it. I grind my molars at the vice-like grip of her cunt, the way it feels like a desperate tug every time she lurches forward. The loud *slap* of her cheeks when she slams down to my base draws my eyes to the sight, and fuck, if it won't be burned into my retinas forever.

I need more of her, her soft skin under my palms and under my tongue. Driven by madness, I pull the belt tighter until she's no longer bent over the sofa, but flush against my chest. With another small tug, her head drops back against my collarbone, exposing her throat to me. She smells so good I don't think twice about sinking my teeth into her racing pulse, then licking the mark I left when she lets out a sharp hiss of breath.

My free hand skims under my hoodie and over her stomach, squeezing one of her tits. 'What about these, Queenie?' I growl against the shell of her ear. 'These yours too?'

Before she can choke out a muffled reply, I roll her nipple between my thumb and forefinger, thrusting into her to absorb the shudder that vibrates through her core.

'I'll get back to you on that one,' she gasps, her pussy clenching around me.

I hold her there, playing with her tits, my mouth giving equal attention to her neck and earlobe, until the flush on her throat darkens a few shades.

'Please,' she gasps over leather. '*Please.*'

My stomach tenses against her spine. 'You want to come?'

Her teeth saw against my belt as she nods frantically.

Fuck. I had to damn-near torture her to get that word out of her mouth this morning, and the fact she's now giving it to me so freely sends an inferno through my veins so hot it could melt steel.

'Good girl,' I mutter against her pulse, sliding my hand between her legs. 'You're such a good girl when you beg.'

She twists her face away from my words and grinds restlessly against my hand, working the length of my dick in a frenzy. I rub her clit hard and fast, watching her profile in fascination as she writhes against my restraint.

'*Fuck*,' is the last thing she grinds out, before her body shudders violently against mine. The sound of her strangled moans, the way her pussy pulsates around me – bring me so close to the edge that I couldn't turn back even if I wanted to. Her limbs go so limp that I cage her in with my forearm and hold her upright. I tug her head back with the belt and bury my face in the collar of her hoodie. *My* hoodie. The last thing that crosses my mind before a white-hot orgasm wreaks havoc through me, is how fucking good her scent smells mixed with my own.

Muscles weakening, I let the belt slide from my grip, my arm leaves Penelope's waist, and I let her slump forward over the armrest. I fuck her with long, lethargic strokes while I catch my breath, then give her ruined ass a light spank of approval.

'You're trouble Queenie. You know that?'

Wordlessly, she slides off me, pulls down the hoodie so it covers her ass, and glances toward the door.

My spine stiffens. The fact I'm still drunk off her pussy, yet she's already scouting out the exit, pisses me off. The irony isn't lost on me – I've been the one zipping up my slacks and scanning for my car keys before the girl can offer me a post-fuck coffee more times than I can count. Doesn't feel as easy when the shoe is on the other foot.

'Going somewhere?' I ask tightly.

'Mm. I'll probably shower and catch a ride back to the Coast. Have you seen my shorts?'

She spots them draped over the corner of a cabinet and stalks toward them. As she passes, I grab her wrist and toss her back onto the sofa. Her ass hits the cushions and she winces.

'Stay here.' Her focus slides to the door again, tightening my shoulder blades. 'I'll tie you to this fucking sofa if you move.'

A few moments later, I come back into the room with a

bottle in hand, and I'd be lying if I said I didn't feel relief at the sight of her perched on the edge of the sofa, even if she looks like she's waiting to see the dentist.

Eyes cautious, she tracks my movements as I sit beside her. Before she can argue, I pull her across my lap, ass up.

'Um, what the fuck?'

'Shut up, Penelope.'

My tone is harsher than I intend it to be, but her desire to be anywhere but here has stirred a layer of unease under my skin. She tenses when I pull up the hem of my hoodie, revealing the fresh bruises that decorate her ass.

Softening at the sight, I exhale a ragged breath and gently run the back of my hand over her burning skin. 'Does it hurt?'

'Wasn't that the point?'

She's right, it was the point. Once again, my rage-fueled plan of dragging her onto this yacht and ruining her has been corrupted by something unwanted expanding beneath my ribs. Ridiculous. I can't stand the girl. Can't stand how her bad luck has bled into every corner of my life. And yet, here I am, a bottle of cocoa butter in my hand, itching to take the pain away.

Maybe it *is* a breakdown.

As I squirt lotion onto her ass, she stops breathing. Her thighs tense against my own.

'Relax, Penelope,' I murmur, slowly rubbing the cream over the curve of her ass. When she doesn't do as she's told, I repeat the command with a harsher tone. Eventually, her muscles soften under my palms and her breathing shallows. *Good girl* is dancing on the tip of my tongue, but I swallow it.

Outside, a storm swallows the sky. Light rain patter hardens against the windows, until it's so loud I almost miss the sweet sigh that escapes Penelope's lips.

She twists her head and looks up at me through half-mast lashes.

'Why are you doing this?'

Irritation tightens my jaw. How can this girl like to fuck rough if she doesn't know what happens after the fact? I bite down the urge to demand to know who has spanked her, and add their deaths to my list of errands. Instead, I turn my attention back to my hands gliding frictionlessly over her thighs.

'If I don't put you back together after I break you, then there'll be nothing to break next time.' My gaze slides up to hers, just in time to see heat burning through the haze.

'Does a massage come with every spanking?'

My lips tilt. 'I'm sure we can come to some sort of agreement.'

'And do I just ignore your dick digging into my stomach?'

Now, I let out a dry laugh. *This girl.* I've just emptied my balls less than five minutes ago, and I'm already rock-hard underneath her again.

I glance at my watch. 'Yes. As much as I'd like you to take care of it with your mouth, I've got a plane to catch.'

Her stomach tenses. 'Where are you going?'

'Why, going to miss me?'

She scowls. 'Like a hole in the head.'

I'm about to give her ass a hard flick when uncertainty shifts through her expression and gives me pause.

I sigh. Despite not knowing whether I want to chain her to my bed and use her as my personal sex slave or toss her overboard, I know it's unfair to expect her to stay here without any idea what's going on.

I pour some more cream on her ass. Massage it dangerously close to her slick slit. Inhaling sharply, she pushes up against my hand, but I press her back down with a flat palm, willing my cock not to get side-tracked.

'Ever since you turned up on the Coast, bad things have happened, Penelope.'

She groans. 'I thought you were joking. Seriously, you can't blame your bad business decisions on me. I'm literally the luckiest girl –'

I give her a light spank to cut her off. 'I don't give a shit how lucky you think you are; you're not lucky to me.'

'It doesn't make sense. If you think just being around me makes you unlucky, what the hell do you think will happen now you've been inside me?'

Laughter rises up my throat, swept away by that newly familiar feeling of recklessness. My gaze trails my fingers as they disappear over the slope of her thigh, grazing her puffy lips.

'I'm past the point of caring, Penelope. Past the point of trying to resist you.' Fuck it, my jet can wait on the tarmac a little longer. I push a finger into her, bending to brush my lips against her ass cheek. 'Let it all burn.'

She writhes out of my grip like a slippery eel, and I catch her by the waist before she ends up on the carpet.

'I don't do this,' she blurts out, clambering to her feet.

'Do what?'

'Men.'

'I don't do men either.'

'No, I mean –' She lets out a noise of frustration, shaking her head. 'I mean, I'm not looking for anything serious. I don't do relationships, or cutesy things like . . . butt kisses and *breakfast*.'

'You didn't like my eggs?'

She moves toward the door. 'Okay, you know what –'

I grab her wrist and yank her on top of me. She fights against my grip for all of three seconds, before meeting my stare and slowing to compliance.

She swallows. Lowers her voice so I can barely hear it over the rain. 'I mean, if there's any chance you'll fall in love with me, you should probably just put me on a boat and send me back to shore right now.'

We stare at each other. Then I burst out laughing.

Penelope scowls, slamming a palm into my chest. 'What, is falling in love with me so hard to believe?'

I tuck a stray red strand behind her ear, ignoring the pressure expanding in my chest. 'Impossible.'

She already knows my biggest secret, that I'm superstitious. She doesn't need to know I chose the King of Diamonds instead of the King of Hearts, too.

Love isn't an option. Let alone with the girl that's ruined my life.

My cell buzzes on the coffee table, reminding me I have shit to do. 'You staying here or not?'

'And if I wanted to leave?'

I bite my tongue. The truth would scare her: I'd drag her back onboard kicking and screaming.

Instead, I run my hands up the backs of her thighs, pulling her onto my erection. 'You don't like being fucked by me, Penelope?'

The muscle in her jaw ticks. Her lids flutter shut. 'Fine. We can be enemies with benefits.'

I arch a brow. 'Enemies?'

'Well, we're not exactly friends, are we?'

I hold back a smirk. 'I suppose not.' Dropping back against the sofa, I hold my hand out for her to shake. 'Enemies with benefits then.'

She glares down at it, like she wants to bite off my fingers. 'Of course, I have some terms and conditions.'

'Of course,' I say in amusement.

'First of all, I need my phone. I think I left it in your car when you turned into the Hulk this morning.'

Of course she needs her phone. How else am I going to obsessively listen to every vapid thought she has if she can't spill it to my hotline? 'Done.'

'And I don't want Laurie or the others to know I'm staying

here. It's . . .' She saws her lip between her teeth, searching for the word. 'Weird.'

I laugh. 'Fine.'

'And I want to be home for Christmas.'

I consider this. It's less than a week away. 'Okay.' *Doesn't mean I don't want you back afterward.*

'And –'

'Jesus, Penelope. Do I need to fly in a lawyer?'

She tugs on my collar pin to shut me up. '*And,* I'm not a floating Rapunzel. If you think I'm going to be holed up here like a woman waiting for her husband to return home from war, then you've got another thought coming. I need to be taken back to shore whenever I want.'

'Yeah, not going to happen.'

A look of disgust dents her features. 'What, worried I won't come back?'

She'd be doing me a favor if she didn't come back, but that's not the reason I don't want her flitting around the Coast right now. Raking my teeth over my bottom lip, I drink in her dark expression with amusement. 'You'll stay here until I'm back, and then we'll discuss this again.'

To my surprise, she drops it, but then when her eyes spark with mischief, I realize there's a motive behind her obedience. She runs her finger up and down my collar pin, biting her lip. 'You know, if we're to be enemies with benefits, you'll have to kiss me.'

I laugh. 'Will I now?'

She hitches a shoulder. 'Yeah, it'd be weird if you didn't.'

'You're right.'

Her eyes slide up to mine, big and blue. 'I am?'

My fingers slide into her hair and grip the base of her head. I pull her face to mine; my mouth is close to hers, I can feel the heat off her lips. Hear the *gulp* in her throat.

'Nice try,' I whisper.

She curses as I slide her off my lap and rise to my feet.

'Chef Marco prepares my meals and leaves them in the freezer. Help yourself to them and anything else on the yacht.' I tug out my wallet and toss my Amex on the coffee table. 'You already have my spare card but I'm guessing it's in my car along with your phone. Use this.' My gaze rises to hers. 'I'm sure you remember the pin,' I say dryly.

'Obviously.' She swoops it up and holds it up to the light. 'Hmm. I don't think they deliver pizza to the middle of the Pacific.'

'They will if you tip well enough.'

As I stroll toward the door, her presence tugs on my back. I have this ridiculous urge to delay my flight another hour. Not even just to fuck her again, but to just . . . do *this*. Talk shit and piss her off.

Instead, I grip the door handle and tell her, 'Try not to burn the place down, Penelope.'

'Rafe?' The way she says my name bounces like an echo in my chest. I pause, glaring at the wood grain on the door. 'All my other fuck buddies call me Penny.'

Violence hits me like a lightning bolt.

'And all your other fuck buddies will be six-feet-under if you mention them again.'

Penny

For the third time in an hour, I float into the forgotten living room at the back of the yacht. Instead of sighing into the silence like last time, I sink down on the window seat and press my cheek against the cold glass, as if it'll extinguish the restless heat underneath it.

After a ridiculously long shower, I've been wandering the yacht like a spirit condemned. A collegiate hoodie instead of a Victorian dress; chained by leather restraints and violent orgasms, rather than the shackles of doom.

I lasted less than two hours before the sound of the decks groaning and the endless grandfather clocks ticking began to grate on me, chafing at my skin.

Now, as I press more of my body against the glass, staring at the rain fracturing the bright lights of Devil's Cove on the horizon, I rattle my brain for something to do.

The answer comes like one of those cartoon light bulbs: I'll work.

I'm not scheduled for a shift, but what else am I going to do tonight? Hide in Rafe's room while the casino vibrates above me? With a quick glance at the Breitling, I realize Laurie and the like will be bobbing over the Pacific in a staff shuttle soon.

Spurred on by new vigor, I dart down to the laundry room and pick up a spare uniform in my size. Brushing the tangled evidence of rough sex from my hair, I paint on a face that looks too innocent to enjoy being gagged by a belt. Within thirty minutes, I'm behind the bar, stocking the mini fridge and loading the dishwasher.

But the start of the shift comes and goes. The hour melts into the next, the solitude tightening like a noose around my throat. No Laurie, no guests. When the dishwasher's three lonely beeps fill the lounge, signaling it's been two and a half hours since I put it on, I drop the rag I'm clutching and stomp up to Rafe's study.

I find Laurie's number in one of those Rolodexes old people have and use the phone on his desk to call her. She answers on the first ring.

'Yes, boss?'

'Laurie, it's Penny. Where are you?'

'Penny?' She pauses, the line filling with the muffled sounds of a bar. 'Rafe's closed up the yacht until New Year's Eve, sweetie. He didn't call you? He said he would.'

Closing my eyes, I sink into the leather chair and drop my head against the backrest. 'No, he didn't,' I say tightly. Although I guess that solves the dilemma of trying to hide the fact I'm living onboard from my colleagues.

'Full pay, of course. And the staff Christmas party will still be going ahead. Wait.' The noise behind her fades, and it sounds like a door slams behind her. 'How are you on the boat? The staff shuttle wouldn't have been running –'

It's stupid and childish, but I panic and hang up on her. When the phone shrills with a call back, I dive under the desk and turn it off by the plug.

Great. Now what?

The silence swells against the walls of the study, dulled only by the footsteps of the ghost crew going about their duties. It's growing darker now, and the only light from outside is the occasional sweep from Rafe's men's torches as they patrol the decks.

The worst part about this seclusion is that I'm stuck with it all night. There's no way I'll sleep before the sun comes up.

I manage to kill another ten minutes rifling through Rafe's perfectly organized drawers and glaring at the photo frames lining his shelves. One of him passing someone an oversized check catches my eye, and I pick it up to study it.

His signature silhouette seeps out from behind the glass. Sharp suit, megawatt smile. Black, gold, green, all the colors so polished, so *refined*, that no other word comes to mind. Perfect.

I knew the moment I met him he was the perfect liar.

A heady thought charges my nerves. Now that I've seen what's underneath the gentlemanly exterior – felt it inside me; heard it in my ear – I'm hot with knowing I've had a glimpse of something no one else has.

Now, he's the perfect liar, to everyone except me.

A slow-moving hum tears me away from his magnetic stare. Frowning, I glance over my shoulder toward the French doors, squinting when I notice a hazy light cutting through the rain.

He's back already?

A Pavlovian response flickers in my clit, and I take the steps down to the lounge two at a time. Realizing I look like a puppy bounding around with excitement at his master returning home, I perch on the edge of the sofa with my back to the doors and turn on the television, staring at a basketball game with plastic interest.

My indifference lasts about ninety seconds before the French doors burst open and an icy chill brings in a bundle of chaotic energy with a familiar female voice at the heart of it.

'The party has arrived!' A blur of blond hair and bags rounds the sofa. My gaze slides up pajama-clad legs and lands on Rory's bright grin. 'I brought candy and card games, Tayce has pizza and wine, and Wren brought a movie.'

'Not just *any* movie – *Mamma Mia!*, the extended karaoke version.' Wren appears and thrusts a well-worn DVD under my nose. I look up at her in surprise. She's a whirlwind of pink, from the glittery scrunchie in her hair to the wellington boots her pajamas are tucked in to.

As Tayce flops down on the sofa and flashes me a sly grin, Rory's attention flicks toward the door, then back to me. 'And *you*,' she whispers, 'will bring the *gossip*.'

'I –'

Rory cuts me off with a flap of her hand. 'Not right now, though. My husband is on the warpath.'

As if the word *husband* summoned a demon, a dark presence heats the nape of my neck.

'Penelope Price.'

I swallow, tracking the black shadow as it shifts over the cream carpet. Shiny shoes come into view, and with a braced spine, I force myself to look up at their owner.

'Where's my brother?'

'Which one?'

Angelo's jaw ticks, and he rakes a look of displeasure over my wrist. 'The one that likes to play games.' He takes a step forward, making my heart jolt. 'Unlike me.'

I stare at him. The expression on his face is one from my memories. He glared at my father the same way all those years ago, when we gatecrashed his parents' funeral. Now that I'm the subject of it, I'm not going to squeal like my drunken father did. Besides, I have this weird feeling of loyalty in my chest – I wouldn't tell Angelo where his brother had gone, even if I knew.

'Rafe? Beats me.'

His eyes thin. 'Then what are you doing here?'

My mind scatters in four directions for an answer. 'Yacht sitting,' I announce.

Tayce snorts beside me, hiding her smirk in the collar of her leather jacket when Angelo cuts her a menacing look. The heat of it makes my resolve splinter, and I find myself muttering, 'Sorry, I know as much as you.'

'And all I know is that Rafe called my wife and invited her to an impromptu sleepover in the middle of the fucking Pacific on a Monday night.'

'And you're ruining the vibe, babe,' Rory groans, sliding in between me and her ever-advancing husband. She mutters sweet words while she plays with his shirt buttons, but I can't hear them over the blood pounding in my ears.

Rafe arranged a sleepover for me? The idea is sweet, sickly even, and it churns in my stomach like I've eaten too much chocolate in one sitting. I try to wash it away with rationale: he probably doesn't trust me to be on his zillion-dollar mega-yacht alone, which is fair, considering the last rich guy that was mean to me got his casino burned to the ground. Besides, it's not like he knows how badly I wanted to have sleepovers when I was a kid.

I look over the top of Rory's messy bun and meet Angelo's suspicious stare. He gently sweeps his wife to the side so there's no barrier between me and his last-ditch attempt at interrogation.

'You know where my brother is, Penelope?'

'Have you tried *Find My iPhone,* Angelo?'

Tayce stills. Wren draws in a sharp breath, and Rory mutters something about flamingos under her breath.

The air heats for a moment, then cools when dry humor softens Angelo's expression.

'I get it now.'

I frown. 'Get what?'

But he doesn't reply. Instead, he plants a kiss on his wife's jaw, tells her to call him before she goes to sleep, and disappears out to the swim platform.

I turn back to the lounge for an answer. 'Get what?'

Rory smirks. Wren turns red and looks away. When I glance at Tayce, she places a hand on my thigh and gives it a squeeze.

'He means, he gets why Rafe is obsessed with you now. You talk almost as much shit as he does.'

***

The interrogation was inevitable. I answered questions about our situation with flippancy – *we're just fucking, chill* – and questions about how long I'll be here for with vagueness – *until I get bored of him*.

Truth is, I don't know the real answer to either.

At least the third-degree was short-lived. When Tayce asked how big Rafe's dick is, Rory got so grossed out she knocked a glass of red wine on the cream carpet. We turned our attention to moving the sofa three feet to the left to hide it, and luckily the conversation never went back to the topic of her brother-in-law's manhood.

The evening bled into night with the unrelenting rain and the soundtrack of *Mamma Mia!* providing the backdrop to a sleepover I could have only ever dreamed of as a kid.

Now, I'm curled up on the sofa in my pajamas, drunk on sugar and wine, and I'm trying to play it cool. Trying not to grin like a maniac as I watch Wren teach Rory the official dance to ABBA's *Super Trouper,* and trying not to ask when we can do this again.

The sofa dips beside me. 'Decide on what you want, yet?'

I glance down at the black box Tayce set on the coffee table. She snaps it open and runs her finger over a silver tattoo gun.

I swallow. 'Depends. Does it hurt?'

'A lot less than getting impaled by Rafe's massive dick, I'm sure.' Cheeks heating, I go to swat her away, but she ducks out of arm's-reach, laughing. 'Nah. It's more a scratch than a stab. And after a few minutes, the area goes numb and you can't really feel it anyway.'

My eyes travel down the length of her arms as she snaps on a pair of black gloves. 'You don't have any tattoos yourself?'

'Nope, that's why they call me the tattooless tattoo artist.' She glances up at Rory and Wren doing the Brooklyn shuffle, then lowers her voice. 'Tattoos make you identifiable.'

The sound of her beer chinking against mine in The Rusty Anchor echoes in my head.

'I hear you're the best.'

She laughs. 'That's what they say.'

'Did you always know you wanted to be a tattoo artist?'

She cocks her head, and for a moment, I watch her unscrew her gun and sterilize each part. 'No,' she eventually says. 'I was studying Art History at college. I wanted to be a museum curator.'

'So why tattoos?'

A dark smirk touches her lips. She flips her long, black hair over her shoulder and pins me with a knowing look. 'I like inflicting pain on men, even just for a little while.'

I knew I liked this girl. My attention drops to the gun. 'It's temporary ink, right?'

'Uh-huh. Will fade in a couple weeks.'

'All right, then I'm happy for you to go rogue.'

She cocks a brow. 'Are you sure?' Leaning in, she adds, 'Because when I go rogue, I go . . . *rogue*.'

The mischief dancing in her eyes gives me pause. 'Okay, maybe put it somewhere I can't see, just in case.'

She chuckles. 'Good idea, red-head.'

We agree on the small of my back. I pretend like Tayce telling me it's an area with thicker skin and fewer nerves is what convinces me, but really, it's because I know Rafe will see it when he next fucks me from behind. The thought of his stomach tensing against my ass and his hot hand grazing over it sends a lethargic excitement through my core.

Tayce was right; the scratching morphs into a light burning sensation. She works meticulously, silently, the ends of her hair brushing against my spine.

When the hum of the gun cuts out, I pop my eyes open. She wipes something cold and wet over the area, then rises to her feet. To my surprise, when I twist around to look at her, she's making a slow retreat.

I frown. 'Is it done? Where are you going?'

She nods to the hand mirror on the table. 'Take a look.'

Rory stops dancing and squints at my lower back. As her eyes widen and her jaw drops, suspicion trickles into my veins.

'Tayce . . .' she whispers, biting back a laugh.

'What?' I snap. I snatch up the mirror and twist awkwardly to see her artwork. When a familiar name in a heart stares back at me, my blood runs cold.

Five heavy seconds pass. I lift my eyes to Tayce, who's staring at me like a deer caught in headlights. 'You told me to go rogue,' she whispers.

I drop the mirror to the sofa. Pull down my top.

'Yeah. And now I'm telling you to run.'

She's out the door before I can finish my sentence. I sprint after her, Rory and Wren hot on my heels.

Tayce's laughter floats up the spiral staircase. 'I'm sorry, okay! You can tattoo anything you want on me as payback!'

'I'm going to draw a massive dick!'

'That's fine, just not on my face, all right?'

She's within arms-reach by the time we run through Rafe's study. Glancing over her shoulder, she yanks open the door to the library. I follow her in and come to a crashing stop.

My breathing slows, but my heart picks up pace.

'Jeez, what an ugly bookshelf,' Tayce mutters, following my gaze.

Rory comes up beside me. 'Are they the *For Dummies* books? Looks like the whole collection? I can't imagine Rafe reading those.'

'He doesn't,' I whisper, my throat going thick.

'Well, who does then?'

I swallow. 'Me.'

In the silence, the wind roars. The grandfather clock ticks on the mantelpiece. My eyes trail the splintered wood, the hammer on the desk, and the Swedish instructions torn into two and dumped next to the trash can.

Wren sighs and clutches her chest.

'See, I told you he was a gentleman.'

Penny

Busted knuckles with a feather-light touch. Silky Italian wrapped around callous words. Slow licks, racing hearts. Sweet and sour, hot and cold; contradictions pull at my nerves in a game of tug and war.

I hate that I love every second of it.

A dull *thud* jolts me awake. I pop my eyes open and realize the sound is *Anatomy for Dummies* slipping out of my hand and hitting the cream carpet. In my post-nap haze, it takes a few seconds for my brain to sharpen enough to realize I'm not alone in the library.

Rafe reclines in an armchair across from the sofa, ankle resting on his thigh as he spins a gold poker chip between his thumb and forefinger. Each spin glints in the midday sun, as blinding as his presence.

I didn't expect him to be back so soon.

His stare traps mine. 'You look like an angel when you sleep.' Before the tug of war can start in my chest again, he swipes the vodka glass off the desk and adds, 'The snoring, though? Not so angelic.'

I sit up, pulling my knees to my chest in self-preservation. How long has he been sitting there? Watching me? Vulnerability and unease grip me, making me want to shrivel up and wilt under the heat of a sunbeam.

Instead, I opt for picking up the book and walking it to the haphazardly-built bookshelf. It's hard to ignore how my heart thumps under the weight of Rafe's eyes tracking me.

I brush my fingers over the yellow spines. 'You bought me all the *For Dummies* books.'

'Mm. Found a career yet?'

'You trying to get rid of me, or something?'

His dark laugh caresses me like silk. 'Or something.'

The room heats with two words left unsaid: *thank you*.

The chair groans. I don't need to turn around to know he's approaching. Each footstep treads up my spine, until his presence brushes my back.

A shudder rolls through me as his hand runs down the length of my braid.

'Did one of the girls braid your hair, Queenie?'

'Why do you call me Queenie?'

His smile is dry. 'Your mama never taught you not to answer a question with a question?'

'No, my mother didn't teach me anything memorable, except that mixing red wine with a whole pack of allergy medicine will make you choke on your own puke.' When Rafe's hand brushes over my neck, I shake the memory away. 'Anyway, Rory did.' I pause. 'How did you know I didn't do it myself?'

The expensive fabric of his slacks touches the backs of my thighs. 'You can't braid, Queenie.'

I frown. 'How do you know that?'

He stills, then skims his nose up the curve of my throat, bringing his lips to my ear. 'Apologies. I'm thinking of one of my other enemies with benefits.'

Jealousy flashes behind my eyelids. I whip around to push him off, but he tightens his grip on my braid, yanking my head back until it rests below his collar pin. 'I'll have to thank my sister-in-law for giving me a leash.'

Sweet, holy hell. All irritation vaporizes, its steam falling to the gusset of my thong. I swallow, trying to slow my breathing as his other hand trails the chain of my necklace. His fingers skim over the four-leaf clover, then carve a path across my breasts.

Something stirs in his slacks.

'My bedroom, ten minutes.'

And then he releases me. I brace my palms on the splintered bookshelf until the violent *click* of the door sounds behind me.

Christ. I exhale shakily, trying to gather my decorum from all four corners of the room. Last night, the excitement of crooning to ABBA and playing *UNO!* loosened the choke hold this man has on me. But once Rory, Wren, and Tayce left this morning, everything that's infinitively *him* soaked through the sudden silence, bled through the wallpaper, and rubbed my skin raw.

We're fuck friends, for now, but I know when all is said and done, his rough touch and smooth voice will be impossible to forget.

I count ten lots of sixty Mississippi's, then follow in his footsteps. The pipes in the walls gurgle and clink, and when I push open the door to the cabin, I realize Rafe's in the shower.

Indecision slows my limbs. I stare at the steam rising from beneath the door and consider what would happen if I opened it. Slid my shorts down, slipped through the shower door, and pressed myself into his wet, naked body. If, under hot rain, I sank to my knees and took him in my mouth. Took control.

Even though I've never done it before, the idea makes my mouth water. But I've taken only one step toward the en-suite when something out-of-sorts catches my eye. My suitcase. It's where I left it, pushed up against the wall in the corner of the room, but it's been opened. Some of my stuff is missing, and I have an awful idea of where it will be.

I slide open the closet door and weaken with dread. White shirts sandwich silk dresses. Crisp, black slacks flank mom jeans. My attention falls to the shoe rack, where his leather dress shoes sit side-by-side with my Doc Martens and heels.

Pulled taut by that damn tug-of-war, I grapple with my stuff, shove it back in my case, and take a seat in the living area. I turn on the television, flicking restlessly through the channels until a news woman talks at me with such intensity, I know if I turn up the volume loud enough, she'll drown out the feeling of unease. At least until Rafe takes me to bed and fills me with something else.

But when I tune in to what she's saying, my blood runs cold.

'For those of you just joining, we have breaking news this afternoon,' she says, shuffling her papers. 'The body found on the bank of Clam Lake in Atlantic City this morning is confirmed to be Martin O'Hare. O'Hare has made headlines in recent weeks after his casino and bar burned down under unknown circumstances.' The reporter pauses, her expression grave. 'It isn't known at this time whether the two incidents are related.'

My head swims in the opposite direction from my stomach. Hot, sticky numbness pins my body to the sofa, and my hand wouldn't be able to pick up the remote to turn the television off even if I'd wanted to.

Martin O'Hare. Dead. The reporter's mouth moves, but I can no longer hear what she's saying over the roaring of my ears. The noise fades when the shower shuts off. Now, I'm hyper-aware of what's happening in the bathroom behind me. The *thawp* of a towel. The turn of a tap. When the door opens and a wet heat brushes against the back of my head, I swallow thickly.

'Martin O'Hare was found dead in Clam Lake.' It doesn't sound like my voice. It's too calm, too at-odds with the violent pulse in my throat.

While my eyes are glued on the screen, my attention is tethered to Rafe as he moves from behind the sofa over to the bar cart. In silence, he pours a vodka.

'Really?' The *clink* of ice cubes rattles my bones. 'That's not where I left him.'

Heat prickles my skin in a way that makes me want to rip my clothes off. Fueled by panic, I clamber to my feet, but when I bump my shins against the coffee table, I realize I won't get very far. I sink back to the sofa, letting the soft cushions drag me down to hell.

'You did this?'

Now, the silence aches. Rafe's calm disposition nips at my edges. Makes me take stock of the exits. Instead of making a run for one of them, I drag my stare to him.

He's back-lit by a window, wearing nothing but ink and a low-slung towel around his waist. His eyes meet mine over the rim of his vodka glass, glittering like the sea behind him. A water droplet trickles down his chest, and he wipes it away before it reaches his navel. I stare at the hand he used. It's even more busted than it was yesterday.

'That reminds me, I brought you back a souvenir.'

My shoulders tense. Rafe disappears from view, and when he approaches the back of the sofa and drops a small box onto my lap, I stare down at it.

And then I scream.

I jump up, roll over the coffee table, and stagger toward the door. 'You're sick,' I choke out, stumbling backward. I've seen this type of shit in films. A horse's head in a bed. A skull on a bookshelf. A fucking *finger in a ring box*.

Aside from the cocked brow, Rafe's the dictionary definition of indifference. He stares at me, then stoops to retrieve the still-shut box from where it rolled under the sofa.

As he snaps it open, I squeeze my eyes closed.

'Penelope.'

When I'm brave enough to pop a lid open, I'm met with dark amusement and a key ring swinging from his finger. He tosses it to me, and it lands at my feet.

I glare at the *I Heart Atlantic City* logo for five staggered heartbeats.

And then my unease rises up my throat and spills out between us. 'I told you not to be nice to me,' I blurt out.

'It was four dollars.'

'You know I'm not talking about the fucking key ring.'

Another heartbeat, and then Rafe's rough laugh touches me. He runs a hand through his wet hair, bitterness clouding in his eyes.

'Christ, Penny. A *thank you* would have sufficed.' He downs the rest of his vodka, then lets the glass clatter to the bar cart. 'I must be fucking mad,' he mutters, wiping his mouth.

I feel so fucking sick, nausea pushes against my seams, leaving no room for other feelings, like relief.

'You killed him for me?'

He looks at me quickly. 'No.'

I let out a tense breath.

'I killed his brother for you. And then I killed Martin because he'd have come to the Coast to kill me.' He fills up his glass with more vodka, pausing thoughtfully before taking a sip. 'Actually, yeah. I killed him for you too.'

'Why?'

'Didn't like the idea of another man putting his hands around your throat,' he says dryly.

I grit my teeth, digging my nails into my palms. 'I set fire to his casino.'

'Semantics.'

I turn away, because I can't stand the way he's looking at me.

'You think I'm bad luck.' I drag a hand down my face. 'You don't even *know* me.'

His laugh is louder this time, tinged with something ironic. 'You have no fucking idea what I know.'

We stand there for a few minutes. Him at the bar cart, me glaring at the clock on the mantel. Every *tick* strikes inside my rib cage, as if counting down to the moment my heart cracks in half.

I'll never let it happen. Never let this man within arms-reach of my heart. Because this is what men do, isn't it? They're nice to you, until they aren't. Until you stop giving them what they want, and then they turn nasty. And then they drag you out to an alleyway and take what they wanted from you anyway.

My necklace sizzles against my clammy skin. Of all the times to think of Matt, it isn't now, but he pops into my head anyway. *You've got to be clear with your intentions from the beginning.*

Rolling back my shoulders and galvanizing my spine, I walk over to Rafe. He watches my approach with a mix of wariness and annoyance, tensing when I step into his hot, wet orbit.

I'm so close his liquor-tinged breath grazes my nose. My nipples glide over his chest through my T-shirt, hardening at the idea of friction.

His gaze falls to mine, melting like the ice in his drink. 'Penny . . .'

There go those busted knuckles with a feather-light touch, skimming over my cheekbone. I turn my head a fraction, because I know what comes next: the silky Italian wrapped around callous words. I don't want the contradictions.

I just want all of the bad and none of the good.

Swallowing in an attempt to slow my pulse, I turn my attention to his chest. We both watch my trembling fingers as I slide them over the serpent's head, down the length of playing cards, dice, poker chips. The walls of his stomach clench when I skim south of his navel and to the fold of his towel.

I lift my eyes to his. He searches them, and then his expression cools with realization.

He lets out a humorless laugh. 'That's all you want, huh?'

'It's all we agreed on.'

His eyes singe like burning embers when I tug the towel. The fabric hitting the carpet sounds so loud, so *final*. Like a signal warning me that, now, there's no going back.

Before I have time to think, he grips my neck, sliding his fingers around the base of my braid. He pulls my face to his; I'm so close to his lips that for the small price of a million dollars, I could taste his last sip of vodka.

He holds me there for what feels like minutes, but can only be seconds. His jaw ticks like the clock on the mantel; his heart beats slower than my own. When I glance toward the bed, it's only because I need a breather from his suffocating glare, but by the way he laughs again, I realize he interprets it as a hint.

He thinks I want him to hurry up and fuck me.

With a curt nod, he releases me and steps aside. Every inch of my body trembles as I walk toward the bed and climb it on my knees.

Behind me, the bed dips with my heart. I drop to my forearms and bury my head in the pillow, as if the tension can't touch me down here. When Rafe's thighs press against my own and his dick grazes my ass, I squeeze my eyes shut, expecting the heat of his hands to sear my skin.

It doesn't come.

Instead, the mattress groans and the drawer beside me slides open. I turn my head just in time to see him take out a condom.

The sight catches in my throat. Of course, safe sex is important and all, but he didn't think twice about fucking me without protection before. Now, I feel like another number, another girl in his bed. The thought makes me want to set his whole fucking yacht ablaze.

I can feel a bitter retort creeping up my throat, but I bite down on the pillow to stop it. *This is what you wanted, remember?* As fucked-up as it seems, sliding into me without a rubber falls into the category of *nice*.

My stomach tightens as he pulls down my shorts. The fabric slides over my ass fast, then the movement slows down my thighs and with a hot whip of embarrassment, I realize why. The *fucking tattoo*. In the storm of dead men and key rings, I'd forgotten all about it. How could I? It's a big red heart with the name *Raphael* swirled through the middle of it.

A ragged exhale slips from his lips and dances up my spine. 'Is this a joke?'

'Tayce . . .' I swallow. 'It's temporary.'

Foil crinkles, latex *snaps*.

'How very fitting,' he says quietly, before plunging into me without warning.

Pain sears through me, but nothing is as painful as the weight of his palm on the small of my back. He's holding me awkwardly, covering the tattoo. I breathe deeply, trying to adjust. Despite the pain simmering to a delicious heat, I realize it doesn't fill the hollowness in my core like it did yesterday, but rather just move it north, so it sits somewhere behind my breastbone instead.

Rafe fucks me like he would a whore he'd paid in advance, before turning up and realizing she looks nothing like her photo. Then he fucks her anyway because she doesn't do refunds.

Each stroke feels clinical, like a step toward an end goal. Devoid of emotion, and it doesn't come with roaming hands or strangled Italian.

He fucks me until I can't bear the animosity. Until I'm on the brink of tears. Just as I turn around to grab his wrist, the words *I'm sorry* brewing on my tongue, his thighs tense against my ass and an animalistic groan escapes him.

My eyes sweep up to his, and he traps in his violent stare as he comes. He doesn't release me from it, not when his breathing shallows, nor when he pushes me off his dick.

It's me who turns away first. As my head falls back to the pillow, the bed dips again and he's gone with the click of a door.

I'm left with silence and another set of contradictions a whole lot worse than the last.

***

The ice-blue sky darkened hours ago, and now my restlessness is lit by moonlight and the floor lamp in the corner of the library. Sleep wouldn't come to me now even if I was narcoleptic.

I've spent the last few hours wearing a path in the carpet from the sofa to the badly-built bookshelf. The routine is well-rehearsed: I pick up a book, crack its spine, gloss over introductions, and glare at diagrams. Then I toss it into the *I don't give a fuck* pile at my feet.

In the silence, the truth is too loud. There's only one thing I give a fuck about right now and he's three rooms over.

He flew all the way to Atlantic City to take the heaviest load off my back, and all he wanted was a *thank you*. The word has blistered my skin all night. I didn't want to say it because the man has already coaxed a *please* from me, twice, but also because . . . why?

Every man has a motive, and Rafe's makes no sense. If I'm so unlucky to him, why not just kill me, instead of someone on my behalf?

Letting out a frustrated groan, I slam *Tennis for Dummies* shut and drop my head to the back of the sofa. I ache in all the places he didn't touch me earlier. There's a persistent throb at the base of my skull, which strengthens every time I close my eyes and see Rafe's violent gaze as he came inside a condom.

I'm hot. *Feverish.* Hoping a blast of December will put my world to rights, I shoot to my feet and fling open the door that leads to the deck. As I stand under its frame, icy wind pushes past me, rippling all the soft fabrics in the room and rustling book pages.

Numbness claws at my bare thighs, and a tremor ripples down my spine. Suddenly, my focus on the black abyss softens. That tremor . . . it didn't come from inside me.

'Oh, no, no, no,' I whisper. But before I can retreat, the night's sky lights up purple, a white flash of lightning streaking through the middle of it.

The only thing worse than a thunderstorm is being trapped on a *boat* in the middle of a thunderstorm. My heart stumbles with every beat, and a clammy sweat clings to my skin. Fumbling with the lock on the door, I press my back against it and squeeze my eyes shut.

Luck has all but left you, I try to reassure myself. *You haven't been lucky in weeks.*

But the next zap of lightning floods the room, bringing all my demons to light.

You know how lucky you are, kid? You're one in a million.
One in a million.

The thunder rumbles under the carpet as I bolt out of the library. It follows me through the study, into a living room. When I crash out into the corridor, I stop short.

At the end of it, Rafe's large silhouette consumes the shadows, his door clicking shut behind him. His gaze finds mine, something too soft to crack my heart dancing in the middle of it.

Somehow, it does anyway.

He steps into the path of light streaming through a porthole, and I realize he's naked. He holds something between his thumb and forefinger. A single die.

'Choose a number.' A strangled noise escapes me. He takes another step forward, voice firmer now. 'A number, Queenie.'

'Five,' I blurt out.

He tosses the dice and catches it. When he opens his palm, he nods in agreement. 'Five.'

'Really?'

His eyes flick back up to mine, glinting humorlessly. 'No.'

A bolt of lightning fissures the space between us. Before the thunder comes, I run toward him. It's not until my face is buried in his neck that I realize he's picked me up, his strong forearms caging me to him as he takes me into his quarters.

A gentle hand runs down my braid. Soothing words touch the shell of my ear, drowning out the next rumble of thunder. He lowers me to his bed, pulls me into his chest, and traps us under the covers.

I press my face against his chest and his fingers find purchase in the base of my hair. His other hand slides down my spine, traces the stupid heart on the small of my back, and a rough noise of approval vibrates behind his solar plexus.

When the next lightning bolt comes, it flashes through the sheets. Rafe brings his palms to my ears, dulling the impending roll of thunder.

'Thank you,' I whisper.

I don't specify what for. For shielding me from the storm, for killing Martin O'Hare. For giving me the two most ridiculous orgasms of my life. For the fucking *key ring*.

But the thunder is loud; my acknowledgment is quiet.

The only reason I know Rafe heard it is that his lips press down on my forehead, giving me the most gentle of kisses.

Rafe

I kill the car engine and turn to Penny in the passenger seat. Amusement warms my chest; she fell asleep an hour ago, and now her half-eaten burger is congealing in the carton on her lap. As I reach to remove it, her hand shoots out and grabs my wrist.

'I'm saving that for later.'

My gaze slides up to the one eye she's opened. 'I swerved to miss a deer earlier, and you didn't stop snoring, not even for a second. But the moment I come for your food, you're suddenly on high alert?'

'Don't fuck with my food,' she says seriously. She pushes herself upright and blinks at the church beyond the windshield. 'What's this? A flying visit to repent for your sins?'

I run my fingers through her hair, before tucking all the loose strands behind her ear. 'No, I'm conducting an experiment.' She cocks a suspicious brow. 'I'm going to throw you inside and see if you catch fire.'

Her laugh is croaky. 'If I burn in the flames of hell, you'll burn with me.'

Don't I know it.

'I won't be long.' My hands don't know how to leave the girl alone; they run over her body like every curve is still a novelty. I guess they are – it's been nearly a week since I sunk my dick into her for the first time, and I've yet to find an inch of her that I'm bored with. I slip one hand under her blanket and skim it up her thigh; the other grips her jaw and forces her to look at me. My voice drops to a mock warning. 'Don't drink my soda. I'll be able to tell.'

She twists her head to bite my hand, then rolls over to face the window when I release her. 'I'll think about it,' she mumbles, yawning.

'Sweet dreams, Queenie.'

The night is a blistering contrast to the warmth of my car, making me begrudge Angelo for calling an emergency meeting in the middle of the night even more. I'm the Visconti with the reputation for theatrics, but Angelo has a dramatic streak when he's pissed. I have no doubt that whatever he wants to bark at me could have been barked over the phone.

As I click the door shut, the headlights casting a glow on my wingtips give me pause. I crunch over gravel and ice to the car parked behind me. After my sharp *rap-tap-tap* on the glass, Griffin reluctantly rolls down the window and stares at me.

'The contract with the Albanians fell through. I'm going to need more eyes on my Vegas casinos. Roen and his men are vengeful little bastards.'

Griffin's stare sours on mine. 'So, you've pissed off the Irish *and* the Albanians. Got it.'

I eye him warily. 'The Irish have been dealt with.' The Irish issue ended when the coroner zipped up Martin O'Hare's body bag. No one else in that family would be stupid enough to come for a Visconti without Martin or Kelly at the helm. They wouldn't survive it. 'But yes, I've pissed off the Albanians.'

'And all in under a week,' he says dryly. His attention falls to my knuckles curled over the window frame. 'Plus, I'm sure Blake's family will want answers.'

Annoyance pulls my jaw taut. Griff has said about ten words to me since I left Blake for dead on the side of the road. Half of them were *yes boss* in the most sarcastic of tones, the other half unintelligible grunts. I let it go for a few days, because I knew he was probably pissed I'd left him a man short, but I think I've been more than gracious.

'Do you have something to say about me killing Blake?' I ask calmly. When he only stares in response, I dip my head into the car and get in his face. 'I don't pay you to have an opinion.'

Without waiting for an answer, I stride toward the church. Somewhere between our parents' gravestone and the wrought iron doors, Gabe's heavy stomps fall into rhythm with mine.

'Angelo's pissed at you.'

My laugh condenses against the night sky. 'What's he going to do? Fire me?'

His attention drops to my knuckles, then he smirks. 'I'm starting to think you like the dark side.'

'Mm. It's kind of fun over here.'

The church doors crack open, and to my surprise something small and four-legged bounds out of it. Angelo emerges soon after, swooping down to pick the dog up. 'Come here, you little shit,' he grunts. He ruffles its head and meets my silent query with a dark expression. 'Don't fucking ask.'

'But you know I'm going to.'

He sighs. 'She's a rescue from the shelter. Rory hasn't stopped going on about her since we visited, so I went back and got her for Christmas.'

'And you're carrying her around because . . .'

'Because every time I leave the house, my wife goes on a treasure hunt for her Christmas presents. The dog's been staying with the housekeeper, but she won't survive Rory's interrogation.'

Biting back a smirk, I regard the panting dog nestled in the crook of my brother's arm. With her golden curls and big brown eyes, she actually looks like my sister-in-law, but I'm in enough shit with Angelo that I think it best not to tell him his wife looks like a dog.

'You bring us all the way up here to pet her?'

Angelo grits his teeth. 'No, we need to talk.'

'Can we talk inside the church? Think my balls are getting frostbite.'

He cuts an annoyed look toward my car. 'I think your balls are getting plenty of warmth, brother. Here.' He turns his wrath to Gabe and shoves the dog into his arms. 'Take her for a walk.'

I cock a brow. 'You never read *Of Mice and Men*? Gabe is Lennie, only stronger.'

He ignores me, glaring at Gabe as he saunters off, comically small dog in tow.

When it's just us, he lets out a quiet, tense breath. 'You've lost the plot, Rafe.'

'Is that an official diagnosis or – ?'

He cuts me off. 'For once in your fucking life, stop talking shit and be straight with me. What's going on? Your head isn't in this war. Fuck, I'm not sure even sure your head is screwed onto your neck anymore.'

The flame of my Zippo cuts across the darkness. I light a cigarette and drop my head against the door of the church. He's got a point. I'd be lying if I said this war had crossed my mind even once in the last week. 'I've been busy.'

Angelo grinds out a sardonic laugh. 'Did you kill the other O'Hare?'

'Yes.'

'How?'

As I bring the cigarette to my lips, I glance over my busted knuckles. 'Messily.'

'Christ, Rafe. What happened to you?'

Something beyond the glowing cherry catches my eye. I tilt my chin to look at my car. Penny's awake now, her face lit by the light of her cell screen. The little brat is slurping on a soda. *My* soda. A smirk pulls on my lips, but I bite it back. *She* happened to me.

I blow out smoke against the night's sky and give my brother a less complicated answer. 'Bad things happened, brother.'

'So, make a plan and fix them.'

My gaze slides to him. 'What?'

'That's what you do in this family, you make plans to fix things. When Tor's last broad overdosed in the bathroom of the Visconti Grand, you drove her back to her apartment and wrote her suicide note. When Benny got held hostage by the Turks because of those dodgy shotguns he sold them, you flew to Istanbul and negotiated his release.'

'The cunt still hasn't said thank you,' I grunt.

'Hell, even when I set fire to Uncle Al's Rolls Royce, you somehow got me out of that mess, too.'

His heavy footsteps echo as he walks up the steps and joins me in leaning against the doors. I pass him the cigarette and he takes a long drag. He's right; I fix things. But that usual fire that burns through my veins when things go wrong has been replaced with a river of acceptance, cold and lethargic. Fate has won, and rock bottom feels solid under my wingtips. Just as Fate promised to give me all the success in the world, it also gave me my doom card. The Queen of Hearts brought me to my knees, and I can't find it in me to care.

Maybe it's because when I'm on my knees, she sits on my tongue.

'I don't even remember you being superstitious as a kid.'

Angelo's remark tightens my throat, sweeping away all thoughts of Penny's pussy. 'And I'm not superstitious now.'

He laughs. 'You think I don't see it? How you side-step ladders every time we check on reconstruction efforts at the port? How you toss salt over your shoulder every time I invite you to my dinner table?' He passes me the cigarette. 'I might have our father's temper, but you have Mama's beliefs.'

I grind my molars together, then blacken my lungs with smoke. 'You only see half the shit,' I mutter. 'If it was happening to you, you'd believe in bad luck too.'

Out the corner of my eye, I see him nod. 'I believe in bad luck, brother. But I also believe what Mama used to say.'

I turn to him. 'The good always cancels out the bad?'

He smiles sadly. 'Nah, the other one. Bad things don't last forever.'

Grinding the cigarette under his shoe, he follows my stare to my car. To Penny, who catches my eye through the windshield. She stills, like a deer caught in headlights, then with a shit-eating grin she takes an extra-long sip of my soda.

Something sweet and sickly blooms in my chest. She can have my drink. Fuck, she can have it all. There's nothing I wouldn't give her, and that's the problem.

The realization stabs me in the gut and twists clockwise. Angelo's been right too many times tonight for my liking, but he's also right about that.

Bad things don't last forever. They can't. Not my game with the Queen of Hearts. Not an enemies-with-benefits relationship – especially not between a girl who believes love is a trap and a man who chose the King of Diamonds.

This won't last forever. And then what?

I'll have to pick myself up from the ashes and start afresh.

'Forget about Dante. I don't need you for that. But I do need *you*.' Angelo's hand squeezes the nape of my neck. 'Make a plan, brother. And then come back to me.'

Penny

Restlessness haunts me like an itch I can't scratch. A disease I can't cure.

Sighing, I drop my forehead against a porthole and watch the raindrops as they race to the bottom of the glass. Is this what it feels like to be a fool in lust? It's *maddening*.

My body hums with an excited electricity, as though I'm forever plugged in at the mains. My mind keeps finding new Rafe-related things to obsess over. As I wait for this stupid lasagna to bake, it's his possessive grip on my hips as he came inside me an hour ago. Before that, it was how he licked me from clit to nipple in one desperate swoop of his tongue.

Shuddering, I pad over to the oven and crack the door to check on my creation again. Cooking isn't what I'd planned to do with my afternoon, and not because I'm shit at it. No, I was meant to go dress shopping with Rory for the staff Christmas party, but the weather is too bad to drive the speedboat.

Shame. I needed that shopping trip like I need air. As if filling my lungs with something other than this man would make the world stop spinning. Throwing the oven mitt on the counter, another more rational thought comes to mind. Maybe I'm so light-headed because the weight of Martin O'Hare was heavier than I'd realized. Of course, I'm going to look at the man who took that burden from me through rose-tinted glasses.

Within our mahogany-clad bubble, we've slipped into somewhat of a routine. We fuck all morning, then Rafe cooks eggs and sourdough toast while making angry Italian phone calls. Afternoons are lazy and lust-fueled, a blur of reading *For Dummies* books and endless games, where the loser succumbs to the mercy of the other. Nights are spent on the mainland in the warmth of Rafe's car. He conducts business while I fall asleep to the low hum of the heater, full of burgers and deliciously sore.

I rise to my tip-toes to grab two plates from the cupboard, and as the inside of Rafe's hoodie grazes against my bare nipples, they tingle from the friction. Breathless, I drop to my heels and lean against the counter, trying let the heat pass without me doing something stupid, like stomping into his office and demanding he puts his mouth on me again.

Fuck, I don't know about love, but lust *burns*. All this fucking is a gateway drug and now I need something more, something more potent.

A kiss.

Not enough to pay him a million dollars I don't have, of course, but still. It'd be nice.

As I'm dishing up the food, my cell buzzes on the counter with a text message.

Rafe: *Hot tub*.

Jesus, for such a smooth talker in person, he sure is stunted over text. But I decide against sending back a sassy message, because he locked himself in his office for the last hour, and I'm just happy he's finished working. I grab the plates and wobble through the yacht, trying to keep upright as the storm rocks the corridors.

When I kick the door open to the sky deck, my heart lurches at the sight. Behind a thin veil of steam and in front of the raging storm, Rafe sprawls in the hot tub, a vision of ink and muscle. His wingspan is ridiculous. His arms stretch out along the back rest, and just out-of-reach from his busted hand sits a glass of vodka. I glance at it, then at the cigar clenched between his teeth.

'What are we celebrating?'

'Me losing four million dollars in a racehorse investment.'

'Is that my fault?'

'Of course.' He glances down to the hem of the hoodie. I'm wearing nothing underneath but a thong and his belt marks on my ass. 'Get in.'

The rain beats on the awning above our heads. The wind whistles past Rafe's broad shoulders and lashes my skin. 'It's freezing!'

Smirking, he takes a slow puff on his cigar, the cherry glowing red like a warning sign. 'I'll warm you up.'

With a shiver entirely unrelated to being near-naked in a December storm, I drop our dinner on the side bar and slide the hoodie over my head and my thong down my thighs. Rafe's wolf-whistle is light-hearted, but ill-intentions swirl in his irises like slow-churning lava.

Under the weight of his molten attention, I step into the hot tub. The heat is like a hug, soothing the ache between my thighs and the bruises on my skin.

In an attempt to play it cool, I settle on the bench across from him, sliding down so everything below my shoulders is submerged in water. 'If it's any consolation, you're not losing *everything*. You've won every game of Mario Kart we've played.'

He lets out a soft laugh. 'Yes, but you're so bad I'm surprised you're allowed to have a driver's license in real life.'

I scowl. 'Fighting talk for a man who owns casinos yet can't grasp the basic rules of *UNO!*'

Biting back a smile, he drops his gaze to my collarbone. 'I'm not concentrating on the rules, Queenie. Come here.'

Letting out a tense breath, I swim into his orbit, coming to a stop when my knees brush against his. Steam rises from his body, like I've opened the door to a sauna. I resist the urge to run my hands down his wet chest and dip them under the water to see whether my fingers find swim trunks or not. Instead, I slide forward onto his lap and find the answer between my thighs.

As I let out a strangled sigh, he studies me with amusement over the length of his cigar. He takes a slow puff, then tilts his head up to blow the smoke over my head.

'Let me try it.'

Before he can protest, I take it from him and put it in my mouth. I take a drag, like I would a cigarette, and immediately start spluttering at the dry smoke filling my throat.

Large hands palm my back, and his chest vibrates against mine. 'Don't choke,' he says.

Opening my eyes, I'm met with the same humor-filled regard as I was the first time he said that to me – in the bar, after I slammed a shot of hundred-dollar whiskey. That feels like a lifetime ago now, and if you'd told me then that I'd be sitting on my mark's mega-yacht, in his hot tub, with his semi-hard dick nestled between my thighs and his watch still on my wrist, I'd have thought you were crazy.

'Here,' he says softly, spinning me sideways so I'm tucked into the crook of his arm. One hand rests heavy on my thigh, while the other slips the cigar back between my lips. Fuck, he makes me feel so *small*. 'Try again, but this time, close the back of your throat. You want to suck, but not inhale.'

My cough is less violent this time, but his laugh still rumbles against my shoulder. I reach for his vodka and wash away the tobacco taste. 'Still grim.'

'Mm,' he says, running his hand up my thigh and over my stomach. 'Tastes better with whiskey.'

I stare at the glass in my hand, flustering with a sudden bout of nervous energy. 'Damn, still drinking vodka?' My eyes crawl up to his. 'You must really want to kiss me.'

Hot, heavy seconds pass. My heart stills when he glances to my lips, but the look is over as quickly as it arrived. He puts the cigar in an ashtray and turns his attention to the plates on the side and changes the subject.

'And what is this?'

I give our dinner a careless glance. 'Slop.'

He smirks. 'Please tell me you didn't attempt to cook a hot-blooded Italian man a lasagna?'

But I'm barely listening. My mind is still stuck on the idea of kissing him, and suddenly, I can't concentrate on anything else.

Fuck this. The art of persuasion has gotten me six-figure timepieces and bulging wallets, and I can't persuade this one man to commit the modest act of putting his lips to mine?

Time to amp up the pressure.

Wrapping my arms around his neck, I twist around so I'm straddling him. His eyes narrow in suspicion, but when I lean back just enough for my breasts to bob out of the water, his expression melts into something more pliable.

'I kiss better than I cook,' I whisper, rolling my hips so my pussy glides over the length of his dick.

My skin dances as he palms my thighs and grips my ass cheeks. 'Yeah?'

I lean in, bringing my face so close to his, our lips are a hair's breadth apart. 'Yeah.'

When he closes the gap even more, my breathing shallows. My ears roar with a mix of heavy rainfall and my racing heartbeat. *He's really going to do it.*

His lips graze against mine. 'Prove it.'

We breathe in each other's air for a moment, the sparks of *what if*'s and *maybe so*'s dancing between us.

I'm buzzing off the anticipation, but I feign enough nonchalance to say, 'Okay.'

He leans back against the side, spreading his arms out like a fucking king. There's that satisfied smirk again, the one I've grown used to over the last week. I see it every time my Princess Peach avatar crashes out of the race. 'Okay.'

Letting out a shaky breath, I follow his retreat, pushing in between his thighs. I slide my fingers into the nape of his hair. The last thing I see before my mouth moves to his is the darkening of his gaze. Before our lips touch, I veer off course and plant a soft kiss on his dimple. Because of his own sleazy tactics, I know full well a kiss anywhere but the lips doesn't count.

His stomach tenses against mine, then releases with a sardonic chuckle. 'You're a fucking tease, you know that?'

Instead of replying, I turn my attention to his throat. Tugging on his short hair just enough to pull his head back, I kiss his pulse how I want to kiss his lips. Slowly, *sloppily*. A soft lick with my tongue and a hard suck with my mouth. As his hot hiss coasts over the shell of my ear, I make a porn-like noise, one I'm not sure is only for theatrics.

His cock stirs between my thighs, and the thought of him getting hard off a school-girl trick makes me drunk on a cocktail of lust and power. I pull away to tease him about it, but his hand shoots out and grabs my neck. He watches me in silence, a tightness to his jaw and a fire in his eye. When he speaks, his tone is calm.

'You're fucked, Queenie.'

Shit.

He chases me to the other side of the hot tub, grabbing my ankle and pulling me back into the water when I try to escape over the side. He pins me against the bench with his hard body.

When I make a pathetic attempt to push him off, he grabs both my wrists, holds them above my head, and presses his nose against mine.

Despite the chill coasting down my arms and breasts, I'm hot all over. Flashing me a look of pure venom, Rafe's head dips between his shoulders and his mouth latches onto my breast, giving it an angry suck before scraping his teeth over my nipple. All the nerve endings in my pussy flare up, desperate for *more*.

I push my tits against his face in a silent plea, receiving his groan of approval. His grip tightens on my wrists, and as I throw my head back, the sight of his muscles and tendons flexing in his forearms as he restrains me drives me *crazy*.

Before I can think about it, I wrap my legs around his waist, lick up the length of his bicep, and sink my teeth into his muscle.

'Fuck,' he hisses, letting my arms fall. 'Did you just *bite* me?'

I look at him seriously. 'You know what they say. Eat the rich.'

He stares at me in disbelief for a beat, then his eyes spark violently. His hands grip my hips. 'That's it, Queenie. Turn around.'

My body reacts before my brain can. Before my brain even knows what the fuck I'm doing, let alone *why*. I tighten my thighs around his waist, but when he twists me harder, I slip off him. The only way I can stop myself from turning is lifting my foot up and slamming it into his chest. My ass slides off the seat and my head dunks under water.

Rafe's hands slide under my armpits and put me back to rights. His amused expression melts into realization when he meets my eyes.

'Turn around, Penny,' he says quietly.

When I don't reply, he tries to twist me again. I put my foot back on his chest. His gaze slides down to it, then flicks back up to me.

'No,' I whisper.

My voice is calm but the insinuation screams.

I don't want him to fuck me like the others. In fact, the very thought makes me want to set the world on fire. At the very least, hunt down those other girls and do things to them that'll put me in prison.

With every silent second that passes, vulnerability rolls off me in waves. The fire between my thighs simmers to a tepid heat. I'm moments away from donkey-kicking him and biting out a nasty remark to protect my ego when he pushes my foot off him and closes the gap between us. With a rough grip on my wrist, he yanks me off the seat and takes my place, then pulls me onto his lap so I'm straddling him.

My high is shaky and impossible to conceal. I let out a ragged sigh and swallow the dryness in my throat. As Rafe's hand dips below the water and gently parts my thighs, he looks up at me with a lazy smolder.

'Is this what you want, Queenie?' he asks, so softly that I can barely hear him over the storm. He cups my jaw, running his thumb over my cheek as he studies my reaction. 'For me to fuck you like this?'

My stomach churns. I feel like I'm standing on the very edge of a cliff, inviting this man to push me off. I protect myself by stepping back from the edge.

Dropping my hand between his thighs and wrapping it around his length, I say, 'Getting railed from behind is getting a little old, don't you think?'

His lower stomach tenses against my knuckles. For the briefest of moments, his eyes blacken with irritation, but they cool to indifference as he releases his grip on my jaw.

He leans his elbows back on the side, as if settling in for a lap dance. 'Show me what you've got then,' he says in a bored tone.

His sudden apathy stings, but in the long run, I know it's

better than anything warmer. Anything that'd be harder to forget when this is all over.

With a flutter in my stomach, I realize I have no idea what I'm doing. I've never been on top, and in the cold light of day, I can't bury my inexperience in a pillow. I swallow my nerves and lift my ass up just enough to grind down on his erection. Fuck. It's so hard, so *smooth,* the sensation spreads from my clit through my veins. He drops his head back against the side, watching me through a lethargic, half-lidded stare as I roll my hips against him. I grow slicker, more sensitive, more desperate for friction.

He hisses when I dip my hand under the water and grip him at the base. He whispers a tight '*fuck*' when his tip pushes inside of me. But every inch I take stings a little more, the pain expanding up into my stomach and denting my confidence.

Fuck. He's so much deeper in this position, and I don't think I can take it. My eyes are watering by the time I'm halfway down. He regards my fingernails digging into his shoulder and his gaze softens.

'You haven't done this before.'

It's a statement, not a question, but I still tense with the urge to deflect it. Before I can, he puts his hands on my hips and slowly pulls me down onto him. 'Relax,' he murmurs, nuzzling into my neck. 'Let me inside of you, Queenie.'

I'd laugh if I thought it wouldn't come out bitter. Truth is, this man is so deep inside me already that I don't know how I'm ever going to get him out.

I wrap my arms around his neck, tilting my head to the storm-ravaged horizon as he rolls my hips for me in slow, cautious movements. The pain simmers to a delicious heat, the wet friction against my pussy making my muscles weak.

Now adjusted, I start moving my hips on my own, chasing my own pleasure. Rafe's groan rumbles against my throat. His hands move to my back and he rakes his thick fingers down my spine, stopping to swipe a thumb over the heart at the small of my back.

'This fucking tattoo,' he hisses, grazing his teeth against my collarbone and kissing a path down my breasts. 'What I'd pay Tayce to ink it on you permanently.'

There's a sarcastic retort about my next enemy-with-benefits probably not being happy about that somewhere at the back of my mind, but it doesn't come to fruition. Instead, I thread my fingers through the back of his hair and pull his face into my chest. My tattoo. *Us.* I don't want to think about temporary things right now.

I pick up the pace, trying to fuck reality away. Rafe adapts to my rhythm, taking over by gripping my neck and fucking me, *hard.* The scrape of his teeth against my nipples. His chest sliding against mine. He's so warm and large and *intense.* Every thrust feels like a stoke of a fire; I want to keep poking it until I burst into flames.

His lips press against the space behind my hair. 'Want to know a secret?' I can only nod in response. 'I've never done this, either.'

His confession slides up my spine and chokes me. I pull his head back and drop my forehead against his. Our mouths are so close, I can taste his last drag on his cigar. 'Really?'

Meeting my gaze, he slows his thrusts. The tiniest slither of unease mars his features. 'Yeah,' he murmurs back. 'Guess I just can't stop breaking rules for you.'

My skin dances in ecstasy. The idea that this is new for him too sends a smug satisfaction through my bones. Feeling a weird need to reward him for his honesty, I push myself down on him and hold myself there. His eyes flutter shut, and when he opens them again, they're filled with a new violence. With a grunt, he carries me over to the other side of the hot tub, slamming my back against the side.

His thrusts are sharp and unrelenting. His grip on my throat inescapable. He braces himself with a hand by my head and grits his teeth.

'I can't stand you, baby. Look what you do to me.' His next thrust feels like a punishment. 'You turn me into a fucking animal.'

When his eyes drop to my lips, I smirk. 'There you go, looking like you want to kiss me again.'

He rasps out a laugh. 'Nah. Just wondering what they'd look like wrapped around my cock.'

Flustered, I try to twist my face from his grip, but it only tightens on my jaw. I've never done *that* before, and the thought of being shit at it for him makes me cringe. It's clearly written all over my face, because his eyes narrow and his hips slow. 'You haven't done that either?'

'I'm saving blow jobs for marriage,' I blurt out.

His eyes flash black, and he slams into me a little harder. 'Liar. You don't believe in marriage.'

'True,' I breathe out, lifting my knees so he can get even deeper. White sparks fly behind my eyes. I'm *so close*. 'Marriage is a losing game, darling.'

His dark laugh skitters over my lips. 'Yeah? What would you lose?'

'My freedom. My dignity. My *pride*.'

He shakes his head again, smirking in disbelief. Glancing at my nails digging into his bicep, he drops his hand to my clit, rubbing in small, taunting circles. My toes curl up, and if it wasn't for his iron-clad grip on my face, I'd tilt my head back and cry to the pouring heavens.

Instead, I can only lock eyes with him as he picks me apart at the seams. His stare is different now, something pensive dampening the lust. 'And what would I lose?'

I swallow. 'If . . . we got married?'

Christ, even in a hypothetical situation, those words taste weird in my mouth.

He slides into me, but halts then holds himself there. Stops teasing my clit. Still and silent, he nods.

I breathe out shakily. 'You'd lose half your shit when I take it from you in the divorce.'

He stares at me for a moment, before grinding out a laugh of disbelief. 'I suddenly remembered why I prefer your head buried in a pillow when we fuck,' he growls, 'You talk too much.'

His hand moves from my jaw to my mouth, muffling my moans with his palm. I struggle against his restraint, only because he watches me with fascination when I do. The unadulterated lust in his expression and the hot, heavy weight of him against me sends me over the edge.

My orgasm is aggressive and bone-shaking, sweeping through me like a hurricane that doesn't care about the destruction it leaves in its wake.

When I float down, my senses sharpen enough to realize he's completely motionless. My next breath wets his palm. He removes it and runs a finger across my bottom lip, his eyes tracking the motion. When he looks back up at me, his expression is somber. Something about it tightens my chest. I don't dare breathe, let alone crack a joke.

Just as the tension starts to scorch, he thrusts into me again, slow and searing. He falls into a rhythm but doesn't pick up pace. Not when I tilt my hips, nor when I tighten my thighs around his waist.

He fucks me slowly. Fucks me steadily. And as his fingers skim a gently path down my side, an awful realization settles on my chest: we're not fucking at all.

There's another name for what this is, and it doesn't belong to us. It's permanent to our temporary; serious to our casual.

By the time his stomach tenses against mine and he fills me

with his warmth, I'm biting down the emotion in my throat. And when his breathing slows back to normal, the realization seems to hit him too.

He glances out at the storm. Runs a hand over the back of his neck. He pushes away and, despite feeling sick, I reach out and grab his wrist before he disappears completely, because somehow, that seems worse.

His gaze hesitates on the watch on my wrist, then skims up my arm and lands on my face.

I swallow. 'Bet you a hundred dollars I'll beat you at Mario Kart.'

We listen to the hammering of the rain. Finally, he nods. 'Make it two hundred and you have a deal.'

I watch his inked back flex as he jumps out of the hot tub and grabs me a towel from the side.

We both know I won't win, but I'd rather lose that game than this one.

Rafe

Twinkling lights pulsate on the Christmas tree; stockings swing above the roaring fireplace. The scent from all the cinnamon and clove candles hangs above the table in a festive haze.

My brother's dining room has been transformed into a fucking greeting card.

'All right, I've got a bet for you,' Nico murmurs, pulling out the chair next to me.

'I'm all ears.'

'Ten grand says Angelo dresses up as Santa on Christmas Day.'

Smirking into my palm, I look to the head of the table and consider this. Angelo's leaning on his knuckles, muttering in venomous Italian at Gabe, who looks like he'd rather be anywhere other than a Visconti family meeting.

My brother is more likely to burn a Santa suit than wear it, and I'm just about to tell Nico so when Rory bustles through the door with a tray of cookies. Angelo's eyes follow her, his face softening. As she drops the tray to the table, he leans over and kisses her on the forehead.

'They look beautiful, magpie,' he says. 'You're getting good at this.'

I flick a glance to the cookies. They're so burnt they look like they've been salvaged from a house fire, but it's then I realize; he'd do anything for her. If Rory asked him to wear a Santa suit, he'd do it. I used to think he'd turned into a simp, but fuck, I'm starting to understand that feeling now.

Swallowing the unease in my throat, I turn back to Nico with a plan. 'Twenty says he'll wear an elf outfit.'

He snorts into his whiskey. 'Everyone's saying you've lost the plot, and I'm starting to think they're right. Is it true you're a vodka man these days?'

I ignore his question and we shake on it. Then Angelo thumps on the table and commands everyone's attention.

'In the spirit of Christmas, I'm going to give everyone a free pass,' he says quietly. 'Get your shit jokes about the Christmas decor out now, or forever hold your peace.'

Silence cloaks the room, then Benny clears his throat. 'Looks like Santa came down the chimney and was sick.'

Everyone sniggers.

'I can see your house from Hollow. Bet you can see it from space, too.' Nico smirks.

Cas leans back, swirling his whiskey. 'You guys are being too harsh. I like it. It reminds me of Santa's Workshop.' He pauses. 'At the Devil's Dip outlet mall.'

Even Angelo laughs at that one, shaking his head.

'All right, all right, I've got one more.' Benny picks up a plastic snowflake off the table runner. 'You're brave having all this flammable shit lying around when your wife starts a fire every time she turns on the oven.'

The smile falls off my brother's face. Cas shifts in his seat. Gabe flashes me a look of lazy amusement.

'Ah fuck,' Benny hisses, sensing the mood shift. 'I've got no more fingers to break.'

With a flick of his wrist, Angelo slides the tray of cookies across the table. 'You wanna make jokes about my wife's cooking, you're gonna eat every single one.'

Benny stares at them in disbelief. 'Okay, I'd rather break my fingers than my teeth.'

Angelo ignores him and sinks down into his chair. 'Right, enough of the shit. We need to talk about Cove. Since Tor has disappeared off the face of the fucking planet, Cove will be left wide open when we get Dante out of the picture.' He smooths a hand down the front of his turtleneck and turns his attention to me. 'My brothers and I have decided we'll give him until the New Year to make an appearance before we implement a plan and take Cove over.'

Bitter humor fills me. *Decided* makes it sound like we had a civilized discussion, when really, we barked at each other in rapid-fire Italian in his office for twenty minutes. He wanted to take it over immediately, while I wanted to give my best friend the benefit of the doubt and wait a few weeks.

He threw a snow globe at my head, I hurled it back with a better aim, and we settled on January 1.

My cell buzzes on the table, and when I glance at the screen and see it's a message from Penny, the conversation around the table fades to background noise.

I snatch it up, open the message, and immediately wish I hadn't. She sent a picture of herself in front of a mirror, stark-fucking-naked. Letting out a slow hiss, I lean back in the chair and zoom in on every perfect part of her.

Christ, she can't be real. I almost wish she wasn't, now that I've shattered yet another rule and fucked her face-on. Usually, I only do doggy because I hate looking into a woman's eyes and seeing my last name flash in lights behind them as they come. It's off-putting. But with Penny, that was never going to be the case. No, I knew if I looked into her eyes as she came undone, I wouldn't be able to look away. Wouldn't be able to forget them, either. I know when she's done with me and I'm left in the ashes of her fire, I'll be looking at another woman's headboard and seeing those fucking eyes on it.

Another text comes through.

> **Penny:** Oops, I sent that to the wrong number. Sorry.

Even though I know she's joking, the thought of another man seeing that body makes a jolt of violence zap through me.

I'd kill him without a second thought, and definitely not with my gun.

My mood darkens the more I ponder it. Then it flashes midnight-black when I remember her words in the hot tub last night. *I'm saving blowjobs for marriage.* If she was trying to piss me off while I was balls-deep inside her, it worked.

I'm deranged. Despite knowing this is temporary, *has* to be temporary, I know I'd give this girl the world on a silver platter, if she just said *please* like she does now when she wants to come.

The ironic thing is that she doesn't want the world. She doesn't even want me to be soft with her. I've killed for her, broken my rules for her. Fuck, ruined my hands for her. Yet while I'm going crazy thinking of ways I can brand her for longer than that temporary tattoo lasts, she's talking about the future with the same kind of indifference as one talking about the weather. Plus, she's flying through the *For Dummies* books I bought her, looking for something, *anything*, to do aside from stay on my yacht and fuck me.

Running my tongue over my teeth, I zoom in on her pussy again, and all my anger runs into a liquid heat and slides south. I adjust my slacks and tap out a response.

> **Me:** You really want me to fuck you hard tonight, huh?

Her response is quick and irritating: a fucking *yawn* emoji.

> **Me:** Those lips are mine, Penny.

I toss my cell on the table in finality. I've decided to stop asking her who her pussy belongs to and just fucking tell her until she believes it.

My cell buzzes and I immediately snatch it back up.

> **Penny:** Which pair?

I pause.

> **Me:** Not the ones on your face.

> **Me:** They're too expensive.

> **Penny:** You can pay me in installments over a six-month period with an APR of 5.8%. How about that, sugar daddy?

I laugh aloud. When I left her a few hours ago, she was in the library reading *Investments for Dummies,* and clearly, she's soaked something up.

My skin prickles with sudden awareness: The room has fallen silent and all eyes are on me. Wiping away my smirk, I glance up at Angelo simmering at the head of the table.

'Griffin and his knock-knock jokes,' I say dryly, putting my cell in my jacket pocket. 'They get me every time.'

Angelo's jaw ticks. 'Were you even listening to anything I just said?'

No. 'Of course.'

'And what do you think we should do about it?'

I pause. 'Rocket warhead.'

Cas laughs into his whiskey, and even Gabe's lips tilt.

'*Cazzo,* if you weren't sexting, you'd know we were talking about the Visconti Grand,' Angelo says tensely. 'I thought you of all people would be interested in what becomes of it, considering the casino alone takes over eight-hundred-million dollars a year.'

'Mm. It wouldn't if I got my hands on it.'

With my current luck, there'd be debt collectors banging on the door after a month. I smirk at the irony of it. I'm the great Raphael Visconti, the king of casinos. Everything I touch used to turn to gold. Now, it just rusts under my fingertips.

Bored with my brother's glare and itchy to get back within reaching distance of Penny's ass, I rise to my feet and rap my ring against the table.

'This meeting could have been an email. Someone send me the CliffsNotes.'

As I pass Angelo, his gaze drops to my hand. 'Make that plan, brother,' he mutters, just loud enough for me to hear.

His words squeeze my throat, but I stroll into the hall like they didn't.

I'm reckless, not stupid. The reason I'm not taking the fate of Cove seriously is because I'm still clinging onto the hope that Tor will come back. That he just went on a crazy three-week bender after the wedding and lost track of time, or something.

Fuck. It sounds ridiculous, even when I only say it in my head.

'Rafe!'

Jingling my car keys in my hand, I turn to Rory running down the stairs, clutching shopping bags. 'Here, give these to Penny.'

I regard them with caution. 'I hope these are clothes and not your leftover Christmas decorations.'

'Is it too much?' She sighs. 'It's too much, isn't it?'

Over her shoulder, a mechanical Santa waves at me from the foot of the stairs. It's twice the size of her and three times as scary. 'I think it's very . . . fun.'

Her face lights up. 'I think so too! Christmas Day is going to be a blast.'

I shake my head, smirking. She's never been to a Visconti Christmas before and it shows. I wonder if she'll still think it's a blast when Cas puts his gun to Benny's head because he cheated at Monopoly, or when Nico's getting sick in the garden because he drank too much eggnog.

'You know what will make Christmas Day even better? Your husband dressed up as an elf.'

She scoffs. 'What? He'd never . . .' Her protest trails off as I pull out my wallet and hand her all the cash inside. She stuffs it into her back pocket, grinning. 'You know what? Maybe he would. Anyway, here.' She thrusts the bags into my chest. 'Tell Penny I picked her out some pieces for the staff party tomorrow, because she couldn't come shopping with me. Tell her the red Chanel looks cute with the Y.S.L heels, but the heels also pair gorgeously with the Bulgari two-piece.'

Amusement pulls at my lips. 'You might as well be talking in Chinese, sis, but I'll be sure to pass the message along.'

It's only early evening, but darkness is already shading the sky. A low mist lingers between the Christmas trees on the circular drive, lit red and green from the glow of all the lights. I almost slip on the way to my car, thanks to the fucking fake snow coating the porch steps.

Cursing Rory and her festive enthusiasm, I slide into the passenger seat. Immediately, something I can't put my finger on gives me pause. It squeezes my nape and sharpens my senses. This survival instinct is why Viscontis live longer than most made men, and I know I should trust it. Key hovering near the ignition, I look through the windshield and lock eyes with Griffin on the other side of it. He and three of my men are in an armored sedan opposite, ready to trail me back to the docks.

I put the key in, but I don't twist it.

I swallow. Sweep the idea out of my head. No, if someone had fucked with my car they'd be dead already. Griff and my men have been out here the whole time.

Still, as I turn the key, my shoulders tense in anticipation. When my car doesn't blow up, I let out a dry laugh and peel out of the grounds, wondering when the fuck did I become so paranoid. The O'Hares are six feet under, and Dante couldn't organize a car bomb even if there was one of Penny's *For Dummies* books on it.

The roads are slippery and silent and familiar. I could take these curves with my eyes closed. Zoning out on the yellow glow of my lights on the tarmac, I become more aware of the inside of the car, where Penny's image lingers like a long-term memory.

Her presence fills the space like she fills my head. Her citrusy scent has permeated my Nappa leather seats; three of her *For Dummies* books are piled up on top of her blanket and pillow on my backseat. Fuck, her fluffy slippers are in the passenger footwell, and her hairbands are littering my cup holder.

As I pick up one of her hairbands and bring it to my lips, my smirk falls as a searing realization bowls through my chest.

The girl is fused to me – every fucking part of me. I don't know how I'm going to cut her out when the time comes. How can I make a plan for the future when I can't see past the length of my dick, especially when Penny's on the end of it?

Muscles tightening, I reach for my cell for release. I have this habit of playing her hotline ramblings through the speakers when I'm in the car alone. I'd never let the thought slide into my head fully-formed, but I have a sad feeling it's because her voice filling the car makes it feel like she's in the passenger seat, talking shit to me until she falls asleep.

I connect to the Bluetooth and click on the most recent log. Her calls have diminished significantly in the last week, from a half-dozen a day to one or less. I don't know if it's because the cell signal on the boat isn't that great, or because I'm around most of the time.

Glancing at the timestamp on my cell screen, I realize the call is from less than an hour ago. I press play, and settle in.

It's pathetic. The moment her voice floats out of the speakers and touches my ears, I'm smiling into my knuckles. She starts off summarizing her morning – *I ate eggs, lost a few games of Mario Kart, then went into the library to read*. She then moves on to bitching about *Weight Training for Dummies*. *I don't know why I bothered picking this one up,* she says dryly, the *thump* of a book hitting a hard surface echoing down the line. *My arms get shaky brushing my hair. How am I going to pick up a dumbbell?*

Amusement fills me, then wilts around the edges. Maybe it's the narcissist in me, but I loathe that she's never mentioned me to the hotline. She ate the eggs *I* made her, lost a few games to *me*. I'd understand if she didn't talk about anyone else, either, but she does. Matt, Rory, Wren, Tayce – they all have starring fucking roles in her calls.

The irritation is making me feel all irrational and hot, so I stab the pause button and fester in the silence. I crack the window, hoping the icy wind will bring my senses back to me.

Because even when she pisses me off I still want to please her, I flick my indicator on, swing onto Main Street, and stop outside the diner. A glance in the rearview mirror confirms Griffin does too.

I put the car in park. Kill the engine. And then there's that hand on the nape of my neck again, only this time it squeezes harder.

Every made man expects death, so why at every funeral do the living mutter that they never saw it coming? I guess no one likes to believe it'll come for one of their own at the most mundane of times, like on a weekday afternoon outside a fast-food joint that sells two-for-one burgers.

I wouldn't see it coming either, had instinct not just turned my head to the right, to the car with the tinted window open just enough for me to see the gun pointing at my temple.

I've no time to do anything but laugh and wonder what the weather is like in hell today. The roar is deafening; the *pop* is familiar. But then it's not my window that smashes, not my head that gets blown off.

The tinted glass shatters, revealing the lifeless body in the driver's seat. Beyond it, a motorcycle helmet with a reflective visor is framed by the passenger-side window. It disappears from view and then four *pops* ring out behind me.

Confusion slows the adrenaline in my veins. The muffled *rap-tap-tap* of a gloved hand knocking on my passenger window pulls my attention. I roll down the glass and the helmet-clad head dips into my car.

The visor flips up, revealing green eyes and an angry scar.

'Now that I've saved your life, do I still need to get you a Christmas present?'

Rafe

The cigar room is dark, and death lingers in the air like a bad smell. If it were my other brother sitting opposite me, he'd demand I turn on a light and crack a window. But Gabe is content in the shadows, relaxed in an armchair and puffing on a cigar.

'How did you know Blake was Griffin's nephew?'

The cherry of his cigar glows red. 'How did you not?'

Huffing out a dry laugh, I run a hand down my throat, feeling it tremble over my pulse. My brother's question gnaws at the one thing I bring to this family: common sense.

Griffin's shouts as I broke my knuckles on Blake's jaw. His coldness in the days that followed. I should have seen the signs and dug deeper. Instead, I muffled them with the weight of Penny's thighs. Drowned them out with her too-loud laugh. I couldn't see them past the girl's heart-shaped back tattoo, even if I'd tried.

Under Gabe's judgmental glare, I pour vodka into a tumbler and down it in one.

'I knew something wasn't right after you killed Blake and I

stayed behind to clean up the mess. Griffin was all over the place, trying to stop me as I dragged Blake's body to the edge of the cliff. Then there were the hushed phone calls in his car.' Gabe's eyes lift to mine, cigar smoke swirling in front of them. 'One of my men did some digging and stumbled across his family tree.'

Another laugh escapes me, this one acidic. I guess nepotism is rife in every fucking industry, then. Maybe Blake being Griffin's nephew was too soap opera-ish for me to connect the dots, but with hindsight being a smug little prick, I can now see something was off. All my men are ex-military, and yet, this kid always acted like he'd just gotten his first gun for Christmas and couldn't wait to shoot it in the yard.

Still, I'd trusted Griff to do all the background checks, and to train them all up to our standard. Fuck, I'd trusted that man with my life.

'I've been following you.'

I pause. 'You have?'

Our eyes clash, and for once I can read my brother's expression like a book. If he was following me without me noticing, anyone could have.

Before my glass reaches my lips again, those awful Visconti traits, violence and impulsion, grip me and I lash out, hurling the tumbler at the wall.

Glass shatters. Liquid splashes. Gabe glances indifferently at the mess and says, 'At least vodka doesn't stain.'

Ignoring the fact that my brother chose today of all days to develop a sense of humor, I rise and pace the room, lacing my hands behind my head.

I've been riddled with bad luck for three weeks, but nothing stings quite as much as being confronted with your own mortality. I guess in the grand scheme of things, everything else I've lost hasn't mattered. Money, bets, business. It's all trivial shit that can be replaced, but my heartbeat can't.

Gabe's gruff voice coasts over the planes of my shoulders. 'As much as I hate to admit it, Vicious is right. You need a plan.'

I stop in front of the French doors and glare out to the ocean. It's ink-black and sparkling. My eyes find the staff speedboat bobbing in the path of the moonlight. Two of Gabe's men heave a body bag overboard; it dips under the surface with a violent splash. The next two lumps are just as heavy. When a fourth doesn't emerge, I frown.

'Where's the fourth body?'

'Griffin isn't dead, only maimed.' His knuckles pop. 'I'm saving him for later.'

Visions of Gabe's cave flash against the window. I grind my teeth; even my brother's sadistic tool box isn't punishment enough for the cunt that betrayed me.

'Plan,' Gabe presses.

I push a rough hand through my hair. A plan? I don't have a plan and I don't know why I ever did. It's clear the second I tapped the King of Diamonds, Fate took over planning my life for me. All I had to do was follow the motions and avoid the Queen of Hearts.

Instead, I let her in, even if only temporarily, and I can't say I regret it. The worst part is that I actually *liked* the reckless thrill of the bottom, but now I realize it wasn't the bottom at all. Just a rest-stop on the way down.

Maybe it's the near-death experience that loosens my tongue, or maybe it's because I've drunk half a bottle of vodka, but I find that I have to confide in my brother or else something else is about to get smashed.

'It's the girl,' I grind out, glaring at my reflection in the glass. 'She's bad luck. Ever since she came into my life, everything's gone up in flames.'

The silence echoes. It's so loud that my shoulders clench when the groan of an armchair interrupts it.

There's a clatter of metal on wood, then heavy footsteps move away from me.

'Then take her out of it,' Gabe says quietly.

The door slams shut behind him.

I don't want to turn around because I know what I'll find, but tonight I've been confronted with all the truths. So, fuck it; what's one more?

Gabe's half-smoked cigar rests easily in an ashtray. Next to it lies a gun, a silencer screwed onto the end of it.

***

The calm before the storm always holds a certain charm. Outside, the waters are at peace, gently rocking the boat to sleep. The moonlight pours through all the portholes and glints off the chrome surfaces in the kitchen.

The digital clock on the oven glows. I was only meant to be passing through, but somehow, hours have passed and I'm still here, palms braced on the counter.

I've smoked seven cigarettes and I can't smoke another.

I swipe up the whiskey glass and bring it to my lips. The bitter smell under my nose gives me pause, but then I slam it in one go. The heat fizzles in my chest until a hollowness forms there. I have an awful feeling it's going to be permanent.

I didn't even want the fucking whiskey. I only drank it because I knew once I did, I couldn't turn back.

The knife makes a menacing *swish* when I drag it off the counter. It's only a paring knife, anything larger would be noticeable, and I can't bear the thought of her being scared in her final seconds. Gabe's gun, even with the silencer, was out of the question for the same reason.

Too much liquor gives me a tremble in my knees as I make my way out of the galley and into my private chambers. The squeeze in my chest has nothing to do with my vodka-whiskey mix and everything to do with her.

Fate fucked me. She assigned the Queen of Hearts as my doom card then sent me a girl I'd never be able to resist. Not only have I let her into my life, I've let her under my skin. She crawls inside me now, does stupid shit to my heart, the shit people make songs and movies about.

But there's no sunshine and rainbows in this story, only losses and near-death experiences.

I can't keep her and I can't let her go.

Turning into the corridor, I see the orange glow seeping out from under my cabin door, and unease fills my stomach like cement. Fuck, although I knew she'd be awake – she still only sleeps in my car – the reality of it makes me nauseous.

I can only hope I make it painless.

I'm hiding the knife against the small of my back, but as I enter the room, I might as well have stabbed myself with it.

Penny's asleep. Curled up on my side of the bed, her hair fanned over my pillow. Her skin radiates gold where the light of the lamp touches her. Her *For Dummies* book is open at the end of the bed; a cup of tea sits half-drunk on the bedside table.

Emotion closes my throat. Fuck, I wasn't expecting this. She's in my bed, my home, asleep. She can't even sleep in her own bed, but now she's sleeping in mine. The sight should make this easier, but it only makes me want to claw my fucking heart out of my chest.

I'm sure it'd hurt less.

Grinding my molars, I take a step forward. The floor creaks under my foot, and Penny jerks awake. Her gaze is unfocused, her hair mussed as she props herself up on the pillow. When her eyes slide to mine, they sharpen.

She bolts upright. 'I've done something awful, please don't hate me.'

My grip tightens on the knife handle. 'What?' I growl.

The covers crumple at her feet as she scurries up to the headboard. 'Say you won't hate me first.'

I glare at her. 'Penny,' I warn.

She sighs, drops her attention to my shoes, and fingers her lucky necklace. 'I found a cheat code on some dodgy website for Mario Kart. But instead of adjusting my score, it just deleted yours. All your trophies, too.' She glances up at my stony expression. 'I'm sorry, okay! I know I said I wouldn't swindle anymore but I just couldn't resist. You're always so smug about being better at it than me. I just . . .' She scowls. 'It makes me want to bite you.'

I stare at her.

Then all my insides crumple like a house of cards.

Fuck. Who am I kidding? I can't kill the girl, even when the only other option is killing myself. Now, I'm looking into her big blue eyes and I actually feel like doing that. Guilt gnaws at me, making me sick and hot.

Her eyes search mine, panic flickering in them. 'Say something.'

My laugh comes out bitter and tinged with disbelief. Fucking Mario Kart. I killed off all her big problems, and now all she has left are soft and innocent worries. Suddenly needing to be near her, *inside her,* I take a step to the lamp and plunge the room into darkness. Then I slide the knife into my top drawer and crawl into bed with her.

'Come here.'

She tenses under my touch, but I slide my hands up under the hoodie – she's barely taken off since I demanded she put it on – and I pull her toward me, until every inch of her warm skin sizzles through my suit. I run my fingers through her hair. It smells like nostalgia and temptation. She's so still, I don't even think she's breathing.

Her lips tickle my throat. 'You don't hate me?'

I smile sadly into her crown. 'Of course I hate you; we're enemies with benefits, remember?'

She pauses. 'But no more than usual, right?'

'No more than usual, Queenie.'

Her little sigh of relief makes her body melt into mine. Now, I can feel her heartbeat against mine, feel her lungs rising and falling under my palm on her back. Fuck, to think I was about to snuff this life out of her.

Before the guilt pounding behind my breastbone becomes unbearable, she wriggles from my grasp and props herself up on her elbow. Backlit by moonlight, she peers down at me.

'Tell me why you call me Queenie.' The tips of her hair brush against my forearm. I twist them around my fist, pulling her head down to mine. My forehead presses against hers. We're so close her lashes tickle my cheeks. 'I know it's not because you think I'm regal,' she says.

'If I tell you –'

'You'll have to kill me, yeah, yeah,' she grumbles, sticking her tongue out and licking my nose.

I choose wiping my wet nose over hers instead of responding. I wasn't going to say I'd have to kill her; that'd be a bit fucking ironic, all things considered.

No. I know if I told her she was my Queen of Hearts, she'd want to leave.

I push her elbow so it falls from underneath her and she comes crashing down on my chest with a yelp. I wrap my arms and legs around her so she can't escape.

Even though she's brought me to my knees and set my world on fire around me, I'm not letting her go anywhere.

Rafe

Christmas Eve on the yacht.

The staff party is fueled by festive cocktails and the type of glitter I'll still be brushing off my suit come Easter. Leaning against the bar, I watch in amusement as Nico cuts through the tables toward me.

I know what he's going to say, because he always fucking says it.

'Whose idea was karaoke?' He swipes an eggnog off the bar and regards the set-up over the glass rim.

Laurie has done a solid job. The stage is lit with Christmas lights and flanked by two towering Christmas trees. A large projector screen covers the wall behind it, displaying the lyrics to whatever song is being butchered by whoever imbibed enough mulled wine to believe they're Mariah Carey.

'Why, not enjoying it?'

He stares at Benny, who's on stage crooning along to Janis Joplin's *Mercedes Benz*. His mulled wine must be super-spiked, because his hip thrusting rivals Elvis. 'Are you kidding? Name a better combination than drunk people and a microphone.' He shakes his head. 'You can't, because there isn't one.'

Laughing, I down my vodka and flick the tumbler across the bar for a top off.

'And I suppose we have you to thank for this glorious show, Laurie?'

'Yes, Nico, you do.' I turn just as Laurie slides in between us. She sparkles in a silver dress, and her reindeer ears wobble when she whips her head around to glare at me. 'Boss, I have a bone to pick with you.' She pauses, cocking her head. 'Only a small one, obviously, I don't want to get fired.'

I laugh and press an eggnog into her hand. 'Hit me with it.'

'You told me to organize a *staff* Christmas party. Why is your entire family here?' She sneers toward the stage. For some reason, Benny's now sliding across it on his knees. It's not even nine p.m. 'And why's that idiot asking the Lord Jesus for a Mercedes Benz? He already has three of them.'

'Uh-huh, and how would you know?' Nico asks, quiet humor tugging his lips.

Laurie doesn't flinch. 'I've fucked him in two, and I keyed the third,' she says simply.

I shake my head. 'I really didn't need to know that. Here.' I pull out a small velvet box from my pocket. 'I was going to give this to you later, but since you're pissed off, it might sweeten you up a little.'

She eyes it in mock suspicion, but she can't hide the excitement dancing behind her glare. 'If it's an engagement ring, I'm not signing a prenup.'

'Good thing it's not an engagement ring then.'

Her annoyance evaporates when she snaps it open and tugs out an Audi car key. 'Oh my god, you're shitting me.'

I raise my glass to her. 'Heated seats, white trim. Already

parked outside your apartment. Now you can fuck my cousin in your car where there's more room.'

She flings her arms around me, squeals her gratitude and insists Benny's sticky fingers won't be allowed anywhere near her white seats, then she bounces over to the other girls to jingle the key in their faces.

As my gaze follows her, it slides left and locks onto Penny's. Man, she's just got this way of making my heart flinch every time she does that – catch my eye from across the room. She's at the side of the stage with Rory, who's studying the karaoke book. Penny grins at me, then pretends to pick her nose. Only when I realize it's her middle finger stuffed up her left nostril do I realize she's flipping me off.

I huff a laugh into my vodka and flip her off back. The heat of Nico's stare burns my cheek.

'Be good to her, Rafe.'

Nico's voice is quiet but it still squeezes my spine. *Good to her?* Fuck, if only he knew how good I am to her. This morning, I stared at her for an hour as she snored beside me. Maybe it was the guilt of nearly slitting her throat or the fascination that she was sleeping in my bed, but I brought her breakfast on a fucking tray. Even put a flower I'd swiped out a vase in the dining room on it. When she tells me not to be nice to her, she no longer says it with a grimace but a smile, and this little eye roll that makes me want to be nice to her all the time.

I drag my hand over my throat. An hour watching her, yet I still don't have a plan to get out.

'What was she like?' I say suddenly. 'As a kid?'

By the way Nico purses his lips, I don't think he's going to answer. He glances up at Penny, who's now impatiently tapping a stiletto and glaring at Benny as he takes an unrequested encore.

'She was a little shit,' he laughs. With a more serious tone, he adds, 'She was lucky. Still is.' I rub my mouth, the irony prickling at my skin. 'All the patrons at the Grand thought it. At first, it was just because of her name. You know – find a Penny, pick it up, all day long you'll have good luck? Well, when they actually started picking her up and letting her blow on their dice, it turned out that old adage was true.'

I frown. 'She'd actually make them lucky?'

'Always. Back then, I only knew her from seeing her around. But then one day she started charging men a dollar to blow on their dice, and I wanted to know why.'

I bite out a laugh. 'She was hustling from a young age, then.' Nico glances at his shoes, but I press on. 'Did you know her parents?'

He cuts me a dark look. 'Alcoholics. She spent more time with me in the cloakroom than she ever did with them. Some nights, they'd forget she existed and one of my father's men would have to drive her home.'

This irritates me beyond belief. The thought of this little red-head sitting on the steps of the Visconti Grand, waiting in vain for her parents, makes my stomach churn and my fingers twitch to break something.

'Who killed them?'

He shrugs. 'No one important. Two men they were in debt to. Not a Visconti.'

Like stills from a black-and-white film, my mind cuts from the little girl on the steps to the teenager cowering between the fridge and the washing machine, a gun that'd never go off pressed to her head.

'And where can I find these men?' I ask, as calmly as I can muster.

He swallows. Shakes his head. 'Both were found with bullets in their heads a few days later.' He gulps his eggnog and grabs another. 'They were unofficial loan sharks in Visconti territory, you can connect the dots.'

Penny's loud laugh touches my ears and draws me back to her. She's going through the karaoke book now, my watch sliding up her wrist with every flip of a page.

'Nico?'

'Uh-huh?'

I turn to him. 'You taught her to swindle, didn't you?'

He pauses for the longest time, eggnog halfway to lips. 'Depends.'

'On?'

His expression turns thoughtful. 'How much it's going to hurt when you swing for my jaw. I've never seen you hit anyone, so I can't gauge it.' He pauses. 'But I've heard you do that now.'

Laughing, I clap him on his back and push off the bar. 'You're a good kid, Nico. I'll let you off this time.'

He's right to be concerned, though. I'm a big believer in cheats getting punished, but I'll give him a pass, because the thought of him being the one stable presence in Penny's childhood instantly bumps him up the ranks to favorite cousin.

Leaving Nico with his third eggnog and a reminder of what happens when he gets past five, I take a seat beside Angelo. Over the rim of his whiskey, he cuts a glance at me, then to the vodka I set on the table. He turns his attention back to his wife stepping on stage and says nothing.

'Where's Gabe?'

'I don't know. Where's Griffin?'

By the tick of his temple, I'm certain he knows where both men are. My former head of security, along with all the men underneath him, are in the depths of our brother's cave. Some to be tortured, some to be interrogated. I'm not sure who of my men I can trust now, but one thing's for sure; Gabe will send only the loyal ones back to me.

In the meantime, his men are surrounding my boat like the

crown jewels are onboard. No doubt they've had a stern warning from my brother, because one of them even followed me into the fucking bathroom earlier.

'Have you made a plan yet?'

That fucking question. It sparks something hot and irritable in my stomach. 'Did you make a plan, brother, when you shot our father in the head? Or when you blew up Uncle Al's Rolls in a fit of rage? Or when you shot his lackey between the appetizers and the entrees at Sunday lunch?' I lean over the table so only he can hear my venom. 'Did you think for a fucking second of the consequences, or were you just living in the moment?'

His stare slides to mine, the heat of it dampened with mild curiosity. 'Is that what you're doing? Living in the moment?'

I run my finger across my collar pin. Glance back up at Penny. Right now, I don't know how to live anyplace else.

Darkness shades Angelo's glare; someone dimmed the lights. He turns back to the stage, straightening when he realizes his wife has taken center stage.

The mic thuds when she taps it. 'Hello, lovely people. Since I seem to be the only person to grace this stage tonight who remembers it's Christmas Eve, I shall be singing a festive classic.' The lopsidedness of her grin tells me she's been on the white-wine spritzers. 'I'll be singing, *Baby, It's Cold Outside.*' Squinting into the spotlight, she spots Angelo and beams at him. 'Obviously, it's a duet, so . . .'

The room starts cheering my brother on.

'No chance,' he mutters, scowling behind his whiskey.

'Pretty please?' Rory says sweetly, clasping her hands together.

He stares at her for a few seconds. The moment his shoulders slump in defeat, I press the heel of my shoe against the toe of his under the table to stop him getting up.

'You are a capo, brother. You command respect from every

man in this room. Do you think that'll be the case when you sing Tom Jones's part to a Christmas song? Sit the fuck down.'

'Fuck,' he grunts, stroking his jaw. 'You're right. Think I need to switch to water for an hour.'

When he shakes his head to Rory, she yells *boring!* down the mic, and Tayce fills in for my brother.

I'm not watching Rory butcher Cerys Matthews' lines; I'm watching Angelo. How he's staring at her like there's no one else in the room. How he lunges over and smacks one of my deckhands upside the head when he dares to talk over the chorus. How he rises to his feet and whistles as she and Tayce take a bow.

When he sits back down, he's still grinning.

'How did you know?'

It slides off my tongue, loosened by liquor and this weird, foreign feeling that's been sitting under my ribs for the last few days. He turns to me. Confusion mars his face but only for a split second, then mild amusement replaces it.

He knows what I mean.

'When you start doing stupid shit, like eating spaghetti with raw meatballs and going back for seconds, because she cooked it. Smuggling a labradoodle out of your house in a duffle bag at three a.m. so it's still a surprise on Christmas Day.' His attention falls to my knuckles and his jaw tightens. 'When you start using your fists because you need to the feel the bones of the man that hurt her break underneath them.' He eyes my vodka and shakes his head. 'When you start drinking like a Russian, even though you own a seventeen-percent stake in one of the fastest-growing whiskey companies in the world.' Meeting my eyes again, he adds, 'That's how you know.'

There's a fresh wave of cheers, but I hear them like I'm underwater. A very un-festive guitar riff pours through the speakers and turns my head to the stage. Penny's standing under the lights, microphone in hand. Fuck, she looks good. Beautiful, even. Wearing a little red dress and heels that both shimmer when she does an awkward wiggle to the beat.

'I haven't heard this song since we were in school,' Angelo says.

'What song?'

When she starts singing, realization spreads through me. I still, looking up at Penny's shit-eating grin as she sings into the mic. Fucking *Kiss Me,* by Sixpence None the Richer. Running a hand over my jaw, I laugh in disbelief. I'm sure there's nothing coincidental about that song choice. *You're a little brat,* I mouth at her. She winks in response.

Angelo's stare heats my cheek. His chair groans, then he's on his feet, his hand on my shoulder.

'When you have private jokes,' he murmurs.

He strolls over to join his wife, while my grin dampens at the edges.

Penny

The night is a holly-jolly blur of bad singing, mulled wine, and risky bets placed on roulette wheels with a *fuck it, it's Christmas* attitude. Condensation mists the portholes, and even the icy breeze trickling in from the cracked French doors does nothing to dull the searing heat burning through my veins.

I'm taking a respite in the bathroom, running my wrists under the tap. As I glance up to check on my makeup, I pause.

I'm *grinning*.

I guess I get it now, why people love Christmas. I've barely drunk but the festive excitement has seeped into my pores and intoxicated me.

Growing up, the holidays were nothing more than a week to muddle through. Some Christmases, I'd receive the most ridiculously expensive presents from my parents, which would then be slowly pawned off throughout the year to fund their binges. Other years, I'd get our DVD player wrapped up in the pages of the Devil's Coast Herald.

When you're surrounded by people you actually like, it feels different. Magical, even.

I'm twisting off the tap when I hear a nasal voice seep under the door.

'Oh, boss! I'm glad I caught you. I hope you don't mind, but I just had to use your private en-suite. Every bathroom on the yacht was in use, and after four glasses of champagne, I didn't have the patience to wait in line for the Little Girls room.'

A bitterness fills my mouth. It's Anna. I glare at the empty row of cubicles in the mirror and brace my hands on either side of the sink.

'Mm. All twelve of them were occupied,' Rafe muses. His tone is cashmere-clad but I catch the irritated undercurrent. 'Such a coincidence.'

'Indeed. Anyway, I couldn't help but notice all the female products. So . . . who's the lucky lady?'

My brain doesn't have time to slow my impulse; I yank open the restroom door and stomp down the hall. Rafe's at the end of it, and Anna with her back to me. His gaze slides to mine over her head, amused and all mine. Deep down, I know why I didn't wait for his response: if he told a lie, something in me would shatter a little.

My shoulder connects with Anna's more aggressively than necessary as I slide in beside Rafe. I put a possessive hand on his chest, and when his hand slides around my hip and brings me closer to him, a warm satisfaction runs south.

I turn my attention to Anna. 'Mine,' I say sweetly. 'Now, fuck off.'

Her shocked expression tastes delicious, but the silence thrums in my ears. I know I'm dipping my toe into bunny-boiler territory but I don't give a fuck. I guess I've learned two things tonight: why people love Christmas and why women do crazy shit like smash up cars with baseball bats over men.

Anna looks up at Rafe as if he's an SOS signal. He only brushes his thumb over my hip and says, 'Happy Christmas, darling.'

She huffs and click-clacks back to the party. When the door slams shut, leaving us alone in the corridor, I twist out of Rafe's grip to face him.

A hint of a smirk pulls on his lips. He swipes at it with a thumb and slides his hands into his pockets. 'Meow.'

Maybe it's only because the heels I'm wearing are a couple inches taller than usual and all this height is giving me new confidence, but I curl my finger around his collar pin and yank him toward me.

'Call another woman darling again, and she'll die crossing the road.'

It echoes what he said to me after I gave him a lap dance in his car. Guess that's why he raises a brow and searches my eyes for humor. When he doesn't find it, he nods, a small amount of satisfaction leaking through.

'If that's what you want, Queenie,' he says quietly.

His compliance is so soft, so intense, that I'm instantly breathless. Suddenly needing air that isn't thick with Raphael Visconti charm, I burst through the side door and out to the deck.

Slow, heavy footsteps follow me to the bow. Gripping the railing, I tilt my head to the ink-black horizon, not caring that the wind is undoing all the hours of work I spent putting rollers in my hair.

My skin prickles with awareness when a silhouette interrupts the glow of the security lamp above me and Rafe's jacket slides over my shoulders. His hands come either side of me, his lips skimming behind my ear.

'Nice song,' he murmurs, raising a thousand goosebumps along my arms. 'Were you trying to hypnotize me?'

I smile into the darkness. 'I don't know what you're talking about; it's the only song I know all the lyrics to.' My attention drops to his hand next to mine. Big and busted to my small and smooth. A sick thrill sweeps through me when I remember his hands didn't used to look like that; every scar is fresh and belongs to me. Skimming my pinky over his bruised knuckle, I add, 'Unless it worked?'

He shakes off my light touch and spins me around so my back is pressed against the railing. It's a stark contrast: the warmth radiating off his body and the icy wind lashing my back. Each feels as dangerous as the other.

Sliding his hands over the lapels of his jacket, he pulls me even deeper into his orbit. Steals my next breath with a brush of his nose against mine.

'It really would be the perfect night to kiss you,' he whispers.

Fuck.

All of my senses sharpen, aside from common sense. I'm suddenly aware of the rhythmic sound the ocean makes when it slaps against the hull. How handsome Rafe looks under the romantic glow of the security light. Wren's sweet rendition of ABBA's *Lay All Your Love on Me* drifts through the glass and grazes my ears.

This is how it'd happen in a film.

Then when this was all over, I'd have to torture myself with the replay forever.

I let out a tense breath and close up my heart. 'Nah. I already told you; I want rain. Like in *The Notebook*.'

A soft laugh escapes him. 'I'll bear that in mind when you write me a check.'

He glances quickly down the deck, then, biting down on his bottom lip, he skims a large hand up the inner seam of my thigh. Christ, his palm sizzles like rain on a hot roof in the height of summer, burning a hole into my lower stomach. When he pushes my thong aside and dips two thick fingers into me, my moan is one of relief.

Sexual tension has tethered me to him all night. Every time his velvet laugh has chafed the back of my neck, every time I've been trapped by his wink over the rim of a crystal tumbler, my blood has heated another degree. I don't know how I've gone four hours now without fucking this man.

His stare darkens at my reaction. 'But I suppose for now, *these* lips will have to do.'

Despite rising on my tip-toes to chase his touch, my tone is defiant. 'Not yours,' I whisper.

Annoyance threads through his features, just like it does every time we fuck and I scramble enough semblance together to tell him this.

Eyes narrowing, he skims his middle finger over my entrance, then further south. 'Then what about this?'

I yelp as he pushes into the entrance of my ass, falling into him. He catches me, his laugh against my chest tightening my nipples.

We're so close now, his scent consumes me like a drug. I rub my face over his neck, desperate for more of it. All of it.

'It'll cost you,' I murmur half-heartedly against his pulse.

'I'll pay it,' he mutters back, resting his chin on the crown of my head. His tone is so simple I know he's no longer joking.

We stay like this for a while, his jacket warming my shoulders and the rise and fall of his chest lulling me into lethargy.

I sigh against his top button. I'm guarded, but I'm not naive. I know I'm obsessed with this man. He makes me want to do stupid shit, like tell him so. Or even tell everyone else by yelling it from the bow like Jack yells *I'm the king of the world!* in the Titanic.

That'd be pretty embarrassing, though, so I'd settle for staying here forever in his strong arms, the hum of a good time barely touching us. Although, when the thought of *forever* comes to mind, it slides down my throat and tightens there like a noose.

There's no such thing. Even if there was, it's not made for us, but it's hard to remember that when his eyes find mine across a packed room. When he puts his hands over my ears during a thunderstorm. When he spends an hour massaging me after he ruins me.

'Tell me why you think I'm unlucky,' I blurt out. *Convince me this can't be forever.*

His stomach tenses against mine. 'You already know why.'

'No, but why do you think it's *me*?' I push off him, tilt my chin, and meet his stony glare. 'You might be superstitious but so am I. And even *I* know coincidences can exist, so why are you so sure it's me causing you all this bad luck?'

His jaw ticks. When his eyes coast over my head to the black horizon, I think he's going to shut me down. But then a reluctant puff of air leaves his lips, and his gaze falls back to mine.

'Mama was as stupid as you.' He flicks an irritated look to my necklace. 'God, fate, karma – she believed in all the things she couldn't see. When I was still struggling with my first-ever casino, she came to visit me in Vegas. Dragged me to this fortune teller on Fremont Street.' He runs a hand over his jaw, shaking his head at the memory. 'She was a cartomancer – read fortunes with playing cards. At the time, I thought it was total horseshit, but my mama was sold. Anyway, I watched on while the fortune teller drew her the Jack of Diamonds, followed by the Ace of Spades.' He pauses, searching my eyes for any sign of recognition, but I only shrug. 'Combined, they're known as the death duo, apparently. Anyone who draws both cards consecutively is destined to die.'

Ice threads through my veins. 'Did she . . .'

His jaw tightens. 'Three weeks later. Poisoned at a fair.'

My vision dims. My hand fumbles for Rafe's, and I bring it to my mouth. 'I'm so sorry,' I whisper against his knuckles. My eyes lift to his. 'Is that why you're superstitious?'

A humorless smirk touches his lips. He stretches out his palm and cups my face. 'Not quite. After she drew the cards for my mama, the fortune teller told me she had a reading for me, too, but I was too pissed to listen. I thought it was all bullshit, anyway. But then, with both parents dead within a week of each other? I needed answers. So, after the funeral, I skipped the wake and flew back to Vegas to get them.' He swallows, tracking his thumb with a pained expression as he runs it over my cheek. 'I don't know what I was expecting, but it wasn't for her to put two cards in front of me and tell me I could choose my fate if I so wished.'

'What were the cards?'

'King of Diamonds, or King of Hearts. She told me that in this life, I'd only have one or the other – success in business, or success in love. The caveat was that it could never be both.'

Something sickly spins my stomach. 'And what did you choose?' I croak, my mouth drier than it should be.

He smiles sadly and stretches his hands to sweep over the menacing silhouette of the yacht behind him. *His* yacht. 'You know the answer, Penelope.'

My heart beats double-time, a question more loaded than a gun shooting up my throat. 'You chose *this* over being in love?' I jerk a thumb to the ship, wave the watch on my wrist in his face. 'Materialistic shit over true feelings?'

The words are desperate and venomous, floating between us like soap bubbles. I wish I could pop them as easily. He regards me with suspicion. 'You don't believe in love either, remember?'

Yeah. Grinding my teeth so nothing else stupid can escape my lips, I wait for him to continue.

'I returned to the fortune teller when I was jaded and confused. My parents had just died; their love meant nothing now.' He pauses. 'Well, it wasn't really love, but I didn't learn that until later. And Angelo had just told me he wasn't returning to Devil's Dip to take over my father's role as capo, which meant I wouldn't be his underboss. All I had was a hotel room in Vegas and a shitty casino that was barely earning enough to keep the lights on.' He shrugs carelessly. 'I had nothing to lose and a lot to gain, so I tapped the King of Diamonds.'

A few heavy seconds pass. The wind fills them with the faint hum of laughter and Mariah Carey's *All I Want for Christmas is You.*

'So, you've explained why you're richer than God himself, and why you don't usually fuck the same girl twice,' I say sharply, 'but I don't get what this story has to do with me?'

Rafe runs his tongue over his teeth, his focus shifting behind me. I swear, he hasn't moved an inch, but he suddenly feels further away. 'As I was leaving, she told me that, just like every action has a reaction, every fate card has a doom card. A card that, if you let into your life, it'll ruin you. Bring you to your knees.' He laughs, like he's just remembered a private joke. I have a feeling I wouldn't find it funny.

'What was the card?' I grind out.

He glances at me quickly. 'The Queen of Hearts.'

The deck spins in a haze of black, gold, and green. 'Queenie.'

I'm brought back to rights by a soft tug on my hair. 'The redhaired lady,' Rafe says pensively, staring at my strands around his fingers. 'Of course, I thought she was talking shit and my mother's death was a coincidence, but then almost overnight my casino had all this interest from investors. My bank balance grew as fast as my reputation, and within three years, I owned most of Vegas. If the fortune teller was right about my mother and about the King of Diamonds, then why wouldn't she be right about the doom card? For years, I avoided red-haired women like the plague, just in case.' He tugs sharply on my strands, his stare hardening as it meets mine. 'Then you stomped down the stairs of the Blues Den. Red hair, stolen dress, an attitude I wanted to fuck out of you.' He shakes his head. 'You were magnetic, and I couldn't resist giving you the time of day. You turning up at my brother's wedding could have been a coincidence. It's a small town, after all. And the port explosion; we had it coming, but when I saw you at the hospital and realized you'd been there, my skepticism began to wane.' He glances along the deck, his jaw ticking. 'I didn't give you a job as a favor to Nico, but to convince myself I was only being paranoid.'

I let out a shaky breath. Fuck, I don't know what I was expecting, but it wasn't that. 'Well, I knew you didn't hire me because of my bullshit resume,' I say weakly.

His smile doesn't touch his eyes. 'The night you started, I lost forty grand on the tables and had to sever ties with one of my most lucrative investments. And then it never fucking stopped, Penny. Every call and email I got was bad news. Shares sliding, stocks crashing. My first casino got hit. Christ.' He runs a careless hand through his hair. 'Griffin tried to kill me yesterday.'

I blink. 'What?'

His hand slides up to the nape of my neck, his squeeze cutting me off. 'A story for another time.' We breathe in each other's air for a few seconds, my pulse beating off-kilter in my ears. With a heavy puff of breath, Rafe drops his forehead down to mine, his imposing silhouette obscuring the outside world. 'I don't care how lucky you think you are,' he murmurs. 'To me, you're the unluckiest girl in the world.' Instinct pulls me away from him, but he only tightens his grip on my neck. 'But you're also the prettiest. The funniest. The fucking *rudest*. You've ruined my life but I'm not strong enough to stop you.'

As his admission tickles my top lip, panic rises up my throat. I can't pin down its source; all I know is that it's deep-rooted and desperate. 'Go back to her,' I whisper. 'Go back to the fortune teller and ask her to reverse it or something.'

Keeping his grip on my neck, he slides his other hand around my waist and rubs a thumb over the small of my back, where his name is fading. 'I can't. You're not the only one who likes to start fires, Queenie.'

Maybe it's just the wind, but now my eyes are stinging. His next words feel like a punch to the throat. 'We always knew this was only temporary, right?' His gaze sparks with bitter amusement. 'We wouldn't want you falling into that trap now, would we?'

My vision blurs at the edges. All I can focus on are his eyes searching mine. I hope he can't see the realization behind them. I take a steadying breath, choke down my emotion, and nod.

'Temporary,' I rasp.

He's right. Despite the ache that pounds in my chest, the common sense beneath it knows this can never be permanent.

I'll ruin his life.

He'll break my heart.

In the end, neither of us will win this game.

Rafe

'My eyes hurt,' Penny whispers, brushing glitter off her lap. She picks up a fake gift off the table runner and rattles it. 'And why do the decorations have decorations?'

Amusement pulls my smirk taut. Somehow, Rory walked into her dining room, saw the festive explosion, and decided it still wasn't grand enough for Christmas Day.

Now, a branch of a fir tree tickles my neck when I lean too far back in my chair. My shirt-cuff almost catches fire on one of the thousand candles every time I reach for my drink.

Opposite me, Benny lets out a loud sigh. Eyes the labradoodle licking Tayce's face. 'If I don't get fed soon, I'm eating that fucking dog.'

Tayce wraps a protective arm around Rory's Christmas present and glares back at him. 'I'll eat *you* before you eat Maggie.'

'Yeah?' Benny licks his lips. 'Sounds like a pretty good Christmas gift to me.'

A lethargic laugh ripples around the table. Dinner was meant to be served two hours ago. The good mood soured when the sun set on the other side of the fake snow-coated windows and plates were still empty. Now, everyone's hungry, restless, and drunker than they should be, including me.

Over the rim of my fourth vodka, I do a scan of the table. Usually, Christmas is a grand affair at the Cove mansion, but for obvious reasons, we've broken tradition this year. Surprisingly, two of the Cove clan actually turned up: the twins, Leonardo and Vittoria. They hammered on the front door an hour ago, Vivi in tears and Leo holding their suitcases. They wanted to be let in, and considering they had all their belongings, I don't think they just meant for Christmas.

Filling the empty chairs are a few add-ons. Tayce sits next to Nico, and Penny's neighbor, Matt, sits on the other side of her. Penny only agreed to spending Christmas with me if he was allowed to tag along. Every time I lock eyes with him, he freezes like I've shot him with a stun gun.

Suddenly, the swinging doors burst open. Everyone sits up a little straighter. Shoulders sag and sighs fill tumblers when they realize it's only Angelo, and he's empty-handed.

He leans against the head of the table and glares at the spinning Santa centerpiece. 'No one eat the turkey,' he murmurs, cutting a glance behind him. 'It's as pink as Barbie's playhouse. There's eight bathrooms in this house, and twelve of us; you do the math.'

The collective groan is loud. Across the table, Matt catches Penny's eye. He holds up eight fingers and mouths, *fucking hell* at her.

My brother cuts off all protests with a thump on the table. 'I'll punch the living daylights out of anyone that mentions this to my wife. Eat the trimmings, put the turkey in napkins, *subtly*, and I'll order us pizza –'

'And dinner is served!' An excited trill cuts Angelo off. Rory pushes through the doors, struggling with a large turkey.

There's a half-hearted ripple of applause, which gets louder when Angelo clears his throat. He takes the bird from his wife and sets it on the table. Beside me, Penny shudders.

I put a hand on her thigh. 'Don't worry, Queenie, we'll get burgers on the way home.'

She flashes me her signature grin. 'No need.'

Before I can ask why, Rory places a nut roast in front of her. 'Here you go Pen,' she sings, before sauntering off.

Penny winks at me. 'I told her I was a vegetarian.'

***

The grounds to the rear of the house are covered in frost. In the darkness, I can't tell if it's real or bought from Party City.

Angelo passes me the cigar and drops his head back against the brickwork. The heat lamp above his head gives his despair a red glow.

'WebMD says I've got about three hours until food poisoning kicks in.' He glances at his watch. Runs fingers through his hair. 'I'm on borrowed time.'

My laugh comes out in a puff of condensation. 'You ate half the fucking bird.'

He cuts me a sideways glare. 'She was sitting right next to me. It's all right for you; I saw you scrape all of yours into Penny's purse.'

'Yeah, now I've ruined it. Apparently, only a Birkin as a replacement will do.'

My brother frowns. 'I don't know what that is.'

'Mm. You better hope your wife doesn't, either.'

Easy silence swirls us, a backdrop of laughter and Christmas classics vibrating against our backs.

'What's the deal with Leo and Vivi?' I ask, passing him back the cigar. 'I'm surprised they turned up. You know, considering you shot their father in the head and all.'

He smirks at the memory, then wipes it off with the back of his hand. 'Think they hated Big Al more than we did. Dante too.'

'You letting them move in?'

He shrugs. 'They're family. I'll interrogate them tomorrow, but they seem pretty genuine.'

'Bet Dante hasn't even put up a tree, the fucking Scrooge.'

We both laugh. 'Leo said the Cove mansion felt like North Korea, but it's slowly become a ghost town.' Angelo turns to me, expression turning serious. 'Dante's the last man standing.'

I take this information in with a puff of tobacco. The burn at the back of my throat is as satisfying as the news. 'Yeah?'

'Gabe will be pleased. He's been climbing the fucking walls.'

I keep my mouth shut, my mind wandering to his sadistic cave. I think Gabe has been just fine.

The wind whistles over the shells of my ears. Behind us, Tayce calls someone a dickhead – probably Benny – and a loud laugh permeates the brickwork and squeezes my shoulders. Warms my fucking chest.

I'd know that laugh anywhere. I slide the cigar inside my bittersweet smile. It's a hollow feeling, loving the sound of something and knowing that one day soon I'll never hear it again.

I glance at my brother's amused expression and nod to the cigar.

'Just doesn't taste the same with vodka. It's true what they say about Russians having no taste.'

He ignores me, takes the smoke from my hand, and takes the two steps into the yellow glow leaking from the living room window. He puffs, watching the scene beyond it.

'You're good together.'

'What?'

He cuts me dry look that suggests I fucking know what. Reluctantly, my legs carry me over so we're standing shoulder to shoulder, looking in the window.

Benny's holding Rory's dog up like Rafiki does Simba in *The Lion King,* and Tayce is jumping to rescue her.

I frown. 'What's that on Tayce's arm? Thought she doesn't have any tattoos.'

Angelo huffs out a laugh. 'It's a dick.'

I turn. 'What?'

'A massive veiny dick. Your girl drew it. Lucky for Tayce, it's temporary. I think. It's fucking awful.'

Your girl. The words come out of my brother's mouth like melted butter. Slide down my spine as easily, too. It sounds so natural, but so foreign at the same time. No girl has ever been mine for longer than a night.

Finally, I let my gaze go to her, and as usual, a hand squeezes around my heart. She's sitting by the fire with Nico, balls-deep in a card game with him. She's got that stern expression she gets when we play Mario Kart and she's on the cusp of losing. She's the only one wearing the ugly Christmas sweater handed to us as we crossed the threshold. It's almost as big as her and just as loud.

I shake my head, melancholic humor filling me. Last night on the bow, I laid everything out in the cold gap between us. I don't really know why. Part of me wanted her to make it easier on me by running away; the other part wanted her to *fix it.*

She did neither, and so we're still here, balancing on the tightrope between the flames.

I almost wish I hadn't demanded she come today, because every moment with her has been perfect. After dinner, we moved to the drawing room to play games. We teamed up, and fuck, I'd never thought I'd enjoy playing games with her as much as I do against her. Maybe it's because we obliterated everyone. After two rounds of Charades and a whole lot of Pictionary, everyone else was mildly resentful of our triumph and got bored with playing.

If only her luck canceled out my bad luck outside of playing games, too.

The back door crashes open, tensing my muscles. Both me and Angelo reach for our guns, our fingers sliding off the grips when we see it's only Cas who darkens the doorway.

'Seems like there's been a Christmas miracle,' he says dryly. 'Guess what fuckwit just turned up?'

***

I stare at Tor Visconti through a haze of cigar smoke.

He stares back.

'Can you get food poisoning from mashed potatoes?' I ask Angelo blankly. 'Because I must be fucking hallucinating.'

Tor regards the vodka in my fist. Confusion sweeps through his gaze. 'Might be the paint stripper you're drinking. And what happened to your knuckles? You fall over or something?'

'Rafe –'

Ignoring Angelo's warning, I set the drink down with one hand and swing for his jaw with the other. His head snaps back as a little *oof* escapes his lips. He rubs his cheek and looks up at me, a mixture of humor and admiration dancing in his eyes. 'Rafe throwing a punch? Fuck, maybe I'm the one who's hallucinating.'

Behind him, Benny gives me a thumbs up of approval.

'Rather Rafe than Gabe, I suppose.' Tor glances to the cigar room door, as if my brother's going to burst in at any minute. 'You gonna set him on me later?'

'Tell them what you just told me,' Cas says calmly. He sinks into an armchair and rests his forearms on his knees.

Tor takes his sweet-ass time. He reclines in his chair, plucks a cigar from the humidor and holds it up to the dim light. With a nod of approval, he slides it into his top pocket and pins me with a half-lidded stare.

'I've been on vacation.'

Beside me, Angelo's temple vein ticks so loud I can almost hear it. He clears his throat. 'You've what?' he asks quietly. Calm-before-the-storm quietly.

'Mm. Didn't want to miss Christmas Day, though. Hey look – I brought gifts.' He grabs a bag from under the chair and sets it on the table. Pulls out three bobblehead figurines in floral shirts, wearing garlands around their necks. 'This one's Rafe, this one's Angelo, and this is Nico.' He flicks mine so it starts swaying side-to-side, then flashes me a lop-sided grin. 'They dance, see? Don't worry; I've got them for all of you.'

I've never been in a room of Viscontis so silent. Disbelief consumes me. It feels like the fucking floor is breathing. My stare rakes over him, trying to make sense of it all. He's got a month-in-the-Maldives tan and is wearing a bright white T-shirt to highlight it. His ink spills out from the collar and the cuffs, and I realize he's not even wearing a fucking watch.

Nico breaks the silence. 'So, just to be clear: when the port exploded, you left the wedding, got on a jet –'

'Believe it or not, I flew commercial,' Tor interrupts. 'That was a fucking adventure in itself.'

'– to a different continent, and have spent the last month sipping on margaritas under a palm tree and getting your dick wet?'

Tor rubs at his smirk. 'I'm more of a mojito man myself. And I wouldn't say I got my dick *wet*. But there was this one girl . . .' He shakes his head, raking his teeth over his bottom lip. 'Fuck, she was something else.'

More silence. This time, it's the click of a safety catch releasing that interrupts it. At the corner of my eye, Angelo's Glock winks in the light. 'That's it,' he growls. 'Get up.'

My hand flies out and pushes down on the barrel, so he's aiming at the dancing figurines instead of our cousin's temple. Tor doesn't flinch; he just slides his gaze up to mine expectantly.

Yeah, seems like he missed the memo about me not being the one that fixes things anymore.

'You better start talking, *cugino*,' I say, as calmly as I can muster, 'because I won't intervene the next time he raises his gun.'

A few heavy beats pass, thick with tobacco and expectation. Slowly, the smirk falls off his lips, and his reddened jaw hardens.

'I had no idea the cunt was going to do it,' he growls. 'You know what he said as I walked out the door to your wedding?' He glances up at Angelo. 'Tell the Dip Clan I want peace. Fuck – he really had me fooled. I'd spent the month after you popped a cap in our father trying to reason with him, and I thought he'd finally come round.' His stare darkens on my brother. 'I told you from the jump, *cugino,* I wasn't going to choose between the two of you. But the moment the port went *boom,* I knew I didn't have a choice anymore.' Falling back against the seat, he rubs absent-mindedly at his jaw. 'And I knew my life was going to change forever.'

'So you sat on a sun lounger for four weeks,' Angelo grinds out.

Tor's indifference doesn't waiver. 'Yeah, I did. I knew I had to choose a side, but I wasn't going to hang around and watch you kill my brother. So, I got out of your way for a little while.' He runs his tongue over his teeth. Curls his fists on the armrests. 'I'm assuming you've . . . taken care of it?'

Angelo cuts me a look; I give him a small shake of my head, signaling not to tell him Dante's still alive. Fuck, Tor is – *was* – my best friend. My best business partner and confidant. Maybe it's because I feel betrayed by his sudden absence, but I'm wary of telling him.

Jerking his chin to show he understands, my brother changes the subject. 'How do we know we can trust you?'

Tor shrugs carelessly. 'You can't, and it doesn't fucking

matter.' He rises to his feet, standing tall, and looks Angelo in the eye. 'But you're looking at the new capo of Devil's Cove. You can work with me, or you can work against me, but I promise you, not only am I better-looking than my older brother, I'm also smarter, wealthier, and better connected. You want a war, bring it on, baby.' He swipes a bottle of Smuggler's Club off the drinks cart and slams two glasses on the table. Liquor sloshes over the rims as he fills them up with vigor. He slides one in Angelo's direction. 'You want to call a truce and help me build Cove back up? Then that's good with me too.'

He raises his glass and waits.

Angelo glares at him for the longest time, then he swipes up the glass and silently downs it in one.

Penny

The Visconti mansion is quiet, save for the whir of mechanical Christmas decorations and the storm battering the floor-to-ceiling windows in the entryway.

'Come in!' Rory calls when I knock.

I poke my head around her bedroom door and am greeted by her tipsy grin and her fluffy dog. 'Please tell me you've come to join the sleepover?'

I glance at the bed, where long, black hair snakes across a cream pillow. Somewhere under the covers, a small lump is snoring. 'Have you swapped your husband out for Tayce?'

She flashes me a guilty smile. 'He's not feeling too well, so he's been banished to a guest room. I thought it might be the turkey, but everyone except you and I ate it, right? And they're all fine.'

I study her big, innocent eyes. Either she's the best liar I've ever met, or she just so happened to choose the perfect day to become a vegetarian too.

'Uh-huh,' I say dryly. 'Maybe it was the humiliation of

dressing up as an elf. How *did* you convince him to do that, by the way?'

She smiles knowingly. 'I was financially motivated.'

I laugh. 'Anyway, I brought you a gift.'

Her eyes light up at the Rolex dangling by its strap between my thumb and forefinger. 'Is that Cas's watch?'

'Yep. Thought you might like it after he told you a bag of frozen vegetables and a self-service bar isn't a replacement for a full catering service on Christmas day.'

'He's such a snob. As if I was going to make my staff work Christmas day – they have families too, you know?' She swipes the watch from me and holds it up to the light. 'I love it.'

Then she drops it in the half-drunk white wine spritzer on her dresser.

'Do you have everything you need?'

I stare at the bubbles engulfing the six-figure timepiece, distracted. 'Uh, yeah. I mean, no. Do you have any pajamas?' I skim an eye down her lithe frame. 'Ones that might fit me?'

The storm came out of nowhere, power-washing all the fake snow off the windows. Rafe got word that the waters are too choppy to head back to the yacht on the shuttle, so we're staying here tonight.

We can't go home, Queenie, Rafe said. His use of *home* fizzled in my chest and burned a hole there.

Rory tosses me an oversized T-shirt. 'Be nice to it; it's my fave.'

I unravel the fabric and read the logo: *The Washington State Birdwatchers Association.*

I catch Rory's eye and she grins. 'Proud member since I was five.'

We say our goodnights, and I pad down the hall with my new sleepwear slung over my arm. At the end of it, soft light seeps out from underneath the door of our bedroom for the night. Every step I take toward it, my heart beats a little faster, knowing the sight behind it will leave me breathless.

Rafe's lying on the bed in nothing but ink and black boxers. He has one arm behind his head, and the way his bicep flexes makes me want to sink my teeth into it again.

He regards me with lazy amusement. 'Hey, cutie.'

Despite the blush heating my cheeks, I roll my eyes. 'Trying out new nicknames?' He rakes his teeth over his smirk and nods. 'How about Doom Card? Or, The Unlucky Charm?'

His gaze sparks. 'Not very catchy. I'll stick to Queenie, I think.'

I flip him off and disappear inside the en-suite. Although I've had the perfect day, dread washes over me. It's been coming in unexpected waves ever since Rafe explained why he calls me Queenie.

The Queen of Hearts. The red-haired lady that'll bring him to his knees. It's an odd mixture of guilt and frustration that haunts me, and the irony isn't lost on me, either.

My fingers find my necklace. I run the pendant up and down the chain, watching it wink at me in the mirror. Maybe I'm lucky because I'm unlucky to others. The more I ponder it, the more it makes sense. I start fires. I steal wallets, watches, or anything I can get my sticky fingers on. If I choose you as a mark, you're bound to have a stroke of bad luck, simply because of what I plan to do to you.

Feeling feverish, I splash my face with icy water and try to wash the thought away. Fuck other men; I don't care about them, but I'd be lying if I said I didn't care about Rafe.

I get washed, brush my teeth, and slip on Rory's shirt. When I step back into the bedroom, Rafe rolls onto his side to face me, eyes narrowing on the logo.

'That better not belong to another man,' he says quietly.

'It belongs to your sister-in-law, actually.'

He screws up his nose. 'Even worse. You better take that off before I fuck you.'

I throw a discarded cushion at his head. He catches it in one hand. 'Who said we'll be fucking tonight?' Though, watching his abs tense as he slides the cushion behind his head, I know it's inevitable.

He treats me to a lop-sided grin, tone all silk and syrup. 'What's the alternative? Talk about our feelings?'

Enjoying the heat of his stare as I stroll across the room, I play into my nonchalance. 'No, but we can talk about something else. Like, why Tor Visconti showed up earlier, and why you punched him.'

He's barely listening, as he's too busy watching me bend over as I put my folded clothes on the armchair in the corner. 'Family drama. Boring.' He lunges off the bed, swiping for my legs. 'Come here.'

Maybe it's the vodka slowing him down, but for once, I manage to step out of his reach in time. 'Nico said you got him good.'

'I did,' he says carelessly. 'Now *come here*.'

Stopping at the foot of the bed, I lift my gaze to his. It's dark and irritated, the look of a king not used to being denied what he wants.

Smirking, I stoop to pick up all my gifts and drop them on the bed. 'Let's go through what everyone got me for Christmas, shall we?' I say sweetly.

His stare blisters. 'No. Also, everyone kept thanking me for presents I'd never heard of. Did Laurie go all-out this year, or did you put both our names on all your gift tags?'

'Both our names.' I flash him my most angelic smile. 'Seemed only fair, considering I paid for them on your Amex, sugar daddy.'

He laughs and shakes his head. 'I bought your neighbor,

who's said three words to me in his entire life, a round-trip to Toronto to watch the Maple Leaves play. How charming of me.'

'Speaking of Matt, you see the welcome mat he got me?' I slide it out and hold it up. 'It's a pun, just like his.'

Rafe reads off the slogan. 'Hi, I'm Penny. I just make cents.' He grimaces. 'That's fucking awful. It's not coming home with us.'

I falter. There it is again. *Home.* The word that sounds too permanent for my heart to cope with.

Our eyes clash, his searching mine with mild confusion. 'It'll come home with *me*,' I say quietly.

For a second, he doesn't understand. Then I see the realization harden his jaw and boil down to indifference just as quickly. 'Ah, yes. I forgot you typically live in a crack den with a busted building door,' he says dryly.

I say nothing.

With a slow exhale, he drops back to the pillows, locking his hands behind his head. 'Go on then, show me the rest.'

I do. I show him the Van Cleef necklace Rory and Angelo got me. The personalized Blackjack set from Nico, and the Charlotte Tilbury makeup hamper from Tayce.

He barely glances at the presents, choosing to stare at me with a soft expression for the whole show instead. 'Lovely,' he says when I'm finished. 'Now come here, or I'll wake the whole house up dragging you here.'

But I'm not listening. There's another gift sitting at the bottom of my bag, one I'd forgotten all about. Not one I received, but one I was of two minds about giving.

Discomfort nips at my edges. I do a shitty job of hiding it, though, because Rafe's brow deepens. 'What's wrong?'

'Nothing –'

But his eyes are already on the bag. This time, he's faster, and he grabs it from me before I can stop him.

He pulls out the gift. Flips over the tag and glances up at me. 'This is for me?'

'Yeah but –'

'From *you* ?'

My cheeks grow hot. 'No, from baby Jesus himself,' I snap back. 'It's nothing though, just a stupid little –'

'Why are you trying to hide it? Is it going to blow up when I open it?'

I glare at him. 'No, but I wish I'd thought of that.'

He tears off the paper and holds my gift up to the light. A pair of puke-green socks covered in four-leaf clovers. When his gaze comes to mine, I can't read the expression behind it, and it makes me feel even more uncomfortable.

'They're just socks,' I mutter, shifting my weight from foot-to-foot. 'Lucky socks, maybe. I know you probably get a rash from just *looking* at polyester, and I know I've probably made you hate four-leaf-clovers, but . . .'

My explanation melts off. The gesture is sweet, and it hangs in the air just as sickly. Truth is, I bought them from a dollar store on the high street when rowing in one of those waves of dread. I thought maybe if he has lucky socks, like I have a lucky necklace, it might stop me ruining his life anymore.

I realize I just said that aloud.

He stares at me. It's so *loud* outside, with the rain beating on the windows like we've done something to piss it off, but in this bedroom, you could hear a pin drop.

Rafe places the socks on the bedside table. 'Come here.'

This time the command isn't lit up with lust, and I'm compelled to obey it. Numb, I crawl onto the bed and lie in the crook of his arm. He props himself up on his elbow and stares down at me, blocking all the light above him.

'You think these lucky socks will work?' he murmurs, running a finger over the pendant of my necklace.

'Maybe,' I whisper, choked. *Hopefully*.

He flicks a glance at my eyes. Searches them. 'When did you buy your necklace?'

'I didn't; it was given to me.'

'By your mama?'

I laugh. *Yeah, right*. 'Someone's mama, probably. But not mine.'

'Why did she give it to you?'

Our eyes lock and he stares at me patiently. I squirm under his body heat, not wanting to bring up that memory, not on Christmas day. Not *now*. But when I go to sit up, Rafe pushes me back down, holding me on the bed with his hand on my hip.

'Tell me.'

I focus on the patterned ceiling and sigh. 'No offense, but men in casinos are assholes.' He doesn't laugh but waits for me to continue. 'Growing up at the Visconti Grand, all the patrons thought I was lucky.'

Now, he smirks. 'Nico told me you used to charge them a dollar to blow on their dice.' His knuckle skims my cheek. 'Why don't I remember you?'

Instead of making a joke about how fucking old he is, I swallow and keep going. I know if I stop, I'll never get it out. 'I didn't charge at first. I used to be a lucky charm for free, until one night, one of the regulars hoisted me onto his lap at the roulette wheel. He was drunk; I could smell the whiskey on his breath.' I glare at him. 'Another reason I fucking hate whiskey. Anyway, he was being reckless. Bet everything he had on black, and because I'd always been so lucky for him before, he thought he couldn't lose.' I swallow. 'My mama was the croupier for that table that night. He'd convinced her to let me blow on the ball and even drop it onto the wheel, although it was completely against the Grand's rules. It spun and spun and as it slowed, I remember his grip on my hip growing heavier.'

My stare slides up to Rafe's. His jaw ticks, and in the shadows he looks demonic. 'What did it land on,' he asks calmly, though not calm at all.

'Zero' I whisper. We stare at each other, and I let out a shaky breath. Fuck, I hate this memory. I've never told it to anyone, not even the hotline. If Rafe wasn't so warm, if his arm under my head wasn't so solid, I wouldn't be telling him either. 'I knew I was in trouble; I could feel it. I jumped off his lap and ran out into the alleyway. Seconds later, he followed me out.' My laugh is bitter and tastes of self-deprecation. 'He was the first man to trap me in an alley; Martin O'Hare was the second.'

'And he'll be the fucking last,' Rafe growls, raking a hand through his hair, glaring out at the storm.

I bring his attention back to me by stroking the head of his serpent tattoo. 'It was then I learned that when you can no longer serve a man, they turn their back on you. Or worse, they turn *on* you. He was angry and wanted to teach me a lesson. His hands tried to go places they should never go on a ten-year-old's body. You know, up my dress . . .'

The emotion clotting my throat cuts my story short. Rafe breathes out, dropping his forehead to mine. 'Fuck, Pen.'

But I keep going. Now it feels like I have to. 'He didn't get very far, thankfully, because a woman appeared from nowhere. I think she was just stepping outside for a cigarette, but her presence was enough to scare him off. She was wearing the nicest dress, and the alleyway was filthy but she didn't care. She sat down beside me and pulled me into her arms. Let me cry there for as long as I needed to.' Fuck, to this day, I still remember her scent. It was warm and welcoming. She smelled like white picket fences and freshly cut flowers and Sunday dinners around the kitchen table. Everything I'd never had. 'When my tears had dried, she took this necklace off her own neck and fastened it around mine.' My fingers fly to it, bringing the memory to life.

'She told me it kept her lucky, and now it would keep me lucky too. At first, I refused – because what if she wasn't lucky without the necklace anymore? What if she suddenly started losing in the casino? But what she said next has stuck with me forever. "Luck is believing you're lucky. This will just give you a little boost when you forget it."'

Rafe's silent, mind simmering and swinging between sadness and violence. Now that my worst childhood memory has left my mouth, it feels like it grew claws and is scraping my skin raw.

'Say something,' I grit out.

Eventually, his large palm engulfs my jaw. 'I'll kill him,' he says tonelessly, and then the bed dips and I'm cold. He stands at the end of it, scooping up his slacks. He takes a deep breath, glaring at the wall. 'I'll find him, and I'll kill him.' He pauses. 'Slowly.'

'Rafe –'

'Nico will know who he is. Maybe that bastard Tor, too. The Grand has security everywhere. I know it was a decade ago but –'

'He's dead,' I blurt out, sitting up on my elbows.

His pauses, lifting his eyes to mine. 'What?'

I curl my hand around my necklace. 'Less than a week later, he was staring back at me on the obituary page in *The Devil's Coast Herald*. That was the first time I realized that, yes, I am truly lucky.' I shrug. 'I've believed it ever since.'

It feels like he stands there forever, slacks in one hand, phone in the other. When his cell screen grows dark, he tosses it on the side table and drops to his haunches beside me.

'Fuck,' is all he says.

'Fuck,' I repeat in agreement.

He shakes his head, a grimace on his lips. 'I have to take a walk or something. I'm too pissed off to sleep now.'

I roll onto my knees, looking up at him. 'Then we won't sleep.'

His gaze falls to mine, softening. 'I'm sorry, baby.'

'I'm sorry too.'

His jaw ticks. 'Don't you dare say sorry.' He shifts over to me, gripping my hair and nuzzling his face in my neck. 'You're not a girl that says sorry.'

'Not even for buying you ugly socks?'

His laugh tickles my skin, and somehow it lightens the mood a few shades. 'They are fucking ugly.'

'Will you wear them?'

'If you want me to.' He pulls away, expression darkening again. 'I didn't realize we were doing presents.'

I laugh at the ridiculousness of his statement. 'Uh, that's fine. I guess your black Amex, your six-figure Breitling, and the shit-ton of cash you paid me to shake my ass in your face will have to do.'

He watches my hand slide down his chest, tensing when I run a finger across the waistband of his boxers. 'Or . . . I'll take this.'

He searches my expression. 'Are you sure?'

I consider this for all of half a second. Truth is, I feel like a weight has been removed from my shoulders, now that I've shared my secret. I want to chase this high with something that makes me feel even better.

'What's the alternative?' I snap his waistband and it slaps back to his stomach with a loud *thawp*. 'Talk about our feelings?'

His eyes narrow, dropping to my lips. 'You think you're funny, huh?' he growls, pinning me down on the bed. 'My Christmas present to you is that I'm going to fuck you so hard you –'

I fake a yawn and put my hand on his face. 'Boring. I've got ten of them. Did you keep the receipt?'

He hisses something about me being a cheeky bitch, then his hands catch mine, and he holds my wrists above my head. As he studies my face, something dark glints in his eye. Self-preservation makes me attempt to twist out of his grip.

His glare heats as he runs a languid path down my chest, stopping at the hemline of Rory's shirt. He swallows. 'I'll fuck you soft, then.'

'What?'

As I sit up in protest, he takes the chance to slide the shirt over my head, tosses it in the corner of the room, and comes down on his side. 'Shh,' he murmurs, tracing the dip where my waist meets my hip. 'Lie down and relax.'

I'm not quiet because I'm compliant, but because I'm suddenly too stunned to speak. Slowly, he releases his grip on my wrists and slides his shoulder under my head, so I'm lying in the crook of his arm.

My body is cloaked in his warm shadow; bathed in the intensity of his stare. He watches my breasts rise and fall for a few moments before grazing a knuckle between them.

A shudder rocks my core, my nipples tightening in anticipation. 'Look at you,' he rasps. 'You're so perfect, Queenie.' We both watch his hand as it glides over the curve of my stomach. 'Every single inch of you. Perfection.'

'I –'

My objection melts into a moan when his hot mouth latches onto my breast. He sucks slowly, gently, giving me so little of his tongue that all my muscles clench for more of it. Eyes lifting to mine, he grazes his bottom lip up my breasts to my collarbone, where he gives the pendant of my necklace a small kiss. 'No talking. Just relax and let me worship you.' His eyes flick to mine again, a heated desperation behind them. '*Please.*'

I'm rigid, confusion and confliction freezing my bones. This is too *nice*. It doesn't sit right with words like *temporary* and *for now*. But then he peels my panties down my thighs, and I watch as his hand disappears between them.

And with every butterfly wing brush against my clit, I start to thaw.

Rafe studies me with an intensity that makes me feel more than naked. He watches his hand play with my pussy; watches my expression when he slides his index finger inside me and presses against my sweet spot.

'Good girl,' he whispers against my mouth when I moan. 'Let me hear it again.'

My blood sizzles like cold water on a hot skillet. My nerves thrum in places I didn't know existed. I'm consumed by ink and cashmere, and, with every satin word spoken against my clammy skin, it gets harder and harder to breathe.

'Come for me, beautiful girl,' he murmurs, working my clit to a low, slow rhythm.

As his head dips to kiss my pendant again, an explosion erupts in my core, spreading outward, down to my toes and up to my fingertips.

My orgasm is violent to his calm. Desperate to his composed. He holds my head to his chest as I ride it. His heartbeat against my cheek is the first thing I hear when my senses come back to me. It's strong and steady, reliable like the ever-present tick of a clock.

He lowers me gently to the pillow. Follows his thumb as he swipes it over my wet bottom lip.

'My Queen of Hearts,' he rasps in fascination, more to himself than to me. 'My beautiful demise.'

Time seems to slow, like it doesn't want to rush to the end either. I feel broken. I guess all that ice was holding me together. We lie like this for what feels like hours, my ragged breathing mingling with the roar of the storm.

And then another sound, this one imagined, scratches down

my spine. The scrape of metal; the clanging of a lock. The *snap* of a trap around my ankle.

Panic grips me instantly. My hand shoots out to grab Rafe's bicep.

'What game are we playing now?' I breathe.

His gaze is everything I don't want it to be.

'The game of make-believe, Queenie.'

Rafe

The sky is the same ashtray gray as the snow on the ground. It meets somewhere in the middle and creates the illusion the horizon rolls on forever. The sprawling hotel in front of it is only a few shades lighter.

Angelo lights up a cigarette. 'You've watched *The Shining*, right?'

'Unfortunately.'

Fucking Gabe. I was feeling equal parts generous, preoccupied, and out-of-luck when I handed him the right to choose the set-up for this month's Sinners Anonymous game. This was way back when I was as oblivious as Angelo, believing our brother was crawling the walls with the mundane task of eliminating Dante's men with slashed tires and laced cigarettes, not torturing them with makeshift weapons in a cave.

We drove for hours, way past Devil's Cove, up to where Canada's terrain and cold weather seep out from its border.

'He only killed a cat,' Angelo grunts.

Begrudgingly, I'm thinking the same thing. Why the fuck

am I standing half a mile from British Colombia, in front of an abandoned hotel, for a cat killer?

'You know I'm not one to dampen the spirit of the game, and I'm always hassling you to be a little more creative, but in this instance a drive-by shooting would have sufficed.' My mind flicks to Penny, back on the yacht, warming my bed. 'I've got better shit to do,' I mutter.

Behind us, three shots ring out in quick succession. Angelo and I whip around in unison, guns cocked. We let them go slack when our idiot brother emerges from the fog, firing an AK-47 at the sky.

'Good afternoon.' He squints up at the falling snow. 'Lovely weather, isn't it?'

I stare at him. 'It's a miracle you've never been to prison.'

'Mm,' Angelo agrees. 'Not even a short stint.'

Gabe ignores us and nods behind him. Two of his men come into view, dragging a large metal trunk across the snow. They pop it open to reveal an array of modified metal implements. Most pieces I recognize from rifling through the iron chest in his cave; some I don't.

By the sharp intake of breath, Angelo hasn't seen any of them before.

'What the fuck is that?' He crunches over the snow and peers into the box. 'Is that . . . Fuck, does that have a *motor* attached?'

Gabe straightens up and regards us both with his signature indifference. 'Listen carefully, because I can't be fucked to repeat myself.' Angelo ducks as Gabe swings the AK-47 up, pointing it at the hotel behind us.

'Black Springs Resort and Spa. Been up for sale for the last twenty-five years, and now it's the latest addition to the Visconti property empire.'

'You bought that thing?' Angelo asks quietly, temple ticking. 'With money?'

'No, with magic beans,' Gabe deadpans. 'I've bolted all the doors and windows shut.' He stoops into his trunk and pulls out an electric drill. 'There's only one way in, and unfortunately for our sinner, no way out.'

I turn one-eighty, glaring up at the hotel with fresh eyes. Through the sheets of snow, I hadn't even noticed the iron grates covering the windows and doors. 'He's already in there?'

'Been in there for three days, brother. No light, no water, no stimulation.' Gabe rubs his hands together. 'He's going to be desperate to get out.'

'Christ,' Angelo mutters, popping his knuckles.

'Choose a number.'

My head snaps back to Gabe. 'What?'

'A number. Between one and twenty.'

'One,' Angelo drawls. He glances at me. 'Can never go wrong with one.'

Gabe's lackey dives into the trunk, checking the small label on the bottom of each weapon. He hands Angelo a fishing spear.

'No,' Angelo says sharply.

'Didn't ask,' Gabe grunts back. His eyes meet mine. 'Number.'

I scrape my teeth over my lip, thinking. Clearly, the number I choose will dictate the weapon I'm armed with. It's all down to luck. A reckless wind snakes down my collar, and the ugly green socks tighten on my ankles.

Fuck it; let's see if they work.

'Thirteen.'

Angelo mutters something about me being an idiot. Gabe cuts me a knowing look. 'Thought you might say that,' he murmurs, handing me my favorite weapon of all.

'Easy,' I purr, slapping the hammer against my palm, adrenaline nipping at my edges. 'Give us the rules.'

Pressing the AK-47 into his lackey's chest, he tightens his grip on the drill and steps between us.

'You don't need the rules, brother, it's just hide and seek.' He nods to the decaying building. 'There's two-hundred-and-fifty-one rooms in there. He's hiding in one, and whoever seeks him out first, wins.'

'What do we win?'

Gabe glances at me. 'A beer from the Rusty Anchor.'

I let out a dry breath. 'How very motivating.'

Angelo stares at his fishing spear in disgust. 'You're going to make us leave our guns out here, aren't you?'

'Yep. Hand them over.'

Unease slithers through my veins as I press my Glock into his lackey's palm. Hunting in the dark with nothing but a hammer feels very primal. Very *Gabe*. Usually, I'd be delighted he's taking the game so seriously. This, plus the set-up he created in the cherry field for last month's game, is an excellent change from the usual concrete dungeons he picks. But with my current . . . problems, it seems as though a lot could go wrong.

Gabe sweeps an eye over us and nods in approval. 'Let's begin.'

We close in on the hotel in silence. Gritty snowfall compacts underfoot as the wind whistles a haunting tune in my ears.

The closer we get, the eerier the hotel becomes. Fuck, it really is something out of a horror film. The mist devours the tops of the fake turrets, and the graying paint has cracked into a thousand spider veins. The thought of clambering around its pitch-black rooms in a fucked-up game of cat and mouse pokes at the sadist in me.

Gabe grinds to a halt in front of the iron-clad door. 'Wanna see something cool?' Before we can reply, he snaps off the walkie-talkie from his waistband and clears his throat. Brings it to his mouth and taunts, 'Ready or not, here we come.'

I hear his voice everywhere but beside me. It seeps out of the mansion, loud yet muffled, and gets swept away by the wind.

Angelo runs a palm over his smirk, shaking his head. 'You rigged up speakers? That's fucking terrifying.'

Gabe gives me a knowing look, touched with dry humor. 'I like the acoustics.'

The sizzle of a cigarette; the screams of a long-lost cousin. I shudder at the memory and turn back to the hotel.

Gabe's drill works through the lock. Angelo mutters something about using a fucking key, but I can't bring myself to laugh. Suddenly, something very unfunny is squeezing the nape of my neck, and the last time I had this feeling, I found myself staring down the barrel of a gun just a few moments later.

My grip tightens on the hammer. 'Is he unarmed?'

The way Angelo sneers at me, you'd think I'd just confessed to pissing the bed. 'Are you?' he snaps back, eyes darting down to the hammer.

With a groan, the door heaves open, revealing the void behind it. Gabe slams it shut behind us, and then the games begin.

The darkness is blinding.

'Come on, cat-killer,' Angelo murmurs to my left. The sound of his easy swagger tapers off into a connecting room.

A hand grips my shoulder. 'Do me a solid, brother. If you find him, maim – don't kill. Griffin could do with some company.'

I squint into the abyss, shaking out of Gabe's clutches. *Griffin's still alive?* Fuck me, he must be in ruins.

He skulks out of reach, and now I'm alone. Devoid of sight, my ears prickle with awareness.

Floorboards groan. Footsteps echo. The tease of a drill whirs above my head. With every room I enter, each blacker than the last, the unease tightens another notch around my neck.

To my right, something rustles. A shadow shifts within a shadow, and without thinking twice, I swing for it. Metal glints and the claw sinks into rotting plaster board.

After wrenching it out, my grip loosens on the hammer handle, and I drop my head to the wall.

Fuck. I'm losing my damn mind.

I don't realize I said that aloud until a reply comes from the shadows.

Gruff. Familiar. *So close.*

'I can't say I ever thought of you as sane in the first place, *cugino.*'

Dante has always worn the most awful aftershave. It's the last thing that assaults my senses before sharpness sears my skin.

Penny

A moonbeam permeates a porthole, projecting the shadows of the storm onto the back wall. I've been staring at it for hours. Awake. Alert. Wondering if Rafe is coming back, or if I'm going to spend a second night hugging his cold pillow.

He said it was a meeting. The period between Christmas and New Year's Eve is always a smudge on the calendar, I know. But *two days*. What meetings last for two days?

My cell hasn't buzzed once with a shit joke, or even a curt, one-word command. Instead, it's burned a silent hole in my pocket as I've wandered aimlessly from room to room, taunting me with the idea of texting him.

My pride won't let me.

My sigh melting into the thrum of rain, I kick the covers off my clammy body and prop myself up on my elbows. I'm hot and restless, and as pathetic as it is, I know only the soft lull of Rafe's voice in my ear and the hard comfort of his body against mine, will soothe me.

I drop back on the pillow. Traps are the worst fucking thing.

I lie like this for a while, contemplating what to do. I'm down to my last *For Dummies* book, and I've called the Sinners Anonymous hotline so many times that my head is devoid of mundane topics. Just as I'm considering doing another lap of the yacht to burn some of this nervous energy, a low hum in the distance makes all the hairs on my arms stand to attention. My eyes slide up to the row of portholes lining the wall and the yellow glow from the boat lights that slowly washes over them.

Relief eases the pressure in my chest. Sliding under the covers, I close my eyes and strain my ears, listening to the movement shift around the yacht.

The engine shuts off. The swim deck groans. Only when the French doors open and slam shut so violently that the headboard shakes against my crown, does a sheet of unease slide over me.

It grows heavier with every irregular footstep that crawls across the ceiling. Almost suffocates me when the sound travels down the stairs and closes in on the cabin door. When the door clicks open and the smell of rain and animosity spills into the room, I squeeze my eyes shut and stop breathing.

Something's not right; I can sense it. There's a venom in the air, and Rafe's breathing too loud. My arms tingle with awareness as he navigates the bed and sits in the armchair by my head.

Danger screams, but the silence is louder. Letting out the slowest, quietest breath I can, I dare myself to crack an eyelid – not wide enough for him to realize I'm awake, but enough to assess him.

His eyes are on me, his elbows propped up on the chair arms. He spins a poker chip between his thumb and forefinger, each turn glinting gold in the moonlight. He's a rumpled version of himself: his hair is mussed, his shirt soaked, and the shadows even make him appear unshaven.

Even if I were wide awake and we were in the cold light of day, I wouldn't be able to read his expression. His attention is unfocused, somewhere else. Somewhere bad luck thrives and heavy decisions have to be made.

I squeeze my eyes shut again.

A few seconds later, the chair groans and deliberate footsteps lead to the bathroom. The pipes gurgle and pop in the walls as he turns the shower on. Water pitter-patters against tiles and steam creeps under the door. The very normal act of him coming in and having a shower almost lulls me into a false sense of security, until a loud *crack* snaps through the room and bolts me upright.

What the fuck?

Heart pounding, I glare at the bathroom door. 'Rafe?'

No answer.

On shaky legs, I slip out of the bed, cross the room, and knock. When there's still no answer, I brace my bones and gingerly push the door open.

Fear chokes me, but nowhere near as much as not knowing what's on the other side of it.

Behind the steamed-up glass, Rafe's got his bare back to me. One hand is braced on the wall, his head dipped between his shoulder blades, while water droplets capture the moonlight, glistening like metal as they glide over his tattoos and swirl down the drain.

'Rafe?' His inked shoulders tense, but he doesn't turn to look at me. 'Are you okay?'

Silence and mist cloak me; I suck it in through my nostrils and almost gag on it.

Unable to take the tension, I yank open the shower door. Duck under his arm and slide in between him and the wall. His eyes are as icy as the water soaking through my T-shirt as he lifts them from the drain to me.

'Your socks didn't work.'

What? Stupidly enough, I glance down at his feet, as if I'm going to find those ugly green socks growing damp. But what I see makes my throat dry. Blood, and lots of it, swirling with the water and disappearing down the drain. I follow the trail up his thigh, over his navel, and to the right of his stomach.

'You're bleeding,' I whisper, reaching out to touch the bloody bandage. Realizing it'll hurt, I curl my hand into a ball and press my back against the tiles. One scrapes roughly between my shoulder blades. A glance at his knuckles, also bloody, and I connect the dots; the *crack* was him punching the shower wall.

'What happened?'

His gaze is lazy and irritated. Blacker than the dark side of the moon. 'You happened, Penelope.'

I blink the water from my eyes and stare at him through the downpour. For once, I'm at a loss for words.

His stare latches onto mine, burning hotter as it rolls over my soaked ponytail and down the length of my plastered T-shirt. He pauses at my breasts, running a hungry eye over my nipples.

'Get on your knees.'

My throat tightens. 'What?'

He wraps his bloody fist around the base of his cock. It grows harder the longer I stare at it. 'You brought me to my knees; now it's your turn.'

I'm frozen, and not just because I'm drowning in a constant stream of ice water.

I don't know this man. He isn't the one who swoops in to steal a bite of my burger, or the one that kisses every mark he leaves on my body.

I don't know him, and I don't like being trapped between him and the cold shower wall pressing against my spine.

He takes a step forward and violence flashes in my veins. For a split second, the tiles are brickwork, the shower's an alleyway, and he's a man hell-bent on revenge. My hand shoots out and slaps him across the face, *hard*.

Rafe doesn't flinch. 'That all you got?' he says lazily.

So I slap him again. And again when his indifference doesn't waiver. Anger roaring in my ears, I curl my hand into a fist, but as I draw it back, he ducks and, in one swift movement, sweeps me off my feet and lifts me over his shoulder.

Blood-soaked tiles, moon-streaked carpets. They pass in a breathless blur, until a sudden blast of ice water flash-freezes my skin.

It's a million degrees colder than the shower stream. I gasp from the shock of it and instantly struggle to escape Rafe's grip, but it's unrelenting, and all I can do is scream as the carpet melts into the decking. He lowers me until wet metal touches the backs of my thighs and the wind lashes my hair.

There's no time to gather my bearings because I'm falling backward. The sensation slows my perception of time, dragging my heart to my stomach, but it's over as quickly as it began, because Rafe's hand shoots out and grips me by the throat.

Wheezing, I sweep a panicked glance over my surroundings. I'm balancing on the railing that separates the bow from the raging ocean below. The only thing stopping me from falling into the abyss is the battered hand choking the life out of me.

I've always told myself I'll stare death in the face when the time comes, not curl up into a ball like my father. One option I never considered was what I'm doing now; flailing my arms and legs, clawing at his inked forearm and screaming for mercy.

'Please!' By his blank expression, I don't think he can hear me over the wind, so I scream it louder.

My stomach jumps to my throat when he takes a step forward, pressing his drenched forehead against mine. He smells like whiskey and looks like a man who has my entire life in his hands. Fuck, he had it anyway, long before he decided to hold me over the edge of a railing.

'If I throw you overboard, maybe this will all go away,' he growls. 'Maybe I'll get my luck back.'

I'm so cold I feel sick. So scared my heartbeat threatens to crack my ribs.

'*You won't!*' I cry.

His hand slips around to the nape of my neck. I arch my back and press my body into his, feeling his hot, bitter laugh skitter down my throat. 'I know I won't. Can't seem to hurt a fucking hair on your head, let alone end your life.' His squeezes, coasting his lips up to the hollow behind my ear. 'You think I haven't already tried, Queenie? I want to snuff the life out in you so badly, but if I do, it'll go out inside me too.'

Numbness seeps into my skin and then freezes everything underneath it. I realize he thinks I meant he won't kill me, not that he won't get his luck back. It's a crack in his demonic facade, and I dig my claws in.

'Please,' I whisper against his forehead. 'I'm cold. We can talk about this inside. We can –'

He pulls back so suddenly my life flashes before my eyes. I grab onto his slippery bicep, my stomach muscles aching from where I'm trying to keep myself upright.

'*I didn't choose love* !' he roars into the wind, eyes black and agitated. 'I chose the King of Diamonds! I didn't choose you!'

His anger sparks my own to life, and suddenly, I forget this man could end my life with a slip of a fingertip. 'And I didn't either, yet here I am, stuck in your fucking trap! Stuck so deep I fear I'll never get out!'

His breathing slows, his eyes sharpening with clarity. I take advantage of it, putting my hand around his throat too.

We stare at each other. Him naked and bloody, me soaking wet and shivering.

We look nothing like the King of Diamonds and The Queen of Hearts.

Just two fucking idiots in love.

I swallow the thickness in my throat and whisper my truth.

'If I drown, you're drowning with me. If you burn, I'm burning too. Pick your route to hell, Rafe. The destination and the company are the same.'

He makes a noise of anger. Grabs a fistful of my sopping ponytail.

And then he makes me a millionaire.

His mouth presses against mine, hot and desperate. My lips only part to let out a gasp from the shock, but he immediately slides his tongue in. As he tastes me, his moan fills my mouth, triggering violent, fire-starting sparks between my thighs. Fuck the storm; I can't feel the freeze anymore. With every animalistic glide of his tongue against mine, with every nip on my bottom lip, my body grows so hot I could melt the Arctic.

His fingers slide down my nape and grip me there. Not only am I in his trap, the chains are pulled taut; he won't let me move an inch. He leans into my hand wrapped around his throat when I pull back for air. Steps between my thighs when I attempt to twist my head from his grip. The warm heat of his groin radiates through the thin fabric of my thong, melting underneath into something pliable. Something that fits in his hands as perfectly as the rest of me does.

As he scrapes his teeth over my bottom lip, his stare clashes with mine through the sheet of rain. A pool of green lava, as angry and as reckless as his kiss. 'Of course I've seen *The* fucking *Notebook*,' he growls, before fusing his mouth to mine again.

He refuses to break the kiss, even as he slaps my thighs so I wrap them around his waist.

Even as he lifts me off the railing and carries me inside. As he drops me on the bed, removes my clothes, and covers me with his hot, bloodied body.

And as he slides himself inside me, I hope he never does.

***

I wake up among damp sheets, swollen with unease. The type that fills all the hollow parts of me and pushes against my organs.

I'm on my side, facing the wall. My crumpled shirt, stained with second-hand blood, lies on the floor drying. A cool breeze taunts my bare back and I know.

But I lie here a little longer, playing my new favorite game: make-believe.

The rules are simple. If I just squeeze my eyes shut and clamp my hands over my ears, I can play it for as long as I like. I can feel the reassuring weight of his arm draped over my hip. Feel his lazy breaths tickling my nape.

But the thing about make-believe is, you can't play it forever. I knew it on Christmas Day, and I know it now.

Movements slowed by dread, I roll onto my back and swipe my hand over his side of the bed. It's as empty and cold as my heart. My fingers slide beneath his pillow and brush against something underneath it.

I prop myself up on my elbow and inspect it. It's a card wrapped in a piece of paper. I unravel the paper and realize it's a check for a million dollars. Then my eyes fall to the business card. To the number I know by heart, then to the written words that I don't.

I own Sinners Anonymous.

I'm sorry.

Rafe.

I stare at it for the longest time. Not an ounce of emotion flowing through my blood. Not a single thought filling my head.

And then I curl my hand around the lamp on the bedside table, and I throw it at the wall.

Penny

Lust burns.

Love cuts.

But betrayal? It fucking *incinerates*.

I stand shaking in the shower, unable to tell whether it's the stream from the faucet or my tears that's blurring my vision. They aren't tears of sadness, but of rage, and the cuts on my hands are the product of it.

Smashed glass, broken lamps. Clothes slashed into a thousand strips. I destroyed everything in my wake, because I couldn't let go of him quietly like he did me. Fuck, I would have set the yacht on fire in a heartbeat if I wasn't on it.

Rafe owns Sinners Anonymous. My oldest friend, my fucking confidant. He might as well have taken my diary, had the pages enlarged, and pasted them all over town. The humiliation feels the same.

The whole time, I thought I knew all the games we played, yet little did I know he was playing the biggest game of all. Maybe it's karma – the swindler finally getting swindled. God, how I wish he'd only taken money from my pocket, and not ripped my entire center from my chest.

Another wave of nausea rolls over me, and I snap on my exfoliating glove to distract myself again. Although I've been scrubbing at it for a half-hour, the remnants of his name still stain my skin.

I want him *gone*. Off my body, out of my heart. I want my ears to forget his silky laugh, my nose to forget his scent.

And I want him to catch on fire, too.

The moment I turn the shower off with an angry bump of my fist, the knocking starts up again.

'Penny!' Matt's muffled call floats through the front door and down the hall. 'I know you're in there, so open up!'

He heard me drag my suitcase up the stairs early this morning and poked his head out into the hall, just in time to catch my tear-streaked face disappear behind my front door. He's barely stepped off my new welcome mat since, even when I sent him a quick text to tell him I had food poisoning. I don't know if he replied, because I swiftly turned my cell off and hurled it at the wall.

Wrapping a towel around myself, I walk into my bedroom and perch on the edge of the bed. The vanity mirror on the dresser reflects my swollen, blotchy face. I'm too embarrassed to let Matt or anyone else see me like this, because now I look like the girl I always swore I'd never be.

Vulnerable. Used. Stupid enough to get played by a *fucking man*. I'm an ungraceful winner, sure, but I'm an even worse loser.

And love really is a losing game.

'Penny, I'm going to see some family up in the mountains for a while. I won't have cell service, so even when you've stopped throwing a fit, you won't be able to get hold of me.' He pauses.

'Fine. You've got five seconds to open this door or I'm going to break it down.'

Fuck's sake. I thought he'd have left by now. I glance down at where Rafe's watch used to be and my throat tightens. It was the only thing on the yacht I couldn't bring myself to smash; I just left it on his upturned bed. Now my wrist feels as bare as the rest of me.

'Alright, that's it, Pen. If you're behind the door, I suggest you step back, because I'm about to go through it.'

Matt's footsteps retreat down the hall. They quicken, and a loud *thud* rattles my window panes. He barks out a pained curse, and I can't help the humorless smirk tilting my lips.

I'll miss him.

The thought slides into my head without context. Then I realize my survival instinct is two steps ahead of me.

My attention slides away from the mirror to the stack of money on my dresser and the million-dollar check.

I'm stubborn, but I'm not stupid. He told me he owns my hotline and he gave me the money because he knew I'd leave. And as much as the bitter side of me wants to stay in Devil's Dip and ruin his life, I know it would hurt me more than it would hurt him.

Passing the diner every day and remembering his food order. Looking out to the horizon and seeing all the lights twinkling on his yacht. Fuck, I can't even see my friends without being reminded of him. Rory's married to his brother and lives in the house he grew up in; Tayce tattooed his fucking name above my ass. And Wren. She was the one who tried to convince me he was a gentleman.

I guess I'll do what I always do when things turn sour.

Run.

***

Cove's bright lights flash and flicker behind the sheets of rain falling from a starless sky. The smooth sidewalks are as silent as they are slippery. In a few days, they'll be abuzz with New Year's Eve celebrations.

And me?

Fuck knows where I'll be.

My necklace sizzles against my collarbone. Yet again, I'm standing at a bus station, with all my belongings beside me, hoping luck will let me land on my feet again. This time, I'm leaving the Coast with more than I arrived with. Heavy pockets and an awful sense of vulnerability gnawing at my chest. It's like an open wound, and I'm not sure how I'll ever be able to stitch it back up.

Rain trickles like melted ice down my collar, sending a violent shiver through me. I close in on the timetable board, rubbing the sleeve of my faux-fur jacket over the screen to wipe the droplets away. The next bus out of town isn't for another hour.

Sighing, I sit down on the wet bench and wait.

What am I going to do now? I don't mean how I'm going to fill the next hour, but the rest of my life. I came to the Coast with the intention of going straight, yet I'd gotten so twisted that I fear I'll be permanently bent out of shape. No *For Dummies* book has sparked a fire in me, and now I'm so bitter and betrayed, all I want to do is shake down every man I come into contact with, in an attempt to put the world to rights again.

A black car turns onto the Devil's Cove strip, its headlights slicing through the rain and washing over my Doc Martens. Its speed is slow and intentional, as if the driver is searching for something along the sidewalk.

I guess my heart can't be hardened in a day, because it lurches into my throat with the hope it's Rafe. Visions of a Hallmark-worthy grovel flash behind my eyelids, and in a moment of weakness, I wonder how many pieces of the moon he'd have to fetch for me to forgive him.

The car slows to a stop in front of me, and I rise to my feet. The blacked-out window rolls down, and I'm met with the eyes of another Visconti.

'Get in, Little P.'

We stare at each other for a few seconds, then he shifts his attention to the rain-streaked windshield, as though my compliance is non-negotiable.

With numbness biting at my veins, I climb in and shut the door. The car fills with warmth and nostalgia, and there I go again, silently thrashing against the need to burst into tears.

We drive in silence. Amy Winehouse's rendition of *Will You Still Love Me Tomorrow?* plays low on the radio. Nico's jaw is slack with indifference as he turns off the main strip.

I can't fight it. An awkward little sob escapes my throat and his gaze warms my cheek.

'Do you want to talk about it, or do you want to be distracted?'

My vision blurs and there's no turning back. The dam opens, the tears flow, and my sobs fill the car, ugly and loud.

Nico lets out a tense breath and swings the car around.

'Distracted it is.'

Rafe

They say if you love something, let it go.

If something almost kills you twice in one week, you should probably let it go too.

As I watched her sleep peacefully in my arms, my blood smeared over her stomach and my come glistening on her inner thigh, two truths solidified like metal in my chest.

The first, was that now that I knew what it felt like to kiss her, I'd never kiss another.

The second, was that I'd never let her go.

She was all mine, and not a soul on this fucking earth could prize her from my cold, dead hands. No, she had to be the one to let *me* go, and I needed to give her a good enough reason to never want me back.

The football game roars on the television; the rain hammers on the bay windows. I'm reclined on my brother's sofa, bringing another chip to my mouth, when Rory appears in the living room doorway.

The night I wrote the check and scrawled a note, I turned up at the house because I didn't know where else to go. Angelo opened the door with a gun, lowering it when he saw the look on my face. He held out his hand in silence, but I only shook my head. I couldn't even keep my breathing steady, let alone my fucking hand.

The next morning, I awoke to his wife standing over my bed, her dog in one hand, a kitchen knife in the other.

'I'm sorry to hear you got stabbed,' Rory said calmly. 'But what the flamingo have you done to Penny, and why is her cell switched off?'

Since then, she's been arguing with Angelo behind closed doors and shooting me death glares from all four corners of the house. I still haven't eaten or drunk anything that hasn't come from a sealed container.

But now, as she runs her gaze down my legs, it's the softest it's been all week.

'Are those my sweatpants?'

'Your husband's.'

She frowns. 'Same thing.' She glances at the bag of chips nestled in my arm. 'Are those my snacks?'

'Probably.'

Stroking the ball of fluff in her arms, she stares at me for the longest time. She sighs. 'You're just a heartbroken little fool, aren't you?'

'What gave it away?' I ask dryly.

Her eyes fall to my feet in sad bemusement. 'The novelty lucky socks. Oh, and the fact you've hardly moved from this position all week.'

New Year's Eve has come and gone, and I barely even glanced at the fireworks on the other side of the living room window, let alone threw a signature Raphael Visconti party.

What would I have done, put on a fucking suit and a smile and pretended like everything underneath it wasn't on fire?

The only respite I've had from the pain was when the captain of *La Signora Fortuna* texted to let me know Penny had gone nuclear.

Good. I hope she's angry. I hope she ruined everything I own. And I hope she feels better for it.

Rory disappears upstairs and comes back in her sweats, her curls piled on top of her head and a paper bag tucked under her arm. 'Therapy dog,' she says, dropping Maggie in my lap. She plonks down next to me, tosses the chips on the coffee table, and with a stolen glance over her shoulder, she upturns the contents of the bag between us.

'Don't tell anyone, but I keep all the good stuff upstairs,' she whispers, letting the candy fall through her fingers like it's a pile of gold coins.

She then reminds me that I've already watched this football game twice this week, and turns the channel to some trashy reality TV show.

***

I pick up a gummy thing wrapped in loud plastic and hold it up to the light. 'Is this strawberry flavor or raspberry flavor?' She sighs. 'Swan, this breakup really has ruined you.'

Rory tears her eyes from the show we've been watching about rich housewives in Beverly Hills. We're balls-deep into season two, and fuck, I guess it's easier to get invested in who's sleeping with whose husband, rather than think of the Penny-shaped hole burning in my chest.

'It's red flavor.'

'Yeah but –'

'Shh. Kim is about to confront Kyle in the limo about stealing her goddamn house.'

Outside, the purr of a super car melts in from the driveway, then a car door slams. Rory sighs, pausing the show. 'Never mind; I know that slam. You're in trouble.'

I turn to her. 'How do you know *I'm* the one in trouble?'

She scoops the sleeping dog off my lap and flashes me a look of disbelief. 'Not going to be me or Maggie, is it?'

The front door slams shut and rattles all the windows. Angelo's voice booms through the foyer. 'All right, that's it.' He appears in the doorway of the living room, bringing in cold air and animosity with him. 'I've put up with a week of this shit; now get up.'

I glance at him. Pop the gummy in my mouth. 'Nah, I'm good.' I turn to Rory. 'Plot twist: I think it's watermelon.'

'Ooh,' she squeals, digging around in the candy pile for one.

Angelo's charred glare flicks between me and his wife. He braces his palms on the sofa armrest and grits his teeth. 'Get up. Shower. Shave. Put on something that doesn't have an elastic waistband, and meet me in my car in twenty minutes.'

'Can't.'

'Why not?'

'Kim's about to confront Kyle about stealing her goddamn house.'

Beside me, Rory nods in approval. 'We've been waiting all season for this.'

His blistering glare scorches my skin, but I hurt too much everywhere else to notice. 'I told you to make a plan.'

'And my plan is to take a break,' I growl back.

'A break from *what*?'

My back molars grind together. A break from *everything*. From being Raphael Visconti. From being an underboss; a CEO. A brother, a friend, a fucking *gentleman*. Anything that requires me stepping outside this house and into the world where she isn't. Through half-lidded eyes, I look back up at him. Now, his irritation is softened by something around the edges.

'Don't do this to me,' he says quietly. 'Gabe's disappeared off the face of the planet again.'

'Good. The cunt almost had me killed.'

His eyes flash. 'You know he didn't mean it.'

Gabe's done a lot of reckless shit in his time, but swapping out the cat-killer for Dante tops everything. I don't know whether Gabe gave him the glass shank or he smashed something to get it; I just know it ended up three inches deep in my stomach, narrowly missing a main artery.

I lost a lot of blood, but in the end, it was a pretty superficial wound. I managed to get a good swing to his head with the claw side of the hammer before hitting the deck. The last thing I remember was hearing Gabe's gruff voice muttering something about how he couldn't take it anymore. How he was going out of his mind.

I glance down at my feet. The lucky socks didn't work, which confirms what I already knew: while the Queen of Hearts is in my bed and under my skin, I'll burn until there's nothing left of me.

Doesn't stop me wearing these ugly fucking socks, though.

'Just give him a few more days, baby,' Rory pipes up, flashing her husband her sweetest smile. 'He's *moping*.'

'Rafe doesn't mope,' Angelo grunts.

'He does now that he's a heartbroken little fool.'

Angelo's eyes slide to mine, narrowing in disgust. I don't care if he thinks I'm pathetic. I just know if he tries to pull me off this sofa I'll put him in a headlock, stomach wound or not.

'Fine,' he snaps, rising to his full height. 'I'll meet Tor in Cove *alone*. I'll be sure to bring back a box of tampons and some ice cream.'

He storms to the foyer. 'Make it chocolate chip,' Rory calls after him.

'Nah, vanilla,' I mutter, popping a Jolly Rancher into my mouth.

***

'Rafe?' My attention falls from the diner's backlit menu down to Rory's concerned eyes. 'Libby asked what you want to order?' she whispers. She glances at the server but says to me, 'Are you okay?'

No, I'm not okay. The lights are too fucking bright and my chest is too fucking hollow. It feels like there's not enough inside of me to prop my bones up, and I'm going to implode at any second. And whose fucking bright idea was it to get burgers?

Her loud laugh. Her wet coat drip-dripping onto the checkered tiles. *Cough up, sugar daddy.*

Violence grips me and I sweep everything off the counter. Rory gasps and steps back. Eyes come to me over the backs of booths, and silence crackles like an electric current.

I run my hand over my throat and glare up at the strip lights. 'I'll wait outside,' I say calmly, stepping over the cash register and pushing out into the cold street. Our security men stare at me like I've lost my mind. I don't know why, because it's not exactly a revelation.

The mist falling from the black sky does nothing to cool my blood. I drop my head against the glass window and light up a cigarette. As the smoke dissipates, my focus sharpens on the phone booth across the street, and I let out a bitter laugh.

This is it, isn't it? What it's going to be like forever? Not a day will go by when I'm not reminded of the red-haired brat who ruined my life. When I don't wonder what she's doing. When I don't have to stop what *I'm* doing, because I suddenly remember how other men exist in this world, and one day, one of them will treat her a lot better than I did.

The door chimes, and Rory falls into step with me, clutching the grease-stained sack to her chest. She's silent and wary as she slides into Penny's seat. Her cell lights up her face. No doubt she's texting my brother about my outburst.

'I'll cover the damage,' I murmur, kicking the car into gear.

She stares straight ahead. 'Uh-huh.'

I inch down the window. 'And don't eat that burger in my car. It fucking stinks.' *And reminds me of extortionate lap dances and sharing milkshakes with my girl.*

She nods tightly.

An awkward tension presses against the walls of the car, swelling when I slow on Main Street. I can't help it: I take my foot off the gas and steal a glance at Penny's living room window. Rory does too, then she lets out a small sigh.

'Me and the girls have tried to contact her every day,' she says sadly. 'I just need to know if she's okay.'

My lungs pinch together. Galvanizing my glare on the windshield, I slam on the gas, narrowly missing a Ford Fiesta coming the other way.

'Me too,' I mutter under my breath. 'So try harder.'

***

Tor's leaning against the pillar propping up the front porch when we pull up to the house. He's just outside the glow of the security lamp, and the only reason I know it's him, is because he tilts his chin when he hears my engine, and his stupid fucking nose stud glints.

'What's this dick doing here?'

Rory spots him a few seconds after I do, and tightens her grip on her dog. 'No idea. We hate him, right?'

I run my tongue over my teeth. Bad blood thins quickly in this family, aside from when certain members do extra-stupid shit, like blow up the port.

'For now.'

My eyes clash with his as I slam the driver's door shut. I don't break eye contact, even when I round the car and open Rory's door. She walks into the house, whispering 'attack, Maggie, attack' in her dog's ear as she passes him.

Tor's face is alight with lazy humor as he drinks me in. He slides his hands into his pockets and strolls into the house after me.

'Sweatpants, *cugino*? Am I seeing things?'

'You'll be seeing stars if you don't get the fuck out of this house,' I reply calmly.

His easy laugh follows Rory and I into the kitchen. She takes her time, peering over the breakfast bar as she grabs us plates and cutlery. Tor leans against the counter like he didn't hear me.

'You ever answer your phone these days?'

'Yeah, because you really did that when you fucked off on vacation for three weeks.'

He lets out a tense breath. 'Come on, *cugino*. I explained myself. What the fuck have I got to do for you to get over it?' He runs a judgmental eye down to the green socks poking out between my sweatpants and my Nikes. 'To get over *this*?'

I ignore him in favor of tossing my burger on a plate and feeding Maggie a French fry. 'The housewives are going to Amsterdam in this episode, right?' I ask Rory.

'Uh-huh. Apparently, they have the craziest fight over dinner.'

'*Gesù Cristo*,' Tor grinds out. He lunges over, grabs my burger, and Frisbees it into the sink. 'Let's just put a pin in your meltdown for a minute. I've got the whole of Cove at my feet. Every bar, club, and casino. I own one-hundred-percent of everything, no Dante in sight. What do you want?'

I palm the counter and look up at him. 'I wanted that fucking burger.'

He ignores me. 'I'll sign whatever complicated contract you want me to, and I won't even read it.'

I'd forgotten how persistent this dick could be. I glance to Rory, and she flashes me a lop-sided grin. 'You're heartbroken, not stupid. Get him in the pockets, Rafe.'

I bite back a smirk. 'What do you think I should do?'

A glint sparks in her eye, like the darkness inside her is knocking to get out. She scoops up Maggie and strokes her, like Doctor Evil strokes Mr Bigglesworth in *Austin Powers*. 'I think you should hit him.'

'And I think that's an excellent idea.'

Tor groans. 'Fuck's sake. Fine.' He straightens up, rubbing his hands together and cricking his neck. He rounds the counter and braces himself on the other side of it. 'Just don't knock out any teeth; my smile is my best feature.'

***

I wash my knuckles in the sink. Blood, both mine and Tor's, snakes between lettuce leaves and a lone pickle, then swirls down the drain. Behind me, I can hear the low hum of our reality show floating in from the living room. In front of me, the rain has started up again, hammering on the kitchen window.

Sighing, I hold my hands up to the recessed lights. Splitting skin doesn't feel anywhere near as satisfying when it isn't for her.

Behind me, Rory clears her throat. I glance up, meeting her reflection in the rain-streaked glass.

'She's gone.'

I swallow. 'Gone?'

'I got hold of Matt. He came back from his trip and saw Penny had slid a note under his door,' she whispers.

My heart climbs up my throat and sits there, choking me.

I swallow, *hard,* and try to breathe like a person who hasn't just had the life knocked out of him.

I brace my bloody knuckles on either side of the sink. Meet her reflection again.

'Tell Tor I want forty-nine-percent. And tell your husband I'm back.'

Rafe

Penny was right.

Love is a fucking trap.

Not because you're lured in by lies and shackled by deception, but because once you're in these damn restraints and your captor walks away with the key, you're fucking stuck here forever.

I'm not stupid; I know it won't get easier. I can only hope I'll get better at hiding the chains.

The flames roar from the fireplace, their heat reaching out and grazing the front of my slacks. I stare down at the burning logs and take a sip of coffee. The finest Colombian blend, but it tastes as bitter as me.

Heavy footsteps echo through the walls, then Angelo darkens the living room doorway, his coat slung over his forearm.

Dry amusement lights his gaze. 'And there I was, thinking I'd never see you in tailoring again.' I stare back at him. As he searches my blank expression, his humor dims like a candle slowly starved of oxygen. 'You ready?'

Gritting my teeth, I turn back to the fire and pull the deck of cards from my pocket. Give them a lazy shuffle.

We both know he's not asking if I'm ready to drive over to Cove, but rather, if I'm ready to be *back*.

Of course I'm not, but I can't fester on the sofa with a bowl of candy balancing on my stomach forever. She's *gone*. Just like I needed her to be.

I just didn't think she'd take my entire center with her.

'Born ready,' I say dryly, brushing my thumb over the deck to create a satisfying *thawp*.

Angelo's stare bores into my cheek for a few moments before he walks out of the room.

I shift my focus to the bay windows. There are three armored sedans and a cluster of well-worn men loitering around them. Gabe got me stabbed by our least-favorite cousin then fucked off the face of the planet. Clearly, his lackeys don't know what to do with themselves in his absence, so they've joined the security team he assigned me.

Now that she's gone, I shouldn't need all the extra protection.

With a steadying breath, I give the cards another shuffle and fan them in my hand, face-down. I select one at random. If it's the Ace of Spades – the luckiest card in the deck – maybe forcing her out of my life will feel like less of a massive fuck-up.

With a flick of my wrist, I'm looking down at a different card.

Letting out a hiss, I toss it into the fire and stroll out the room, leaving the Queen of Hearts to melt into the flames.

'There you are!'

I stop in the foyer and glance up the stairs. Rory stands at the top of them, dog in one hand, a bundle of fluffy fabric in the other. 'Guess what? I bought us wearable blankets! Look!' She lowers Maggie to the ground and holds out what looks like an oversized hoodie. 'They've got pockets! I can put Maggie in mine, and you can put the snacks in yours.' She pauses, watching her dog bound down the stairs and paw at my feet. 'Or you can carry Maggie. She likes those ear scritches you give her.'

'Sorry sis, our snacking and binge-watching days are over.' Stooping down to ruffle the dog's curls, I flash Rory an apologetic smile. 'I'm back to work, and back on the steamed broccoli and chicken.'

She frowns. Runs an eye down the sharp crease of my slacks, like she's only just noticed I'm not in sweatpants and ugly socks. Her confusion melts into delight. 'Penny's back?'

My throat tightens at the sound of her name. 'No.'

'Then why the flamingo are you in a suit?'

'What?'

She glares at me like she's hoping I'll catch fire in the middle of the entry. 'I've watched three seasons of *Real Housewives of Beverly Hills* with you. Let you eat my good snacks, let you pet Maggie. Do you think I was doing that to help you get over Penny?'

I shake my head in disbelief. 'I have no idea what you're talking about.'

'That's because you're an idiot. When you first showed up at our door, I told Angelo I wanted you *out*. But then I walked in on you watching the same football game on repeat, and I realized you were just in that in-between stage. You know, the bit that comes after deciding you can't be with her, but before the part where you realize you can't live without her?'

She crosses her arms, sneering at my suit. 'The only reason you should be dressed nicely and leaving this house is because you've had that realization. And, like, now you're rushing to the airport to stop her boarding a flight. Or, I don't know, running to the church to stop her from marrying another man.'

My eyes narrow. 'Penny's getting married?'

Rory slaps her palm against her forehead. 'Christ, Rafe. You're really testing my patience this morning. Have you never watched a romance movie? You *going back to work* is not your Happy Ever After. You're missing a few steps. Like, realizing that against all odds, you'll still make it work, then doing a big dramatic declaration of love. Only then do you get your Happy Ever After.' She pauses before adding, 'With Penny.'

I let out a bitter laugh. 'Sorry to break it to you, but life isn't like how it is in the movies.'

Her gaze shifts over my shoulder, and I'm suddenly aware of my brother's presence in the doorway behind me. 'Yes, it is,' she says quietly.

I run my hand down my throat. Swipe a finger over my collar pin.

She's right about one thing: going back to work isn't my Happy Ever After, but I was never meant to have one of those, anyway. And no one makes romance movies about men who fall in love with girls who ruin their lives without even trying.

I tilt my chin, meeting her glare with a tight, humorless smile. 'I guess you got lucky, then.'

Before I put my fist through a wall, I turn and stride out to the driveway. The sky is as gloomy as my mood, and the wind is as cold as my heart.

Angelo's lazy footsteps crunch over the gravel behind me.

'I've got to drop off some paperwork at the port first, so we'll take separate cars.' His focus drops to my curled fist. 'Don't drive yourself off the cliff now, will you?'

'You better hope I don't, brother. You'll never navigate Tor's sleazy contracts without me.'

Despite the January frost creeping across the windshield, I pull out of the grounds with all four windows rolled down, partly because Penny's scent still seeps out of the walls of my car, and partly because I'm hoping the sharp wind will slap some sense into me.

No more fucking moping. I told Angelo I was back and now I just need to convince myself that I mean it. Gripping the steering wheel, I force myself to focus on what lies in wait for us in

Cove. I wasn't joking about Tor's sleazy contracts. My legal documents might be confusing, but his are just one big, fat loophole, designed to trip up anyone who's stupid enough to sign on the dotted line.

Last night, he agreed to handing forty-nine percent of Cove over to us, but I know in the cold light of day, he'll blame that on the concussion, then shove some terms and conditions, loaded with a million get-out clauses, under our noses.

A weak zap of energy crackles down my spine. This is exactly what I need – to bury myself in business. Heated meetings, spreadsheets, plans for bigger and better events. Anything that makes the memory of red hair and deep blue eyes fade.

The drive is uneventful, except for when I spot a copper-haired girl walking down Main Street and I slam on my brakes. Or when my fingers twitch to connect my cell to my car's Bluetooth because listening to Penny's calls while driving alone has become second nature.

Even if I caved and opened the Sinners Anonymous inbox, I know there'd be nothing new for me in there. I've been obsessively checking, and, unsurprisingly, she hasn't called the line since I told her I owned it.

As my car climbs the hill to the church, a familiar Harley winks at me from underneath the willow tree. Frowning, I glance at the sedans in my rear-view mirror and slow to a stop.

What the fuck is Gabe doing here?

I feel out-of-sorts walking up to the old building, like I'm going to find something dark and depraved behind its heavy doors. Guess that's why I slip my gun out of my waistband as I step inside.

The dust has been disturbed, dancing in the small slivers of light that have broken through the boarded-up windows. It takes a few moments for my eyes to adjust to the shadows and hone in on the imposing silhouette sitting in the front pew.

My footsteps echo off the vaulted ceiling as I walk down the nave, but Gabe doesn't turn around.

I sit on the opposite end of the pew. Gaze up to the Virgin Mary judging us from above the altar.

'You're a massive cunt. You know that?'

No response.

I let out a tense breath, running my palm over the wound on my stomach. It's barely tender anymore, and the physical scar will be no bigger than the length of my thumbnail. But the mental scar of being stabbed by *Dante,* of all fucking idiots, is large and gnarly.

It's not like I won't get over it, though. Besides, only a week before, Gabe saved my life.

'Well, I accept apologies in check-form only.'

As my joke prickles the silence, my words feel hot against my own ears for two reasons. First, it sounds like something Penny would say, and second, my brother *still* hasn't moved.

He sits with his hands resting on his thighs, spine rigid, his face fully concealed by the shadows.

And suddenly, seeing him like this, I realize how much progress he's made over the last month. Ever since the port went *boom,* I've seen glimpses of his old self, the brother he used to be before that one Christmas. He's spoken in full sentences, even learned how to use his phone. And I swear, I've even seen him smirk from the other side of a dining table when I've told a shitty joke.

I've been so wrapped up in everything Penny, I haven't realized how big a deal it is.

I clear my throat. 'Anyway, it's old news. Wanna come to Cove with Angelo and I? He's worried about you, man. Besides, we'll come to an agreement with Tor a lot quicker if you're playing pit bull.' I pause as the silence snowballs down the pew. 'I'll even let you punch him. Not with full power, though. The bastard won't get back up.'

Finally, his gruff voice comes from the shadows.

'It was meant to be fun.'

I grit my teeth. 'And it would have been, had I had my Glock, and had you turned on a fucking light.' When he doesn't reply, I rake my hand through my hair, shaking my head. 'I should have let you deal with Dante and his men your way.' I glance down at my knuckles. 'Combat is your thing, not mine. Besides, I should have known you were more likely to torture the chess pieces than play them.'

The boards on the windows shudder. Jesus and his cross sway from a rusted nail behind the altar.

'I still have him. Griffin too.'

Christ. I let out a slow hiss, my thoughts filling with that fucking cave. The shadows from the fire dancing on the craggy walls. The screams that echo off the sweat-drenched ceiling. Dante's been in there for *two weeks,* Griffin even longer. It's like something out of a horror movie.

I know why my brother is telling me this. 'I appreciate the offer, but it's back to regular programming for me,' I say dryly. 'Give them both a good kick in the nuts on my behalf, though.'

I stand, and the silhouette shifting in the darkness tells me Gabe does too. As he walks toward me, something about the uneven patter of his footsteps instantly raises the hairs on the back of my neck.

When he steps into the dim light, my chest clenches. 'What the fuck, Gabe?' I mutter, instinctively reaching for the grip of my gun. 'Who did this to you?'

He only stares at me through the swollen slits of his eyes. He's a bloody, bruised mess. Busted lip, blackened cheekbones. Fuck, looking like this, I wouldn't recognize my own brother in a police line-up.

As I search the empty pews for an answer, the realization

hits; he's Gabriel Visconti. No one could get close enough to him to do this much damage.

Unless he let them.

'Why?' I grit out.

The thick trunk of his throat bobs. He avoids both my stare and my question. 'I'm going away for a while. I need . . .' He shakes his head, like he's ridding his brain of noxious thoughts. 'Dante will be dealt with, and my men are all yours.'

He pushes past me and limps down the nave. I've gotten used to my brother leaving without warning over the years, but after everything that's happened over the last month, it doesn't feel as easy to watch him go.

Suddenly, he stops. 'You didn't deal with the girl.'

My shoulders tense. Fuck, I don't know what's worse, hearing Penny's name, or hearing her reduced to *the girl*.

'I did.'

'You didn't.'

'I *did*. Just not in the way you suggested.' I swallow. 'She left town.'

'No she didn't.'

The fuck? 'Christ, Gabe –'

'She's in her apartment watching that film that makes everyone cry.' He glances back at me. 'On repeat. At all hours. With that scruffy kid from across the hall.'

Confusion and something hotter bites at my edges. 'What?' I shake my head. 'And how the fuck would you know?'

'Our apartments share a wall.'

I stare at him. There's too much to unpack in one brain dump. I'd love to know why the fuck my millionaire brother lives in a shitty walk-up on Main Street, but I'd like to know how, and why, Penny is still in town more.

Didn't Rory say she left her neighbor a goodbye note?

Before I can respond, Gabe pops his knuckles at his side and continues walking. 'You must have really liked her to give her the watch Mama gave you when you opened Lucky Cat.'

I'm too distracted. Can barely hear him over the pounding in my ears. 'I didn't give it to her; she won it.'

'Did she win Mama's necklace, too?'

My gaze slides down from the rotting beam to his. 'What?'

'The four-leaf clover necklace. Did she win that off you too?'

But by the dry humor dancing behind his swollen eyelids, I know he already knows the answer.

Penny

Matt glances up from his cell to the television just in time to see Ryan Gosling wading through the lake. 'Shit,' he mutters, swiping the remote off the coffee table and stabbing the fast-forward button. 'Close your eyes for five seconds.'

I do as I'm told. It's pointless though, because we've been watching *The Notebook* on a loop for hours, so the kiss is burned into the backs of my eyelids anyway.

When it came on screen four showings ago, I let out a whimper so loud it woke Matt up from his nap beside me. He hasn't let the scene play through since.

Keeping my eyes closed, I choke back the swell in my throat and pull the duvet I swiped from my bed over my face. 'You're such a good friend, Matty.'

He sighs. 'Ah, we're back in the feeling-sorry-for-yourself stage. You're much more fun when you're angry. Leaving scathing reviews on *Yelp* for all of Raphael's casinos? Calling a premium sex hotline for three hours using his credit card? Great times.'

The last two weeks have been a tilt-a-whirl of emotions.

On the highs, I want to burn down the planet simply because Raphael is on it, and on the lows, I want to curl up under this duvet and sob.

My plan to leave the Coast didn't last long. I didn't get farther than the Devil's Cove bus station before Nico swooped me up. My guttural sobs filling his Tesla answered his question. I wanted – *needed* – to be distracted.

He took me to Hollow and put me to work at The Grotto, an elite casino buried deep within the cave network. It makes the Visconti Grand look like a bingo hall, and like most of the people above-ground, I never knew it existed. He sat me in his office, in front of a bank of security camera feeds, and patted me on the shoulder.

'You know every trick in the book, Little P. If you see any of our clients play dirty, you let me know.'

For the first hour, I stared past the monitors, disinterested and sullen. I believed Nico had done what desperate parents do to their annoying toddlers – dump them in front of a screen in the hope they'll stop wailing.

But then I saw it. A roll of a wrist, a playing card sliding out from a shirt cuff and entering the player's poker hand. My spine snapped straight, and Nico appeared over my shoulder. He rewound the footage and let out a dry chuckle.

'Good spot, Little P.'

Then he yanked on a pair of leather gloves and left the office. Only a few moments later did he appear on screen, dragging the man off his chair and out of view.

A dull thrill vibrated through me, then all night I stayed glued to the cameras, watching and waiting to catch another swindle in real time.

It was the best distraction I could have.

A week passed, my nights at The Grotto filled with CCTV and muffled screams coming from the next room over, my days spent in restless sleep at Nico's cliff-side manor. When I rode the lows, I couldn't stop the tears from falling. But on the highs . . . Fuck, I was *angry*.

I was glad Nico'd stopped me leaving town, because fuck that. It was exactly what Rafe had wanted, and I'd rather have carved my kidneys out with a rusty spoon than give that man what he wanted. The Devil's Coast was my home as much as it was his. I was born and raised here too. Plus, I had friends who cared about me now.

And when I began to think of my friends, I started to feel sick with guilt.

After everything he'd done for me, Matty deserved better than coming back from his trip and seeing a goodbye letter on his punny welcome mat.

He was confused and a little grossed out when I came home and gave him a teary grovel, and that's when I found out he wasn't the only friend worried about me.

Rory, Wren, and Tayce had apparently been blowing up my phone, the one that lay shattered on my bedroom carpet. Apparently, they'd also been hammering on my front door and swinging by the diner late at night to see if I was there.

But they are one fewer degree of separation away from Raphael, and although I feel awful, I can't bring myself to reach out yet.

Darkness seeps through the crack in my curtains, shading the stark white walls purple. When the movie credits roll, Matt snatches up the remote before I can reach for it.

'No. No more.' He flicks through the channels and settles on a World War II documentary. 'Ryan Gosling's abs have traumatized me. I swear, I'll never eat junk food again.'

'Fair enough.' My attention roves around the living room for something to do. It's too late to nap; Nico will be picking me up for a shift at The Grotto in an hour. 'Wanna order pizza?'

Matt sits up. 'Hell yeah.'

I swipe his cell off the coffee table and twirl Rafe's black Amex between my fingers. I order two large pizzas with all the trimmings, plus every side on the menu.

'Anything else, ma'am?' the teen on the other end of the line asks.

My eyes slide up to meet Matt's, and the embers of fury glow red in my stomach again. 'Yeah – I don't have any cash. Can I put a tip on my card?'

Matt's eyes light up.

'That's very kind, ma'am. How much?'

I pause. 'A thousand dollars.'

'What?'

Those embers burst into flames. 'Make it two.'

When I hang up, Matt high-fives me. These petty acts of revenge are what's keeping me sane, but he takes even more delight in them than I do. Turns out, he has his own grudge against Rafe.

On Christmas Day, Matt got drunk and confessed to him that he has a crush on Anna. Rafe told him to just text her. *The worst that could happen is that she says 'no.'*

He was wrong. It turns out her replying to my friend's heartfelt paragraph with seven laughing emojis and nothing else was the worst that could happen.

'Fuck Raphael Visconti,' Matt mutters, flopping back on the sofa and putting his feet up on the coffee table. 'Fuck him, and fuck his shitty dating advice. What does he know, anyway? He couldn't even keep *you* around, and you probably drop your panties for the right candy bar.'

I only gave Matt the half-baked truth when I turned up on his doorstep. I didn't tell him about the hotline or the milliondollar check, or the fact that my heart was too soft for that whole enemies-with-benefits bullshit.

I'm about to snap back with a shitty retort, when two flashes of light illuminate my curtains. My heart leaps to my throat but sinks back down to my chest just as quick.

It'll only be Nico; he's chronically early to everything.

I haul myself off the sofa and go to the window with the intention of beckoning him up for pizza, but when I slide the curtain open, my throat goes dry.

It's not Nico's Tesla, but a familiar G-Wagon. One I've slept in, eaten in, and fucked in. And behind the windshield is the silhouette of the man I did all those things with.

Numbness makes my limbs heavy. *What the fuck is he doing here?* I stare blankly at the headlights as they flash again.

'What's going on?' Matt asks.

'It's Rafe.'

The sofa groans under him. 'Shit. Do you think he heard what I said about him?'

'What? No –'

The headlights flicker again, and this time, they don't stop. My retinas burn and orange spots dance on the window pane. A sudden fury sweeps through me, charging my blood. I don't care what he wants – after everything this asshole has done, does he seriously think he can rock up to my apartment, flash his lights, and I'll trot down to greet him like a grateful puppy?

Fuck off.

I want to ask Matt if he has any kind of heavy, blunt object in his apartment that I can throw at Rafe's windshield, but instead, I settle for flipping him off – with *both* hands – and dramatically drawing the curtains.

Matt watches me as I stalk back to the sofa and glare at the television. I snatch up the remote and turn up the volume.

'Cover your ears.'

'Huh? Why – oh, fuck!'

I don't even flinch at the sound of Rafe's horn blasting from the street below; I can barely hear it over the roaring in my ears. He can lay on it all damn night for all I care. Out of all the games we've played, this is one I'm certain I'll win.

'For the love of god, make it stop,' Matt moans after a few minutes, sandwiching his head with two cushions.

Maybe Rafe *can* hear what Matt says about him, because we're plunged into sudden silence. He lets out a sigh of relief, and I sigh too, but for a different reason.

'It's not over,' I say.

The door to our apartment building flies open so violently, that the window shudders. The sound of heavy footsteps echoes from the direction of the hall, and we both turn to look at my front door.

Matt tenses. 'He's coming up?'

I'm too busy scanning the room for something pointy to reply.

'Eh,' he continues shakily. 'It's not like he'll be able to break your door down. I tried the other week, remember? Almost broke my foot. It must be made of steel or –'

Bang.

The door flies open, and fluorescent light from the hall washes across the carpet. Unadulterated rage jolts me to my feet, but Matt has a different survival instinct: making a weird, girlish noise and pulling my duvet over his head.

And then he's *right here*. Darkening my doorway. His wild eyes search the room until they clash with mine.

Gah. The sight of him tightens my lungs then makes my throat burn. It's been two weeks since I woke up in his bloodied bed next to a million-dollar check and a cowardly confession written on a Sinners Anonymous card. And for two weeks, I've been a deranged mess. Alternating between sobbing, plotting his demise, and scrubbing his name off my lower back.

But here he is, in his blackest of suits with the sharpest of creases. *Two weeks* I've spent writhing in his damn trap, and all the while he's been strolling around like he couldn't care less that he lost the key.

Fuck him. Fuck him twenty-times over. '*Get. Out.*'

His attention turns down to the lump on the sofa and sparks black. One hand reaches for his gun, the other rips the duvet away.

He points the gun in Matt's face. 'Are you fucking my girl?'

Matt squeals and holds his palms up in surrender. As soon as Rafe realizes it's just my Golden Retriever neighbor, he rolls his eyes.

He flicks the end of the gun barrel in the direction of the hall. 'All right. Get out before you piss yourself.'

Matt doesn't even glance back at me before bounding out of my apartment.

Fucking traitor.

The slam of the door reverberates around the room, then tapers off into a heavy silence.

We stare at each other for three stuttered heartbeats before I find my voice. 'You have some nerve bursting in here. And I'm *not* your girl –'

He takes a sudden step toward me, and I lose the breath needed to finish my sentence. I'm not quick enough to dodge the hand that flies to my nape, but I wish I were, because his proximity makes my head swim. He brought the winter chill in with him, but his hand is hot and the weight of it bitterly familiar.

'Penny.' His eyes soften as they search my face. Then they slide south and harden on my collarbone. 'Who gave you that necklace?'

Ah, for a split-second, I almost thought . . . Christ. I'm embarrassed to admit what I thought. I should know by now love isn't like it is in the movies. Raphael Visconti didn't pop my front door off its hinges because he suddenly realized he couldn't live without me.

My jaw tightens, and I focus on the wall behind his head. 'Let me guess; you're still unlucky even though you shoved me out of your life, and now you're hoping if you buy a necklace of your own, it'll help? You know, I'm starting to think your luck had nothing to do with me, and everything with you being a massive ass –'

'The woman, Penelope. Describe her to me.'

I try to yank out of his grasp, but he only tightens his grip. There's a desperate edge to his tone and it pricks my curiosity. I look back to him, and realize it's mirrored in his eyes now, too. 'I don't know.'

'Think about it,' he growls.

'Dark hair, in her fifties, maybe.'

'Give me *more*.'

'I said I don't know, Rafe. She looked expensive. Nice dress, high heels. Had this big rock on her finger. What's that purple gemstone called?'

His lids flutter shut. He releases me and walks to the window. Laces his fingers behind his head and glares down at the street. 'Amethyst. An amethyst wedding ring.'

The room swells with the sound of his heavy breathing.

'Who was she?' I whisper.

His shoulders tense. 'My mother.'

The floor under my feet goes soft. My fingers fly to my necklace, as if making sure it's still there.

'How . . .' I falter, shaking my head. 'How do you know? How can you be sure?'

He lets out a huff. 'I'm sure, Penny. I can see it now, as clear as anything. Fuck, I don't know how I never connected the dots before. There's nothing unique or special about the design, I guess. And seriously, what are the chances? But she never took it off, not even for fancy dinners and balls. She'd just layer her diamonds or her pearls over it. I remember . . .' He clears his throat and runs a hand through his hair. 'I'd always untangle them for her in the car ride home.'

My heart cracks in two, right down the middle. As I take a step forward, his gaze meets my smeared reflection in the window. We stare at each other, a stillness cloaking the room.

He's right. What are the chances? All the anger in my body has evaporated, and I'm left with this awful, hollow ache behind my solar plexus.

'That sounds like fate,' I choke out.

His laugh is humorless. 'Yeah, it does.'

He turns and looks at me. *Really* looks at me, like he's committing every angle of my face to memory. He breathes out, rubbing his jaw and giving his head a shake. 'Fuck, Penny. Look at you.'

Dazed, I stupidly look down at my sweats and fluffy socks combo and frown. 'What about me?'

When I glance up for an answer, my pulse flutters in my throat. He's closed the gap between us, finding my hips and drawing me so close my body fuses with his. The heat of his stomach burning through my hoodie thaws the ice in my chest. And when he drops his forehead to mine, blocking out the light in the room, it unlocks memories of violent love-making and gentle massages, and fuck, the damn butterflies that always came with them.

'What was I thinking?' he murmurs, brushing his nose over mine. 'How did I ever think I could let you go, Queenie?'

Before my thoughts can solidify, he grabs a fistful of my hair and brings his mouth to mine. The rough grip is at odds with his soft kiss, spinning my common sense off its axis.

He captures my bottom lip between his, tugging it slowly, like he's savoring the taste. The move sparks a fresh flame in my lower core, and for the first time in two weeks, it isn't anger or rage but *need*. All I can think as he works his tongue into my mouth and groans with approval when I let him, is that he's *kissing me*.

There's no icy rain numbing my skin and I'm not slippery with his blood, but it feels just as dramatic. My heart beat drums so loud it drowns out all my thoughts, and now I'm nothing but my senses. I'm seeing stars on the backs of my eyelids, flashes of green when I dare open them. Tasting his mint flavor, smelling his masculine scent. I don't even realize we've moved until I feel the backs of my legs meet the side of the sofa.

Rafe yanks my head back and scrapes his teeth along the curve of my throat, before sucking where my pulse beats. 'Come home, Queenie. Come home and let me worship you every day for the rest of your life.'

I groan, palming his chest. Maybe because his lips aren't assaulting mine, I manage to reply with a somewhat coherent answer. 'I *am* home.'

His palm skims down my spine and spanks my ass. 'Our home,' he growls into my collarbone, planting violent kisses along it. 'The yacht, baby. Hang your stolen clothes up in my closet, make your god-awful lasagnas in my oven. Light your girly candles in every room. I want all of it, all of you. Just come *home*.'

He drops me to the sofa and comes down on top of me. The rickety frame of my Craigslist purchase cracks under our weight. Rafe glances up at me, eyes darkening.

'Our home has sturdy sofas and doesn't look like a smack den.'

I bring my knee up to his groin, but he catches it and roughly pushes it to the side, lowering himself between my thighs.

'Are you really cracking jokes when all I want to do is put my fist through your face?'

My words melt into a whimper as he pulls up my top and licks along the waistband of my sweats. 'And all *I* want to do is find out if you still taste as good as I remember.' He looks up at me with a dangerous heat, pulling my waistband between his teeth like an animal. 'You can put your fist through my face later.'

I almost ask, 'Pinky promise?' but then his hot tongue sizzles against my clit, and, oh well, I guess I'll just have to take his word for it.

Penny

Raphael Visconti's enormous frame spills out over all four corners of the single bed. The sight would be comical if the bed wasn't mine, and if he wasn't *naked*.

I can't stop staring at him. Haven't stopped since the white sun pierced through my blinds and woke me up. Its colors have warmed in the hours since, and now wash his tanned skin with a golden glow, giving a vibrant sheen to his tattoos.

He's lying on his side, one thick arm disappearing beneath my pillow. The slack of his jaw deepens the contour of his cheekbones; the gentle rise and fall of his chest makes the serpent on his collar slither.

He looks so peaceful.

He looks so heartbreakingly handsome.

He looks like such a douche.

I draw back my foot and kick him in the shin.

His body moves before his eyes open, flipping me onto my back and coming down on top of me with a hot hiss.

'Did you just *kick* me?'

'You got lucky, I was aiming for your dick.'

He finally pops an eye open, pinning me with a bleary yet blistering glare. 'Fuck was that for?'

'I'd give you three guesses, but all of them will probably be right.'

His frown softens when his gaze drops to my lips. He shifts his weight to cup my cheek with one hand, and lowers his mouth to mine. 'Good morning to you too,' he murmurs, kissing me gently. 'Let me get one kiss in before you bite my head off.'

Melting into the mattress is an involuntary reflex. So is the pathetic sigh that rises in my throat. Rafe takes it as permission to kiss me again. 'All right, maybe two,' he says, scraping his teeth over my bottom lip.

I can feel him hardening against my inner thigh, and my nipples tighten in anticipation. We fucked last night – all night. A lot. On my now-broken sofa, in my too-small shower. With his lips against mine a novelty, and his silky sweet-nothings in my ear, I was weak-willed and pliable – the girl on the yacht who threw everything that wasn't nailed down into the raging Pacific was nowhere to be seen. I bailed on work. I sent away pizza, for Christ's sake.

Rafe's kiss travels south and so does his hand, gripping the base of his erection and rubbing it along my slit. My eyes roll damn-near to the back of my head.

No.

I clamp my thighs shut. 'Stop it,' I hiss, twisting to glare out the window. 'I'm pissed at you.'

He holds my jaw in my place and dips to suck on a nipple. *Fuck*. 'I know, baby,' he says, after a sloppy *pop* as his mouth releases my breast. 'Let me make it up to you.'

My toes curl and my back arches. I clench my teeth together to stop myself from moaning. 'Another orgasm isn't going to cut it.'

He moves up to my throat again, smiling against it. 'No? Then what do you want? Diamonds? A car? Two cars? An island, Queenie? A Birkin in every color? Fuck,' He licks the sensitive spot behind my ear. 'I'll give you the world in every color if you want it.'

I can't help but grunt a noise of approval. It's the hustler in me, I guess. 'Yes.'

'Yes to what?'

'All of it.'

His chuckle vibrates against my pulse. 'Deal.'

'And one more thing.'

'Anything, it's yours.'

I grab a fistful of his hair and yank his head back. 'I want you to leave.'

His stare is half-lidded and confused. 'Leave what?'

'My bed. My apartment.' I swallow. 'You've got to go.'

It takes Rafe three heavy seconds to register what I'm saying. When he does, he leans his weight on his palms and glares down at me. 'What?'

I take advantage of the distance he put between us and escape, jumping out from underneath him and wrapping the bed sheet around myself. I run to the window, where I'm far enough away from him that those large hands and that expert tongue can't sway my decision.

'What did you think was going to happen, Rafe? Did you think you could pop my front door off its hinges, lick my pussy, flash me those abs, and all would be forgiven? Over a tiny twist of fate? What type of sponge-brained idiot do you take me for?'

Sitting up on the corner of the bed now, he stares at me blankly. 'Why did you fuck me last night then?'

'I was horny,' I snap back. When he frowns in confusion, I bite out a noise of frustration. 'I don't even know where to begin, honestly. Let's start with the fact you own Sinners Anonymous. I've been confiding in that hotline every day since I was thirteen. It was my fucking diary, Rafe! When did you realize I was calling it?'

I tap my foot, waiting for a reply. Eventually, he palms his jaw and grinds out an answer. 'After the thunderstorm in the phone booth. I reversed-called the number.'

I feel sick. I haven't come to terms with the fact he's behind the soothing robotic voice that has listened to me for all these years. Every time I let my brain go there, I squirm with embarrassment, thinking of all the cringy stuff he must have heard. I also feel stupid as hell; looking back, he'd dropped so many hints. He knew my favorite breakfast, the cocktail I like. That I can't braid my own damn hair.

'A game is only fun when both people know they're playing it. Anything else makes you an ass,' I grit out. 'You had a million opportunities to tell me you owned it, but you didn't. And when you did tell me, it was only for selfish reasons.' A fresh wave of anger burns the lining of my stomach. 'And the *way* you told me? Jesus Christ, don't even get me started.' I storm over to the dresser, snatch up the million-dollar check and wave it around. 'What the fuck is this? I'll tell you what it is; it's a coward's way out. You thought I'd take the money and run, and then you wouldn't have to break it off with me. Newsflash –' I toss the check at his feet. 'I'm still here!'

We both stare at the crumpled piece of paper on my carpet. I sweep it up and put it back on my dresser. I'm manic with anger, but I'm not stupid.

Sucking in a deep breath, I tighten the bed sheet around myself and try to steady my voice. 'It's crazy, actually. I've been ranting at you for five minutes, and yet I haven't even touched on the fact you dangled me over the side of your yacht like a fucking fish on a line.'

We stare at each other, my glare hotter than hell, his unreadable. Eventually, he nods, dropping his elbows to his knees and rubbing his hands together.

'I'm sorry,' he says quietly.

'Sorry isn't good enough,' I whisper back.

His eyes flash. 'Then what will be, Penny? Because one thing's for sure; I'm not walking this earth without you.' He laughs bitterly, running a paw over his chest. 'I tried it. Didn't like it.'

Silence trickles down the walls like syrup. Suddenly, I realize something: I don't know what I want from him. He doesn't know what to give me. We're just two idiots who don't know how love works.

My throat feels like sandpaper. 'Well, then. Figure it out.'

He groans, rolling his neck. 'Rory didn't tell me about this bit.'

'What?'

He rises to his feet, shaking his head. 'Nothing, baby.'

I avert my eyes as he gets dressed, knowing that if I watch those biceps flex as he tightens his belt, I'll be back face down on the bed, waving my ass in the air, and my monologue will have been pointless.

I follow him to the front door, which is flapping against the frame, thanks to his donkey kick. The only reason I haven't been robbed is because two burly men stand outside it. My cheeks heat when I realize they definitely heard my entire outburst – and worse, me screaming Rafe's name in a different way all night. But as we walk to the entryway, they politely turn away and stare at the walls.

Rafe turns, gripping the bed sheet and yanking me toward him before I can dodge his reach. When I try to twist my head, he cages my jaw with his hand and presses his mouth to mine. 'I really am sorry, Queenie,' he murmurs in a way that makes my knees go jelly-like. 'I'll figure it out, I promise.'

I don't dare breathe; I'm too scared something cute will come out. Instead, I fist the fabric at my sides, and watch him cross the threshold.

'Wait,' I blurt out.

He turns at the top of the stairs, hopeful eyes clashing with mine.

'Black.'

They narrow. 'What?'

'That's the color I want my Birkin.' I pause. 'The first one.'

Then I slam my broken door shut.

Rafe

'Grovel.'

I stop spinning my poker chip and frown. 'What?'

Rory stares at me from across the breakfast table, like she just discovered I only have one brain cell, and she's wondering how I survive day-to-day. 'She wants you to grovel, Rafe.' Her lip curls into a sneer. 'And rightly so. Goose, no wonder she disappeared off the face of the planet, you absolute weirdo.'

I cut a knuckle over my jaw and stare at the marble countertop. I wonder if I smack my head against it, if it'll knock some common sense into me. The worst part about Rory's reaction is that I've only told her the super-sanitized version of the story. Losing the kiss bet, the check, and the necklace. I skipped over the whole hotline thing, the wild enemies-with-benefits sex, and of course, the fact that I dragged Penny out to the yacht bow in the pissing rain. And she's reacting like this?

Yeah, I'm a grade-A cunt.

I was so blinkered by the bad luck Penny brought me, I didn't stop to think about how I hurt her. I'd thought the million-dollar check would be enough to sweeten the blow, but fuck, seeing it still crumpled up on her dresser this morning was a knife in the chest. She hated me so much, she didn't even cash it in?

The kettle squeals and Rory jumps up to grab three mugs from the cabinet. As I watch her, a rare surge of panic nips at my nerves. 'Well, what the fuck do I do?'

'Apologize, for starters.'

'Tried that, didn't work.'

Beside me, Angelo laughs into his eggs. I turn to glare at him. 'How did you grovel?'

He looks up at me lazily. 'I killed her seventy-year-old fiancé with a bullet to the head. What did I need to grovel for?'

Rory hums her approval. I roll my eyes, a cocktail of bitterness and jealousy filling me. My brother and his wife are a sickening picture of marital bliss. They're still wearing their matching jumpsuits after an early morning flight. Angelo made breakfast; Rory's making the tea. Christ, I used to pity made men who've walked down the aisle, and now I'm possessed with the thought of standing at the top of one, waiting for Penny. Bet she looks hot in white. She looks hot in everything.

But first, grovel. Right.

'Your first issue, is that it looks like you only came back for her because you found out the necklace belonged to your mama.' Rory scoops a heap of sugar into a mug and stirs it thoughtfully. 'She's probably thinking if that wasn't the case, you'd have never bashed down her door.' She glances at me. 'Very Gabe-ish of you, by the way.'

Angelo laughs again. He's in an annoyingly good mood today. 'You kidding? Anyone with eyes could see Rafe was always going to go crawling back. I was so certain, I've got three different bets going on how long it'd take.'

I frown. 'You don't bet.'

'And you don't wear sweats and watch trash TV with my wife. I made an exception.'

Groaning, I run a hand over my face. My shirt cuff smells like Penny's perfume, and it makes me want to claw my eyeballs out. Truth is, Gabe telling me Penny's lucky necklace was our mama's was the excuse, not the reason. Sure, it's the most perfect twist of fate, one that makes me not give a flying fuck that she's the unluckiest thing to ever happen to me, but I was at the point where any excuse would have sufficed. Hell, once I discovered she hadn't really left town, I'd have kicked down her door over leaving a paperclip in her apartment.

Rory places a steaming mug in front of me. 'Here's your tea, Rafey,' she says sweetly. Too sweetly. As I look down at the steaming liquid, Angelo nudges it out of reach. 'Don't drink that,' he mutters, chomping on a slice of toast. 'I need you sharp today.'

'*Gesù Cristo.*' I glance up at Rory's back as she makes teas for her and Angelo. Using a different spoon, obviously. '*Your girl's a psycho,*' I bite out in rapid Italian.

'*So's yours,*' he grunts back. '*I overheard Gabe's men talking about the state of your yacht.*'

I grimace. I haven't been back there since I left Penny in my bed. Not because I knew it'd be inhabitable, but because the thought of being in rooms she once filled makes me feel violent.

'Fuck it, I'll just force her to be with me. That's what everyone else does –'

Angelo's fist reaches out and clamps over mine. I hadn't even realized I was spinning my poker chip again, this time at a million revolutions per minute. 'All those spreadsheets and contracts, and you're still stupid. It's easy. All she wants is for you to prove to her that you're not the massive cock you've made yourself out to be.' He lets go of my hand and stabs at his bacon. 'You'll fix this, because that's what you do: fix things. Even if you have to drag your balls over a bed of burning coals while serenading her, you'll do it.' He pauses, a smirk tilting his lips. 'I'll rip the shit out of you for the next ten years, but you'll do it.'

My jaw works. Unfortunately, I know he's right. He takes my silence as agreement. 'Good. Have you finished being a whiny bitch? Because we need to talk about more pressing issues.'

I'm still distracted by red hair and slamming doors. 'Like what?'

'Like Gabe. He's gone AWOL again.' He eyes me. 'You just had to go and get stabbed, didn't you?'

My stare hardens on his. I haven't told him I saw Gabe at the church yesterday, let alone the state of him. 'You know what he's like – he'll be back.'

'Yes, but where has he gone and for how long? He's not just our brother now; he's our *consigliere*. He's got a job to do. Just because Dante's been dealt with, doesn't mean he can fuck off on vacation whenever he likes.' He glances over his shoulder into the hall, and lowers his voice. 'Besides, I don't like dealing with his men. You've read *Lord of the Flies*, right?'

'Don't worry about Gabe,' Rory chimes in, sliding a mug in front of Angelo and taking her seat at the breakfast bar. 'He's fine.'

I swipe a slice of toast off my brother's plate before he can reach for it. 'Yeah? And how would you know, Psychic Sally?'

'I spoke to him last night.'

We both stare at her. Angelo clears his throat. 'You what?'

Her eye roll disappears behind a veil of steam as she lifts her mug to her lips. 'Jeez, you two are such *men*. If you're worried about him, just call him.'

The silence is tinged with disbelief. Rory takes a lazy gulp, eyes darting between me and my brother.

'You know where Gabe is?' Angelo asks her calmly.

'Yeah, but I'm not a snitch.' Her cell vibrates on the counter, and her eyes light up. 'Oh my goose, it's Matt, which means it might be Penny!'

My heart thumps on the double at the sound of her name. I

sit up straighter, suddenly not giving a flying fuck about Gabe's whereabouts. 'Answer it.'

Rory looks at me like I've gone mad. 'In front of you? As if!'

She flounces out of the room and up the stairs, cell clutched to her ear.

Angelo lets his fork clatter to his plate. 'I knew I shouldn't let her hang out with Gabe in the garage so much. He's a bad influence.'

I frisbee the half-eaten toast at him. 'Your wife just tried to poison me; I think she can handle herself.' Rising to my feet, I tighten my cufflinks and stride toward the door. 'I'm off. Got shit to do.'

'Like what?'

'Like Googling what the fuck groveling means.'

Angelo calls my name as I cross the doorway. I turn and meet his half-grin.

'She was calling the hotline, wasn't she?'

Jaw tight, I nod.

'And you were listening to her calls, weren't you?'

I nod again, and my brother bursts into the loudest laugh. 'Fuck me, I can't wait to see how this pans out. When I found out Rory was calling the hotline, I just didn't listen. If you'd just done the same, you'd be getting your dick wet right now.'

I glare at him. 'You didn't listen to any of Rory's calls?'

'Nah. I'm not nosy, like you.'

'Don't worry; you weren't missing out on much, brother. Her confessions were shit.'

Before he can jump up and swing for me, I stroll out to the entryway, flipping him off over my shoulder.

Penny

The diner is lit yellow, the compressed chatter humming between its walls lulling me into lethargy. It's gloomy outside – perfect nap weather. I can barely see the sky on the other side of the condensation-streaked window, but when I press my cheek to the wet glass, I can hear the wind whistling down Main Street.

My lids flutter shut. Man, I'm tired. Now that I know how it feels to sleep through the night, I don't know how I ever used to stay awake.

The bell above the door chimes and a flurry of activity follows. I smile before I even open my eyes, because that's one thing I've noticed about Rory, Wren, and Tayce. Every time they enter a room, a chaotic energy chases them in. The good, contagious kind.

'Oh my god, Penny! Are you okay?'

I crane my neck to see Wren click-clacking between booths, a flurry of baby-pink and blond hair. She slides in beside me and slings her arms around my neck. Her bubblegum scent makes my throat tight. 'I'm fine, Wren. How have you been?'

She yanks off a glittery glove and swats me with me. 'Worried sick, that's how I've been.' Her eyes dart around my face, like she's searching for something. 'Why didn't you call me?'

'Because anytime anyone calls you with a problem, your advice is to listen to ABBA's greatest hits on repeat.' I turn to see Tayce shimmying into the seat opposite. She lunges over and plants a kiss on my cheek. She always looks so cool, and with her boyfriend blazer and oversized sunglasses pushing back her black hair, today is no exception.

'I get why you didn't call Wren, but why didn't you call *me*?' she says, dragging my milkshake toward her. 'I'd have taken you on a crazy night out in Cove. We'd have danced on tables, slammed too many shots. Hell, I'd have got you so drunk you didn't remember your own name, let alone Rafe's.'

I laugh, but Wren doesn't find it so funny. 'Ah, lovely. And then at the end of the night, I'd be the one handing you flip-flops and holding your hair back while you're sick in a trash can.'

'Probably shouldn't volunteer to look after drunk people in Cove then,' Tayce muses, slurping from my shake.

'The kindness of volunteers keeps the world turning, honey,' Wren huffs. She glances up at the cash desk. 'What's Rory doing?'

I follow her gaze and see Rory handing an over-stuffed envelope to the girl behind the desk, an apologetic smile on her face.

'Rafe lost his shit in here a few days ago and trashed a few things. I'm guessing Rory's doing damage control on the Viscontis' behalf.'

I snap my attention back to Tayce. 'What?'

She laughs. 'Love makes you crazy, right?'

My cheeks grow hot thinking of Rafe coming in here and trashing things. So ungentlemanly, so *uncouth*. A sick thrill sweeps through me, but I play off the shudder as being cold. He's not the kind of man to go off because they got his order wrong.

Maybe he didn't find it as easy to ditch me as I first thought.

Rory walks over, buttoning up her purse. She stops at the head of the table and pouts at me. By the pity swirling in her eyes, I know I'm about to get asked the same question for the third time.

'Oh, Penny. Why didn't you call me?'

This time, guilt inflates my chest. I let out a slow breath, hoping to relieve some of the pressure. Technically, I did call her, just two weeks later than she means. After all my anger spilled out over my messy bedroom floor this morning and I kicked Rafe out, I felt fearless. Like I could face anything, even picking up the phone and calling the girls.

I stomped over to Matt's and used his cell before I changed my mind. Rory picked up on the first ring. She didn't ask questions, just told me to name a time and a place and she, Wren, and Tayce would be there.

I saw on my bottom lip with my teeth and tell them the truth. 'Because you're Rafe's sister-in-law,' I say to Rory, before turning to Wren. 'And every time anyone mentions the name Raphael Visconti, you clutch your chest and call him a gentleman.' I glance up at Tayce, who's almost finished my milkshake. 'And with all those tattoos he has, you've seen him naked more times than I have.'

'What's your point?' Tayce asks.

'My point is that I thought you'd all be on Team Rafe because you know him better. And also . . .' I swallow. 'I guess I was embarrassed about what happened.'

Silence sweeps the table. I feel like such an idiot with all my vulnerability on show like this. I clear my throat, getting ready to crack an awkward joke, but Wren grabs my hand.

'I'll screw up my nose and call him an asshole from now on. Or dickhead, or prick. Whatever you choose.'

'And then I'll tattoo that on him the next time he comes into my shop,' Tayce pipes up.

Rory slides into the booth beside her. 'This morning, he told me how he left you on the yacht like that, so I dropped a laxative in his tea. He didn't drink it, but I'll try again tomorrow. He might be my brother-in-law, and yes, of course I love him, but you're our friend.'

'Friends call friends when they're sad,' Wren says, giving my hand a squeeze. 'You talk to us, cry to us.'

'Plot revenge with us,' Tayce says with a wink.

I nod tightly. It's all I can do, because I know if I talk, an awful noise resembling a sob will come out. I can already feel it brewing in my throat.

Tayce's face softens with realization. 'Oh, no. When Wren said you can cry to us, she didn't mean now.'

But it's too late. A tear runs down my face, sizzling against my hot cheek. I swipe at the napkin dispenser and hide behind a scratchy tissue. 'Ah, ignore me. I'm just tired; that's all.'

God, this is mortifying.

It's the first time in two weeks I've cried for a reason other than because I'm hurt. No, I'm crying because I'm suddenly overwhelmed. My whole life, I've only really had one friend I could confide in, and it was a hotline voice that couldn't answer back. I'm not used to being surrounded by girls that care about me.

Wren whimpers in solidarity, because apparently seeing anyone cry sets her off, too. Rory jumps up to shuffle past her and hug me, while Tayce makes a beeline for the counter, with the promise to bring back something extra-chocolatey.

As I sniffle into the shoulder of Rory's hoodie, something dawns on me that makes me cry even harder.

These girls would share their jeans with me in a heartbeat.

Penny

The blackened sky finally breaks, just like I did in the diner a few hours ago. The rain falls freely from the heavens and hammers on my living room window. I glance up at the sudden downpour, then turn back to the television.

I swapped out *The Notebook* for a *Friends* re-run. The canned laughter echoes off my bare walls, but I've never really found Joey walking around with a turkey stuck to his head very funny. I'm not really watching, anyway; I'm just wasting time until Matt finishes hockey practice. Partly so I can eat all the left-over pizza in his apartment, and partly because I'm dying to rip the shit out of him for squealing like a little bitch when Rafe pointed a gun in his face.

Rafe.

There's been a twinge in my chest every time I've thought of him today. I guess it's what uncertainty feels like. When I screamed him out of my apartment this morning, I kicked the ball into his court. It's up to him what he does with it now, if anything at all.

I absentmindedly brush my fingers over my necklace. I can't believe the woman who gave it to me was his mother. Now, my memory of her in that dark alley is tinted rose pink. She's not a nameless guardian angel, but Maria Visconti: the woman who gave birth to the man I'm ridiculously in love with.

But still, it's not enough.

Sure, my heart wants to dance to the tune of stars aligning, but my head is bitter with betrayal. A man fucking me over is a song all-too familiar, and I'm not able to let it go so easily.

I know it's only been a few hours, but I haven't heard a peep from Rafe yet. The closest I've had to contact is coming home and finding I have a new front door. I wish he'd replaced my sofa while he was at it; I'm currently sitting on a cushion on the floor because my Craigslist purchase lies in tatters behind me.

Late afternoon bleeds into night, the time passing to a soundtrack of unrelenting rain and endless health insurance commercials. My ass starts to go numb, and as I rise to stretch out my stiff limbs, there's a sharp knock on the front door.

About time. I pad down the hall, stomach grumbling at the thought of cold pizza. But when I open the door, my heart leaps a few inches, then beats a little faster.

It's not Matt, but Rafe.

He's all sharp suit and suave silhouette, looking down at my welcome mat in amusement.

'It's not even a funny pun.'

I can only stare at him. 'What are you doing here?'

His gaze climbs my sweats and traps me. 'I'm groveling.'

I blink. 'Groveling?'

'Mm.' He produces a bouquet from behind his back. 'Grovels start with flowers.' I frown at the roses in his hands. They're blood red and confusing. Rafe takes advantage of my disbelief by sliding me to the side and strolling into my apartment. 'According to Google, anyway,' he continues, before disappearing into my kitchen. 'But Google also thinks I'm thirty-eight and own a Rottweiler named Cookie, so who really knows?'

I follow him in and hover awkwardly in the kitchen doorway. He sets the roses down and opens cupboards and drawers like he owns the place. 'Do you have a vase?'

'What?'

He glances at me, amused. 'For the flowers.'

'Um, no?'

'Figures. A jug?' He surveys my off-white counters, squinting in displeasure. 'A bong?'

His passive-aggressive dig at my apartment brings me back to my senses. 'I have a trash can you can use. You can throw yourself in it too, if you'd like.'

With a smirk, he twists my Nutribullet off its stand and brings it to the sink. He palms the counter as he waits for the tap to run cold, then puts the smoothie-glass under it. 'Go get dressed.'

'I am dressed.'

He glances back at me. 'Not for dinner, you're not.'

'I've had dinner,' I lie.

In the reflection of the window, I see his jaw tighten. 'I'm sure you'll fit in another.'

'Are you calling me fat?'

He practically punches the tap off. 'Baby, I'm calling you a girl who eats two dinners every single night. That's just a fact. I've seen it with my own eyes.' He turns, leans against the sink, and studies me. 'You're not going to make this easy for me, are you?'

My throat dries up, and I shake my head slowly. 'You don't deserve easy.'

We stare at each other, rain hammering glass the only sound filling my kitchen. Then his chest caves as he lets out a tense breath. 'Come here.'

I don't move. First of all, why the fuck should I? He's got legs too. Second of all, 'come here' means I have to go 'over there' and 'there' is where bad decisions are made. External factors, like his hot hands that know exactly where to touch me, make all rationale bleed out of my brain.

I'm safer over here.

I've got a higher chance of keeping my panties on over here.

With a sharp hiss, he pushes himself off the counter and stalks toward me. I retreat for two steps but I'm not quick enough to dodge his reach. He pulls me into his orbit and carries me over to a counter, sliding my ass back on the surface. I struggle to jump down, but he steps between my legs and cages me in.

He stares down at where his hands grip my thighs. 'I'm trying to make it up to you. Trying to show you how much I care about you.' His eyes lift to mine, soft and tinged with something that doesn't suit him. Desperation. 'I'm *groveling*, Queenie. But you need to let me.'

My heartbeat slows, as if dunked into syrup. The butterflies in my stomach take flight, but it feels like they've come out of hibernation too early. I'm still too bitter and hurt to take his promise at face value, which I guess is why my next words slip out of my mouth.

'Say please.'

His gaze darkens. 'Please what?'

'Ask me out to dinner, but say *please*.'

His nostrils flare, and by the way he glances at the ceiling, I know he's wondering if I'm worth the humiliation. But then his stare falls back to mine, his jaw tight. 'Penny, would you do me the honor of letting me take you out for dinner?' He grits his teeth. '*Please* ?'

Despite not being able to decide whether I want to claw his eyeballs out or not, pleasure skates down my spine. I think I enjoy it when that word slips from Rafe's lips. 'Hmm,' I muse, leaning back on my palms and pretending to weigh up my options. 'Are you paying?'

He laughs. 'What kind of question is that?'

'Will there be dessert?'

'Of course.'

'Can I have two?'

'You can have anything you like.'

I scrape my teeth over my bottom lip. 'I don't know. I have other options –'

'Your only other option is getting bent over my knee and spanked,' he snaps, dragging his hand off my thigh and reaching for his belt buckle. 'You can have two of those, too.'

'All right, all right,' I squeal, wriggling out of his grip. 'I suppose I have time for dinner. I'm not changing my clothes, though.'

He sweeps a look of disbelief over my gray sweatpants, hoodie, and messy bun. 'It's a nice restaurant.'

'Are you saying I don't look nice?'

He pauses, then flashes me a plastic smile. 'You'd look beautiful in a potato sack,' he says insincerely. He hoists me off the counter and sets me on my feet. 'Come on.'

Less than five minutes later, we're crossing the road under the shelter of Rafe's umbrella, his men trailing our shadows. Excitement hums under my skin, and there's a reckless taste on my tongue. Maybe I'm a sadist, but I love the idea of Rafe groveling. It feels like the ultimate game, and it's one I get to set the rules for. Hell, I don't know if he'll win or not, but I'm sure as shit going to put him through his paces to find out.

He holds the passenger side door open for me. I glance at his men getting into the convoy of sedans behind. There's more of them than usual, and there's not a single face I recognize. Then I remember Rafe saying something about Griffin trying to kill him, and shudder.

That would explain the sudden change in lackeys.

The moment I slide onto the seat, my excitement sours. The smell of warm leather entwined with Rafe's cologne. The way the backrest perfectly hugs my hips. My slippers are still sitting in the foot well. The familiarity that lives between these four vehicle walls punches me in the gut.

Rafe must sense the switch in my mood when he slides into the driver's seat, because he tenses. There's a *click-thud* as he locks my door. 'You're not changing your mind. I already said please.'

I stare at his profile, emotion swelling in my throat. 'Why are you bothering?'

His gaze is lazy, trained on the windshield as he pulls out onto the road. 'Because I love you,' he says simply.

Another hit to my gut, but this one feels more like a jack knife. *Because I love you.* Even though they were said so flippantly, so *indifferently,* his words ricochet around the car and deafen me. Despite suddenly struggling to breathe, I manage to shake my head.

I understand how and why I love him, despite hating him with a passion. But that's because I didn't rip myself away from him. He *chose* to tear us apart with a million-dollar check and a confession.

And despite his betrayal, I can understand his reasoning.

'But I'm unlucky,' I blurt out, thinking about his blood trickling over his abs and swirling down the shower drain. I still don't even know what happened to him, just that it was yet another notch on his belt of bad fortune. 'You'll be unlucky for the rest of your life.'

He changes lanes, then steals a glance at the silver chain disappearing under the collar of my hoodie. 'I'm trying to take my mama's advice.'

'Which was?'

'Luck is believing you're lucky,' he says. 'That's what she said to you, right?'

My heart clenches at the memory, and I can only nod.

'So from now on, I'm believing I'm lucky.' His hand slides over my thigh and floods warmth through my core. 'I'm lucky that you let me take you out on a date, aren't I?'

He chuckles when I swat his hand away. Touching leads to fucking, and fucking leads to me saying silly shit I shouldn't, like, *I love you, too.*

As we turn off of Main Street and climb the hill up to the church, there's a sudden, sharp *crack*.

I scream. Rafe swerves the wheel with one hand, while the other flies across my stomach and cages me into the seat. I open my eyes as we roll to stop between the trees.

Rafe flicks on the interior light and grips my chin, eyes scanning me. 'You okay?'

'Y-yeah.' I breathe out a shaky exhale, then nod at the windshield. There's a pebble-sized crater on the right-hand side, and a spider web of cracks fissure out from it.

He glances at it. 'Must have been a piece of loose gravel or something,' he mutters insincerely.

'You're not believing hard enough.'

He runs his thumb over my bottom lip and gives me a humorless smirk.

'It's a work in progress, Queenie.'

***

After swapping out Rafe's G-Wagon for one of the sedans driving up our ass, we end up in Hollow. A lift takes us closer to sea-level, and when we step out of it, I have the urge to turn around and smack my head against its closing doors.

Dammit. This restaurant is fancy. The type that has too many forks on either side of the plate, and not enough food on top of it. The type you don't wear sweatpants and a milkshake-stained hoodie to.

I wish I wasn't so damn stubborn.

Rafe palms the small of my back and pushes me into the main cavern, where a server rushes over to greet us. 'Mr Visconti, Mrs Visconti,' she says, nodding at us politely. She makes more pleasantries but they swim around my ears, wobbly and incoherent. *Mrs Visconti?*

As Rafe's hand finds my back again and guides me to a table, I glare up at his profile. 'Why does she think we're married?'

His dimple deepens. 'Because I told her we were.'

'What? *Why*?'

He doesn't reply until he's sliding a chair underneath me. Then he lowers his lips to the soft bit behind my ear and whispers his answer against it. 'Because I felt like playing our favorite game.' He plants a kiss on my neck. It's so gentle, but it racks my insides like an earthquake. 'Make believe.'

Stupefied, my eyes track him as he rounds the table and sits opposite me. There's a flurry of servers with smiles and napkins and leather-bound menus, but how can I focus on trivial things like the daily specials, at a time like this?

Once we're left alone, Rafe's gaze heats on mine. I break away from it for safety purposes, and do a survey of the space.

The cave is hauntingly beautiful. A small, oval room with minimal human touch. There are only six tables, all empty except ours, and all are cut from rock. The bar is, too – nothing more than a craggy ledge jutting out from the far wall, with enough room to show off special edition Smuggler's Club bottles in a back-lit case.

My gaze sweeps upward to the ceiling. It looks like it's dripping. Each icicle-shaped rock is wrapped with fine fairy lights, dousing the cave in a romantic glow.

'Stalagmites,' Rafe says, watching me. 'Produced by precipitation of minerals from water dripping through the cave ceiling.'

'Stalactites.'

'I'm sorry?'

'Stalagmites rise up from the floor, stalactites hang from the ceiling.' Rubbing my sweaty palms on my joggers, I add, 'You bought me *Petrology for Dummies*.'

His laugh is beautiful and drives into my chest like a key, unlocking memories of other times I've made him laugh like that. I harden my jaw and shoo them away.

'Of course.' He waves a careless hand around him. 'Well, do you like it?'

'Did your other dates like it?'

Irritation moves across his face like a shadow. 'You're the first woman I've taken here.' His attention drops to my lips, and he licks his own. 'You'll be the last, too.'

I try to keep my breathing steady. Try not to fall for his charm. It's crazy how easily I saw through it when we first met, yet now it mists my vision and threatens to veer me off track.

I run my finger over the embroidered border of the napkin, ignoring the weight of his stare. 'So, you're back to playing the perfect gentleman.'

'Would you prefer it if I wasn't a gentleman, Penny?'

I slide my gaze up to his, just as a server appears at our table.

'May I suggest a wine pairing for your meal?' she asks.

Rafe's eyes never leave mine. 'Fuck off, Julia.'

I don't know who the gasp comes from, me, Julia, or both of us, but when she scurries away, embarrassment heats my cheeks.

'That was fucking *rude*.'

Rafe is the dictionary definition of unfazed. He acts like he hasn't heard me, then tightens his cufflinks and leans into the light of the flickering candle between us.

'Would you like to know a secret, Queenie?'

'No.' *Yes.*

He abruptly reaches around the table, then there's a

sickening scraping noise as he drags my chair over the limestone floor so I'm sitting right next to him.

I stare down at our thighs touching. My soft sweats beside his sharp slacks. Tatty to his suave. My next breath stutters. Fuck, how I want to hate this man.

His familiar scent weakens me as he snakes his arm over the back of my chair and brushes his lips against my temple.

'You were right all along.'

'About what?' I breathe out.

'About me pretending to be a gentleman.' The backs of his knuckles graze over the nape of my neck, raising all the goosebumps there. 'But only to other women, never you. There's never been any pretense with you, Penny. When you talk, I listen because I enjoy what you have to say. When I fuck you from behind, it's because I know I also have the privilege of fucking you face-on. And when you leave my bed, I can't bear the thought of it being forever.'

I can't do anything but stare down at our legs touching. I fear if I move, the burning behind my eyeballs will morph into something more. I'm torn, ripped right down the fucking middle. Half of me wants to scream at him some more, the other half urges me to tilt my chin and kiss him, if only to taste the confession that just came out of his mouth.

I do neither of these things. Can't. I only stare at our legs until another server comes over in place of Julia and timidly asks us about wine pairings again.

***

The drive home is cushioned by Nappa leather and the familiar purr of the engine. Rafe's windshield had been fixed by the time I finished my third desert, and I kind of wish it hadn't. There's no way I'd be so close to dozing off if I were in a stranger's sedan, even if Rafe was driving it.

I'm full of food, wine, and contentment, and my lids grow heavier with every passing streetlight. I'm not so far gone that I don't notice Rafe glance at me then turn down the radio and turn up my heated seat.

He's transparent. I know he thinks if it's warm enough, and if he's quiet enough, I'll fall asleep, just like old times.

The night has been tinged with a hopeful glow. Despite my best efforts, I've laughed a lot tonight. Felt things in my chest and between my thighs that I wish I didn't. Christ, it'd be so easy to fall asleep here and wake up in the morning to Rafe stroking my forehead, but I have way too much pride and bitterness inside me, and he still has so much to prove.

Squinting through the windshield, I take stock of where we are. In less than a minute or so, we'll be pulling up outside my apartment. But then the turn for Main Street passes on the left and I roll my head to look at Rafe. 'You're going the wrong way.' When I'm met with silence, my stomach clenches. 'Hey, where are we going?'

Rafe's knuckles tighten on the wheel, at odds with his indifferent tone. 'Home.'

'My home is back that way.'

He speeds up, ignoring me.

'Rafe,' I say as calmly as I can muster, 'Turn around.'

'The yacht's ready.'

'Turn the car around!'

Cursing in Italian, he swings into a pull-off. The engine cuts out, plunging us into tense silence.

He drops his head against the headrest. Runs a hand over his throat. 'I groveled,' he says quietly. 'Now. Come. Home.'

I stare at his sharp profile, watching the muscle in his jaw twitch. 'You groveled for three hours and twenty minutes.'

He rolls his head and pins me with a soft look. 'You still hate me, Queenie?'

Despite my throat being thick with the truth, I nod.

He thinks for a moment, then gives a careless shrug and reaches for the ignition. 'Hate me on the boat, then.'

'I'll hate you from my apartment.'

'Or, you can sleep in the car –'

'Rafe.'

Something about my tone cuts him off. He glares out the windshield for the longest time before giving a tight nod and driving me home in silence.

By the time he parks in his signature asshole way outside my apartment, his annoyance has softened. He shifts in his seat to study me, eyes sparkling. 'Invite me up for coffee, at least.'

I laugh. 'No chance.'

He smiles, reaching out to play with a lock of my hair. 'You probably only have that instant shit, anyway.'

I'm about to tell him I don't even have 'that instant shit' – there are no drinks in my apartment besides tap water and a multi-pack of orange soda – but then his focus moves to my mouth. The car heats, and the topic of coffee is suddenly irrelevant.

His grip on my hair tightens. 'I'm getting a goodnight kiss, and that's non-negotiable.'

I sigh, resisting the urge to twist my face into his palm. It'd be so easy to kiss him. To let his hands roam where they want, then let them yank me into the back seat when the sexual tension spills over.

'It'll cost you.'

He shakes his head in amusement. 'I already paid you a million bucks when I lost the bet. Surely that'll cover all kisses in this lifetime?'

A hot venom whips through me at the mention of the check. 'We both know you didn't pay me because you lost the bet.'

My heart thumps, echoing in the silence. The memory of waking up to an empty bed strips my throat raw. Fuck, how will I ever not feel sick when I think of it? Rafe can buy me roses I don't know how to care for and let me eat three desserts on his dime, but how will I ever forgive him for paying me to go away? For only admitting he owns Sinners Anonymous in the hope it would seal my decision to leave?

Rafe frowns, sensing the shift in mood, then realization softens his brow as he skims his thumb over my cheekbone. 'Fine, how much?'

'Fifty bucks.'

He laughs, tossing his wallet on my lap. 'Sold.'

As he leans in, I press my hand against his chest. 'I meant a hundred!'

'Jesus. For a hundred, I want some tongue action.'

Before I can negotiate, his fingers slide up to my skull and draw me in. His lips touch mine, as soft as a whisper in the wind. It's the lightest brush, but it cracks open my core, leaving me hollow and desperate for more.

Fuck it. He paid, right?

I grip his jaw and pull his lips harder against mine. His growl of approval vibrates against my mouth, and I slide my tongue over his to taste it. He sucks on my bottom lip, glancing up at me with half-lidded, dangerous eyes as he releases it from his mouth with a visceral *pop*.

Fuck. The sound is a carnal sin, and the way it heats my blood only makes me want to hear it again. I chase his retreat, kissing him more violently. Each kiss hotter and wetter, each frictionless touch of our tongues steaming up the windows a little more.

I'm so lost in his taste that I barely notice his palm burning a path up the side of my thigh until he's tugging at my waistband. As the air touches my hip, sudden clarity grips me.

I swat him away and press my back against the door. He lunges for me again, but I bring my foot up on the central console, my knee creating a physical barrier between us. 'Enough,' I gasp, wiping his taste off my lips with the back of my hand.

His eyes are black and hungry as they climb down my hoodie and watch my chest rising and falling. 'How much to kiss your other lips?'

Despite him being deadly serious and the thought making my clit thump, I huff out a laugh. 'No more. Goodnight, Rafe. Thank you for dinner.'

He groans, dropping his chin to my knee. 'Don't be such a stubborn little shit. At least sleep in the car.' I shake my head, awkwardly reaching down for my bag. 'Well what else are you going to do?' He glances up at my living room window like it's his worst enemy. 'You won't sleep. You gonna sit and play chess with the roaches all night?'

No, I'm going to touch myself to the thought of where this would have gone if I were weaker-willed, then pretend to watch twenty episodes of *Friends*, while really obsessing over each detail of the night.

Of course, I don't tell him that. I don't rise to his insult about my apartment, either. 'Sounds like the perfect night in.'

'I'll be parked out here all night, in case you change your mind.'

I twist around and pop my door open. As the cool air whooshes in and bites me, Rafe's hand grips my wrist. I turn around, expecting a final plea, but I'm met with a hard set of his jaw.

His eyes search mine, something vulnerable dancing behind his serious expression.

'Just tell me I have a chance, Queenie.' His thumb skims over my pulse. 'That's all I need to know.'

My heart drops off its axis and beats somewhere above my

navel. I stare back at him, taking in his brooding stare and every sharp plane of his face.

Emotion threatens to choke me, but I won't let it. Not in Rafe's car, anyway. I take what I'm owed from his wallet – plus a little extra for a tip, of course – and toss it into the cup holder.

I stare down at it while I answer his question.

'I told you to choose your route to hell, Rafe,' I say quietly. 'It's not my fault you chose the long way 'round.'

His stare blisters my back as I cross the road and disappear into my apartment building.

Rafe

Rory's yelp fills her dressing room. 'Not so *tight*. Goose, you're holding the strands like a Neanderthal.'

I meet her glare in the vanity mirror. 'Last time, you said it was too loose. Now, it's too tight. Maybe it's your knotty hair that's the problem.'

She's impressively quick, swiping her brush off the dresser and reaching back to crack my knuckles with it. I hiss, tugging on her wonky braid.

'If you were anyone else, brother, I'd snap those fingers off.'

I give a careless glance toward the door, where Angelo's leaning against its frame, expression as sour as his voice.

'Almost lost them in your wife's bird's nest, anyway.'

Rory shakes out the braid and ruffles her curls. 'Same time tomorrow?'

'Unfortunately.'

I wink at her reflection, then sling-shot her hair band onto the dresser. Angelo's expression melts into amusement. I feel it following me as I shrug on my jacket and stoop to give Maggie a goodbye scritch. By the time he steps into the hall to let me pass, that smugness is starting to piss me off.

'Say it now instead.'

He does a shitty job at hiding his smirk behind the back of his hand. 'What?'

'Whatever smart-ass remark you're saving until I'm halfway down the stairs. Say it now, while you're within reach of my right-hook.'

He purses his lips. 'Wasn't gonna say shit.'

'Good.'

But the bastard's a liar, because I'm three steps from the entrance hall when his gruff voice chases me.

'It's been three weeks.'

I slow to a stop, glaring at the pink glitter hearts dangling from the chandelier. Apparently, Rory had so much fun decorating for Christmas, she's getting started on Valentine's Day two weeks early.

'I'm aware,' I grind out.

'Three weeks is a long time to be an ass-kissing simp, isn't it?'

Irritation slithers along my nerves, but more so because I know he's not wrong.

Three weeks of groveling. Three weeks stuck in redemption purgatory, playing a game only Penny knows the rules to. Three weeks of taking her out, paying her a hundred dollars – plus tip – for every kiss. Three weeks of staring at her living room window from across the street all night, every night, in case she changes her mind about not sleeping in my car.

Oddly enough, I'd be lying if I said I hated it. Fuck, at least it's been three weeks with her in my life. Besides, I've become weirdly obsessed with finding out what makes her happy. With every beautifully wrapped box I slide over a candle-lit dinner table, I watch her tug off the bow with baited breath, hoping it'll make her eyes light up in that way that makes my cock hard.

'The Birkin didn't work then?'

I glance behind me to see Rory has joined her husband at the top of the stairs.

'Which one?' I grunt back. Aside from being one unsatisfying fist-fuck away from breaking my dick, the only frustrating thing about living in simp-mode is that I haven't found that thing that makes her eyes light up yet. No, the fucking Birkin didn't work. The next three didn't work either. Or the Cartier bracelet, or the Benz that's been collecting parking fines outside her apartment.

'Ah, the shit you do for love, eh?'

My gaze hardens on my brother. He's got his arm around Rory's waist, a smugness to his expression that I want to pour acid over. It's hard to believe this is the same miserable cunt that'd sneer in disgust any time talks of him taking a wife would fly over the dinner table.

'The shit you do indeed. Like, oh, I don't know, secretly telling all your dinner guests not to touch your wife's turkey because it's as pink as Barbie's playhouse, then proceeding to eat half of it and ride out a bout of salmonella instead of just telling her to shove it back in the oven for another forty-five minutes.' I hold my hand on my heart, enjoying the way Angelo's expression turns dangerous. 'That's true love right there.'

Rory's jaw drops open as she turns to her husband. 'You told everyone not to eat my turkey?' Her eyes slide to mine. 'Really? No one ate my turkey?'

I smile at her and keep moving toward the door. 'Guess Gabe was right – I am a snitch.'

Much to my satisfaction, my brother's entreating words follow me out to the driveway. At least I won't be the only Visconti groveling tonight.

The drive to Penny's apartment is slow and painful. I've hit the rush hour, joining the convoy of cars heading into Hollow or Cove for the night. Before I met my doom card, I'd have just driven like an asshole – up on the curb, the wrong way down one-way streets – to get there faster. But these days, there's a higher chance that if I do that, I might not make it at all.

By the time I pull up outside Penny's building and flash my lights against her window, I'm itching to see her. Her curtain twitches, but she takes her sweet-ass time coming down. I'm halfway through tapping out a warning text to her new cell when she breezes out of her apartment building and stops me mid curse word.

Holy fuck. She looks unreal.

I let my phone drop into the cup holder, and step out onto the street. I'd be lying if I said it was only to open her door – really, I want to get a good fucking look at her.

She's wearing a dress. A pink, sparkly one, with feathery trim around the hemline and cuffs. Her white heels are so high, they're going to make stealing kisses from her even easier.

The sight fills my chest for a reason other than her looking ridiculously hot. She's refused to wear anything but sweats every time I take her out, no matter how fancy the destination.

Maybe I'm finally getting somewhere with her.

As she crosses the road, her gaze slides up to meet mine. She tries her best to feign indifference, but as always, a slight movement ruins her shitty poker face. Tonight, it's the way she swallows when she glances at the space below my belt.

'You're late,' is all she says.

I open the door for her and study her ass as she climbs into her seat.

'And you're beautiful.' I rest my palms on the top of the door frame and eye-fuck those thighs. I haven't had them pressed against my ears for so long, I'm starting to hallucinate about it. 'Nice dress.'

She smiles sweetly. 'Thanks, you paid for it.'

Laughing, I slam her door a little too heavily.

She studies her nails as I slide into the driver's seat. 'Where are we going tonight?'

'McDonalds.'

I smirk at the heat of her stare on my cheek. Pulling out onto Main Street, I slide my hand over her bare thigh. Of course, she swats it away immediately, but God loves a trier.

'I'm a little underdressed for such a classy establishment, don't you think?'

I glance down at her tits in that corset bust. I want to burn the image into my retinas and add it to my spank bank.

'You can always take it off; I wouldn't mind.'

She lets out a laugh. I know it's a real one, because her real laughs have this way of clawing to my heart and squeezing it.

I turn back to the road. 'I've booked an eight-course molecular gastronomy experience at *Le Salon Privé*. I'm sure your attire will be fine, Queenie.'

'That's a whole lot of words, and not a lot of sense.' Her cell buzzes in her purse, and she fishes it out too quickly for my liking. She giggles at a text, and my eyes narrow.

'Care to share?'

'Nah.' She places her cell face-down on her lap and stares straight ahead. 'I need to stop off somewhere before dinner.'

'Stop off where?'

'Somewhere in Cove. I'll direct you.'

Suspicion bites at my edges. I'm too unlucky for things like *stop-offs*, and too neurotic about this girl for her to be giggling at unknown texters.

'No,' I grind out, tightening my grip on the wheel.

Her fingers brush lightly over my forearm resting on the center console. They snake down to my wrist and give my hand a squeeze.

'Please?' she asks, tone all cloud-soft and sugary sweet.

Fuck's sake. The car heats with all the other times she's said *please,* like when she's begging me to let her come. She knows as well as I do that I'm so under her fucking thumb, I can taste her fingerprint.

I clamp my hand around hers so she can't pull it away. 'Fine, but it better be quick.'

The drowsiness of Dip morphs into the tranquility of Hollow, which is then washed away by the bright glow of Cove. The strip is Friday-night frenetic. It passes in a blur of lights and laughter, and despite being pissed about the detour, I can't ignore the hum of excitement that sweeps through my blood.

I fucking love the atmosphere of Cove. I'll love it even more when I finally get the shareholder stake I want from Tor.

Penny glances down at her cell again. 'All right, turn left at the bottom of the strip.'

I frown. 'You taking me up to the north headland?' Christ, I haven't been up there since we were kids. There used to be a funfair that teetered on the edge of it, but Angelo burned it down after our mama was killed there. 'Penelope –' My voice lowers to a mock warning. 'If you're planning on shoving me off it, give me a head's up. I'll have to cancel all my meetings tomorrow.'

There's that laugh again, licking my skin with its delicious flames. I squeeze her hand, hoping the positive reinforcement will encourage her to laugh some more.

She tells me to pull over in what was once the fair's parking lot. Now, it's little more than a concrete slab claimed by towering hemlock trees and their twisted roots.

I glance to the three cars parked up on the far end.

Claimed by doggers too, by the looks of it.

She tries to jump out of the car, but I tighten my grip on her hand. 'Blanket,' I demand, reaching into the backseat and bundling her up in it before she can protest. It's early February, and she's dressed like she's going to a summer ball.

She guides me through the trees and through the charred remains of the fair after I drape my arm over her shoulders and press my lips to her temple. 'I just realized, you neither confirmed nor denied you were planning on throwing me off the cliff. We're certainly heading in that direction.'

'I have no plans to push you off it,' Penny drawls, smiling up at me sweetly. She shrugs out of my grip and teeters ahead in those ridiculous heels. 'Who else will take me out for dinner?'

'I'm sure you'd have plenty of men lining up to take you for dinner.'

'Mm, I'm sure I would too, actually.'

The zap of violence that shoots down my spine is irrational, but it's violence nonetheless. Without thinking twice, I twist my fist into the base of her hair and yank her backward, until her back is flush with my chest.

'You'd be stupid to mistake my obsession with you as me being a limp-dick little bitch, Queenie. I'll play your games and jump through all your hoops until you blow the whistle on full-time. But what I *won't* do is tolerate you mentioning another man, hypothetical or otherwise.' When I glance up, I notice the white puffs of condensation leaving her lips have ceased. 'Do I make myself clear?'

A shudder rolls down her back, and I feel it against the wall of my stomach. The proximity of her body mixed with the familiar smell of her shampoo spreads that shudder further south.

I give a small tug on her hair when she doesn't reply. 'Well?'

'I know you're not,' she whispers.

'Not what?'

'A limp-dick little bitch.' She shifts her ass over my groin, and I grip her even tighter. 'This blanket is so thick, yet I can still feel your erection poking me.'

I bite out a laugh, and gently push her forward. 'When you resign yourself to the fact there's no getting away from me, I'm going to give you one spank for every hoop you've made me jump through.'

As we reach the edge of the cliff, she glances up at me, her eyes dancing with a cocktail of mischief and something a little more uncertain. Hair dancing in the wind, she looks out to the horizon. 'I think you're going to want to give me more than that.'

Confused, I turn to follow her attention. It takes me precisely half a second to see it. Fuck, the whole coastline can see it.

The billboard that looms on the cliff above Hollow has always been there, but it usually displays a 'Home of Smuggler's Club Whiskey' advertisement. But not tonight. No, tonight, it features a very large, back-lit picture of me. An enormous sharpie-style cock has been drawn on my head – one mid-jizz – and on the left, a slogan is printed in big, black capitals.

'Raphael Visconti is a massive dickhead,' I drawl, reading it out in my best bored tone. 'Wow, how long did it take you to think of that tagline?'

'The advertising agency said I wasn't allowed to use "cunt".'

'I'm surprised they let you put it up at all.'

'Mm. Nico pulled a few strings. Oh – but he insists I tell you it wasn't his idea.'

I glance down at her, amusement filling my chest. 'Whose idea was it then?'

'Tayce's, obviously.'

'Obviously.'

In my suit pocket, my cell starts to buzz. Then it buzzes again and again, and I have no doubt it's everyone within a ten mile radius asking me about the coast's latest landmark.

Penny shifts beside me, pressing her quilted body into my side. 'Are you mad?'

I laugh, wrapping my arm around her. 'I'm impressed, baby. You even found a picture of me mid-blink. I thought my PR team erased all of them from Google.'

'They have. I had to take a screenshot from a video of you at some fancy gala. It's blurry, if you get up close enough.'

I mutter a light-hearted curse in Italian, but Penny tenses. 'Are you really not mad?'

The wind picks up speed, whistling between us. I tuck a wayward strand behind her ear and brush my knuckle over her cold cheek. 'Do you want me to be mad?'

She swallows. Opens her mouth to say something, but then clamps it shut with resolve. It's dark up here on the headland, but not dark enough that I miss the suspicious sheen coating her blue eyes.

My heart clenches. 'What's wrong?' I drag her into my chest, sliding my hands under the blanket so I can feel more of her. Fuck, she's shivering, even with all the extra padding. 'Talk to me, Queenie. Do you want me to be mad?

'I don't know what I want,' she grits, her hot breath seeping through my shirt. 'None of it's working.'

'What do you mean?'

'Spending all your money isn't making me feel better, Rafe. I don't care for any of your gifts, either. Fuck, when you stopped for gas last night, I took three-hundred dollars from your wallet and felt *nothing*.' She tilts her chin to look up at me. 'I put it back.'

'Jesus,' I mutter, rubbing her nape. 'Really?'

She jerks her head toward my enormous face on the billboard. 'I thought maybe revenge would be what I needed. I thought we'd come up here, and I'd see your phallic face in lights and I'd feel like all was right between us. But it's not.'

I drop my forehead to hers, pain swelling inside me. 'You don't want money; you don't want gifts. I've apologized a million times. How do I make this right, baby?'

She's trembling. Fucking *trembling*. I want to crawl inside her and make it stop.

She sucks in a steadying breath and rests her cheek below

my collar pin. The walls of my stomach tighten. I swear; if her answer to my question is, 'Nothing,' then I'm ninety-nine percent sure I'll tug the Zippo out of my pocket and burn the world down.

Instead, she curls her fingers into my shirt pocket and lets out a sigh big enough to melt her body into mine. 'I need to know you're not like the others.'

We stand there for a few minutes, my chin resting on her crown, her hot breaths skating up my neck. Despite the bitter chill, my skin burns hot and impulsive. I can't fucking think through all the noise in my head. I hate that it's my brother's smug-ass tone that trickles through the chaos and brings me my answer.

I slide my forearm around her waist and gently pick her up.

'Come on, we've got another detour before dinner.'

Rafe

Penny rips her hand from mine and slowly backs out of the church doorway.

'If you think I'm going in there, you must be insane.'

I pin her with a look of lazy amusement. 'If Gabe doesn't get smote when he steps inside, I'm sure you'll be fine.'

'God isn't my concern. Ending up as the subject of a true crime documentary, on the other hand . . .' She glares at the black abyss behind me. 'You go first and turn some lights on. I'll wait here.'

There are two things I could point out at this moment. The first, is that there hasn't been electricity in this joint for years. The second, is that it's far more spooky standing outside in the graveyard alone than coming inside a dark church with me, even with my men watching on from the road.

Nevertheless, I head into the sacristy, blow the dust off some old votive candles, and scatter them along the altar. Penny's gaze scorches my back as I light them with my Zippo. When a hazy orange glow eats away enough of the darkness, her reluctant footsteps echo down the aisle.

'Why are we here, Rafe?'

Her warmth brushes my back as I stare up at the Virgin Mary.

'My father owned this church.'

'I know. I grew up in Dip too, remember?'

'Did you also know he was a fraud?'

Penny huffs out an awkward laugh. 'I suppose I've always found it suspicious that the head of the mafia was also a deacon. I figured it was a tax evasion thing.'

I smile. 'It was partly a tax evasion thing, partly a blackmail thing.'

'What do you mean?'

I turn around and look down at her. She's fucking adorable, bundled up in her blanket with nothing but her big eyes and a few strands of red hair showing.

'My father became a deacon because Roman Catholics love nothing more than a good confession.' I shift my gaze to the confessional in the corner. 'He had dirt on everyone and their mama.'

Penny follows my eye line and cocks her head. 'That's quite smart actually,' she admits.

Of course *she'd* think that, the fucking little grifter. 'Come.' I take her hand and pull her toward the booth. With the light from my cell phone, I illuminate the narrow eaves behind it, making the cobwebs glisten like strands of glitter. 'My brothers and I would hide behind here and listen to all the locals confessing their sins.'

'Ah, so you've always been a nosy shit,' she snaps, yanking her hand out of mine. Behind us, the door groans in the wind, and she quickly clings onto me again.

'We wouldn't just listen, Queenie. Our father would get us to decide on the worst sins we'd heard through the week, and then . . .' I chew on the inside of my lip. Sure, Penny is no saint, but I still hate being so fucking crude with her. 'Eliminate them.'

Her eyes pierce through the shadows. 'What?'

'We'd kill the worst sinners.' I shrug, recalling the fond memories of my childhood. 'The ones who'd admit to raping their wives when they'd come home too drunk from the bar. Ones who hit cyclists on Grim Reaper road driving home after a night shift and left them for dead.'

Penny takes a deep breath, processing my words. 'So, you were basically choir-boy vigilantes?'

I can't help but laugh. 'More like Viscontis-in-training. Violence is a way of life for my family, and I guess my father wanted us to start early.'

'Did you hate it?'

I glance at her. 'No. Truth is, we loved it – me more than my brothers. It started my fondness for games, I suppose.'

She tightens the blanket around herself, glaring at the confessional like it'll suddenly come to life and tell her all the secrets spilled within its oak walls. 'You loved it so much you started the hotline.'

'Yes. After our father died and my brothers and I scattered to different corners of the earth, I decided to bring the game back on a more . . . *professional* level. It gave us a reason to stay close. Now it's bigger than Dip.' I reach out and stroke her cheek with my knuckle. 'Bigger than you, Queenie.'

Her gaze touches mine, dancing with confusion. 'You choose the worst confession from the hotline, hunt them down and kill them?'

'Mm. Once a month.'

'Jesus Christ.'

'Shh, he'll hear you.'

She doesn't laugh at my joke. Instead, she studies me like she's seeing me for the first time. 'Why are you telling me this?'

Angelo's words bounce between my ears. *Prove to her that you're not the massive cock you've made yourself out to be.*

'Because I need you to know I didn't set up the hotline because I'm some weirdo that gets off on listening to people confess their sins.' I pause. 'Sure, some of them are juicy, but being nosy was never my end game. We choose the dregs of society, and we kill them. Of course, I'm not some sort of savior, and yes, it's ironic because killing them also makes me a bad person, but there's no denying the world is a better place without them.' I take a deep breath. 'You weren't using the hotline for its intended purpose. And, sure, when I first heard you call, I was thinking of all the petty ways I could fuck with you –'

'The tuna subs,' she says dryly. 'Ripping the page out of my *For Dummies* book.'

I flash her a sheepish grin. 'You telling me you wouldn't have done the same if it was the other way around?' Only a beat passes, but it's enough to know the galvanized wall around her heart has fissured. I move closer to her, capitalizing on the progress. 'There was never a malicious intent. The novelty of fucking with you wore off so quickly, baby. Soon, I just became obsessed with hearing you talk. About anything and everything – I didn't care. As long as your voice was in my ear, I was happy.'

There's a thunderous silence between us, set to the backdrop of the wind rattling the boarded windows. When she finally speaks, it's nothing but a tiny, one-worded question. A whisper in the dust-filled air.

'Why?'

I run my thumb over her pillowy lip. The truth slides from my mouth like warmed butter. 'Because I love you.'

She stares at me for a few more moments, her expression stiff and unreadable. My heart drops as she suddenly pulls away and walks around the confessional, running a finger over the intricate woodwork and latticed doors.

With a quick glance back at me, she dips inside the penitent compartment and shuts the door behind her. Without questioning it, I slide into the other compartment and shut the door, plunging us into darkness.

Penny's slow, heavy breaths seep through the latticed opening that divides us.

'Do you really love me?' she whispers.

I press my temple against the iron grate. 'Yes.'

There's a pause. 'That night in the phone booth, you told me you'd never been in love before. If you've never felt it, how do you know?'

I close my eyes. I've got too many words and not enough ways to order them. How do I know? Because saying it aloud is as easy as breathing. Because even the mention of her name lights my skin on fire. Because she's my first thought in the morning, and my last at night.

Because I just. Fucking. Know.

I swallow. 'Because even though I'm unlucky with you, I feel even unluckier without you.'

Her breathing grows denser, filling the hollows in my chest. I suddenly remember why I brought her here: *I need to know you're not like the others.*

As her body trembled against mine on the headland, I realized all the money and the gifts and the fancy meals would never bring her reassurance. Only my actions and my words will. She's damaged. Broken by men from our world, and it's my responsibility to patch her back up and make sure she never shatters again.

When I hook my fingers onto the latticed grate, my fingertips brush against hers on the other side. 'I'm not going anywhere, Queenie. Not ever.'

'Even if you almost get killed again?'

My laugh filters through the grate. 'I've just accepted that near-death experiences are a hazard of being with you.'

The grate rattles softly. She must have put her head against it too, because I can feel her warmth and smell her perfume. I squeeze my eyes shut, fighting against the urge to punch through this wall and grab for her. Instead, I take all the restraint I can muster and slip a hundred dollar bill out of my pocket, then push it into the grate.

'Kiss me.'

After a few seconds, it slides back the opposite direction and drops back onto my lap. Then there's a shuffle and hinges groan, and soft candlelight fills my booth. My gaze slides to Penny darkening the doorway. She stoops to clamber inside and sits on my lap.

Her cheeks are wet and warm against mine. She brushes her lips up my jaw and over my mouth, and whispers against it.

'This one is free.'

Penny

The office is filled with the sound of crunching and cogs whirring. Nico crams another handful of chips in his mouth and chews thoughtfully.

'He's card counting.'

'He's too stupid to card count.'

More crunching. We've been studying who we've dubbed 'red shirt dude' on the monitor for three-quarters of an hour, and we're still no closer to agreeing on whether he's a cheat or not.

Nico swipes his feet off the desk and taps the keyboard, zooming in on him. 'Look at his lips moving, Pen. He's counting.'

'He could be saying anything. Humming the National Anthem, reciting his favorite Bible verse. Only beginners count aloud.'

He glances at me in disbelief. 'You really wanna win that fifty bucks, huh?'

I laugh. 'Sure do.'

As we fall into an easy silence, a burst of happiness spreads through my chest. I *love* coming into work. Not only do I get the thrill of swindling-by-proxy, but I get to hang out with Nico.

Sitting here, eating snacks and talking shit, it feels like we're kids hiding in the coat room of the Visconti Grand again.

Nico cracks open the heart-shaped box of chocolates I bought him. It's not the usual type of snack I bring into work for us, but it is Valentine's Day, after all.

'Got a hot date after work, then?'

He huffs quietly, like my question isn't worth an answer. 'Unfortunately, you're the only girl in my life, Little P.'

'Jeez, that's sad.'

'No sadder than you actually having a Valentine, and coming into work, anyway.'

His words make my chest constrict, but a deep breath and a few rational thoughts put me back rights. I've come into work as usual, because neither Rafe nor I have brought up the holiday in conversation.

We've been in this weird-yet-perfect limbo that doesn't have a name or a rule book. Everything shifted about two weeks ago, after the night he took me to the church. Something about him opening up has made me more relaxed and a lot less bitter. We've swapped fine dining for the diner, and my couture dresses for pajamas. I don't torture myself by heading upstairs to my apartment after our dates and curtain twitching all night, either. I sleep in his car, and sometimes, when his goodnight kiss breaks my resolve, I even invite him upstairs to fuck.

Okay, all of the time.

'Valentine's Day is just a money-making scam, anyway,' I mutter. As the holiday drew closer, Rafe's radio silence on the matter made me a little uncomfortable. I guess there's no point celebrating, anyway. We do go on dates every single night, and I did tell him to stop buying me gifts. Besides, apart from Rafe insisting every restaurant worker call me Mrs Visconti, we haven't put a label on what we are yet.

Nico gives me a patronizing pat on the shoulder. 'Well, we can both be lonely losers together.'

I smile to myself. Nico's always been here for me, done things he's never had to. I suddenly remember something that's been playing on the back of my mind. Something I need to ask him. My smile fades and my palms grow sweaty.

'Nico?' He glances at me sideways. 'My parents never had some off-shore bank account with enough money to buy an apartment, did they?'

He stills, a heart-shaped chocolate halfway to his mouth. 'How would I know the state of your family's finances?'

'It was you, wasn't it?'

He's so transparent, tilting his head from side-to-side as he weighs up the pros and cons of telling me the truth. 'It was my college fund,' he says quietly.

The sharpest of knives twists in my chest. 'Nico –'

'Shh,' he grunts, tapping on the keyboard and bringing up random camera screens with the pretense of studying them. 'You did me a favor. I actually had to *work* in school to maintain a scholarship. And that, Little P, is why I'm so smart today.'

The backs of my eyes burn at the thought of a teenage Nico emptying his trust-fund for me. 'Thank you' will never be enough.

'Do you two actually get any work done, or do you just sit around and gossip all night?'

The voice that slides in from the door behind us is pure silk, but it still makes me jump. I turn to see Rafe leaning against the door frame, all sharp suit and smirk. His eyes lock on mine, and he winks.

My throat squeezes. Fuck, he's breathtakingly handsome, even in the low lighting of the office. I wonder if I'll ever get to a point where I look at him and don't have a visceral reaction. If one day, my head won't swim and my cheeks won't heat when he walks into a room.

I mutter a weak greeting, then clear my throat and turn back to the monitors. Out the corner of my eye, Nico rolls his eyes.

'Are you here to steal Penny, or to give me a lecture?' Nico asks Rafe, holding out the chocolate box to him as he approaches.

He looks down at it in amusement, and shakes his head. 'I think I've given you enough lectures, *cugino*.'

Rafe has made it very clear that he disapproves of me working here. It took me longer than it should have to realize The Grotto isn't a regular casino. All the patrons on the other side of the cameras haven't been invited to play here because of their social status or net worth. They're here because they've all been suspected of cheating in other casinos across Hollow and Cove. Turns out, some of them are super dangerous, and Rafe hates that there's little more than a craggy wall and a hallway separating them from me.

But he doesn't need to sweat it. Not only could I probably throw a mean punch if I really had to, but I know Nico can handle these men. While he might be calm in the office, indulging me in games, like seeing how many marshmallows he can fit in his mouth, I've seen what happens when he snaps on those leather gloves and strolls out the door.

He's a quiet beast.

Rafe's warmth crackles against my back. His hands come down on either side of my soda can and cage me in, sparking mini fireworks in my stomach.

'Ready to go, Queenie?'

'Go where?' Nico asks. 'Her shift doesn't finish for another hour.'

'Not tonight, it doesn't.'

Nico's gaze slides to mine, amused and cynical. 'Oh, the power of nepotism.'

I say my goodbyes and meet Rafe at the elevator. He's got my coat slung over one arm, and is watching me with a certain heat as I walk toward him.

'Yes?'

He doesn't say anything until the doors ding. He steps aside to let me in, and we stand shoulder to shoulder, watching the mirrored doors slide shut. The moment the elevator jerks to life, he glances at my distorted reflection, then suddenly presses his palm into my stomach and pushes me against the wall. His mouth captures my gasp, and his rough grip on my throat keeps me in place.

He steals a deeper kiss. Nips at my bottom lip. I'm melting under his wet mouth and burning under his hot hand as it slides up my inner thigh and cups my pussy so hard that I'm brought to my tip-toes.

The elevator slows to a stop. His tongue skims up my neck and flicks against my ear. 'Been dying to do that all day,' he murmurs, giving my mound another squeeze before pulling himself away from me.

I'm high off his touch and breathless from how quick he ripped it away from me. The elevator doors slide open and the bitter February air pours in. Rafe smooths down his shirt and grabs my hand, stepping out into the night as the perfect gentleman.

By the time we reach his car, I'm buzzing with excitement. *He didn't forget.* My mind races with all the possibilities the night holds. A romantic walk on the beach in Cove, a private dinner in the back room of a fancy restaurant. He's probably made an exception for my no-gifts request, too. But my mood dampens around the edges when I twist around and see no beautifully-wrapped box on the backseat.

There's nothing in the glove compartment, either.

Rafe starts the engine and looks over at me. 'Looking for something?'

My mouth moves before I can stop it. 'It's Valentine's Day,' I blurt out.

He rests his elbow on the center console, rubbing at his smirk. 'Is it? Burgers on me then, I suppose.'

My cheeks burn. *They're always on you, asshole.* But I don't say that. Instead, I steel my jaw and glare at the falling sleet dancing in the headlights. Surprisingly, my annoyance melts quicker than the ice landing on the car's heated glass. Maybe it's Rafe's thumb rubbing circles on my thigh, or the fact he remembers to get me extra ketchup when he collects our order from the diner.

Warmth floods my stomach and blooms outward, heating my heart. *This* is what I want. Not the gifts or the money, but *this*. This comfort, this stability, this *love*. It's everything this man gives me, every single day without fail. I'm suddenly so full with it that by the time we're climbing the hill to the church, I have a soppy grin on my face.

Rafe's gaze meets mine, confused. 'Fuck you looking at me like that for, Queenie?' He sweeps the horizon, as if looking for another billboard with his face on it. 'What are you planning?'

'Nothing.' I bite my lip. For some reason, the word *love* has lingered, and now it's bubbling on the tip of my tongue. I'm trying my hardest not to let it slip out.

Rafe's eyes narrow in suspicion, and I feel the urge to throw him a bone, at least. I slide my hand over his and bring his knuckles to my lips. 'I'm just happy; that's all.'

His expression softens. He watches me rub my mouth over his hand, and gives a small noise of approval. 'Want to know a secret?' he whispers, uncurling his palm against my cheek and swiping my bottom lip with his thumb. A shudder of excitement rolls through me: every time he asks me that question, I always like what follows it.

I nod.

'I didn't forget it's Valentine's Day.' His hand skims down my side and squeezes my hip. 'Come here.'

I frown. 'Where?'

He reaches down and slides his chair all the way back. He pats his thigh. 'Here. And don't say there's no room. If there's room for you to shake your ass in my face, there's room for you to sit on my lap.'

With a slight tremble that I always get when I'm about to enter Rafe's orbit, I unclick my seat belt and let him tug me onto his lap. I let out a shaky breath, resisting the urge to melt into his chest and drink in his soothing scent.

He presses a light kiss to my temple, reaches into the side door pocket, and drops something on my lap. It's the weight of a money stack, but when I look down, I see it's a perfectly wrapped rectangle.

'What is it?'

His chest rumbles against my back. 'You'd find out if you opened it.' I rub my sweaty palms over my thighs and gingerly tug at the ribbon. Rafe lets out an impatient huff. 'Jeez, Penny, it's not a bomb – just open it.'

'All right, all right.'

I peel away the wrapping and squint down at it. It's a book of some sort. When Rafe reaches up to click on the overhead light, an orange glow spreads through the car, and I realize it isn't just *any* book.

It's bound in mustard-yellow leather with a title embossed on the cover.

Penelope Price for Dummies.

My throat grows thick. 'What is this?'

Rafe doesn't reply, instead, he slides his arm through mine and gently opens the cover to the front page. I read what's printed on the thick, cream paper:

Penelope Price in Numbers

> **Height:** Comes up to the third button of my shirt. Reaches the second button in heels

> **Weight:** Perfect

> **Age:** I try not to think about it

> **Alias:** Queenie, Little Shit, Brat, Good Girl (note: this is rare; she's never good)

I choke out a laugh, the backs of my eyes burning. The next page is titled: **If Penny Goes Missing.** Underneath, there's my fingerprint, a small lock of red hair, and a piece of tissue with a kiss print on it. It takes me a moment to realize it's the tissue I left in his private bathroom the very first time he let me use it.

'You kept it?' I murmur, running my finger over it.

He huffs out a quiet laugh and rests his chin on my shoulder. 'You're more concerned about the tissue than how I got a lock of your hair?'

When I laugh again, it comes out as a weird sob. 'Yeah, that's weird as shit too,' I squeak.

The next page is all my favorite things. Recipes for a passion fruit martini and for the breakfast he made me every morning on the yacht. My regular order from the diner, the films I love, the songs I listen to on repeat. Some he'd have learned from listening to my calls to Sinners Anonymous, others from just listening to *me*.

I pour over page after page. My hobbies and dreams. My well-worn expressions, my clothing style. By the time I reach the final page, tears are streaming down my cheeks.

'Why?' It's all I can manage.

Rafe turns me to look at him and kisses a tear before it drips off my chin. 'You know the answer,' he whispers against my jaw.

Because he loves me.

And there's no doubt in my mind that I love him too.

'Look at me.' Through blurry eyes, I meet his soft, green gaze. 'I'm your hotline now, Queenie. All your mundane thoughts, all your ramblings: they're mine. I want them all, no matter how trivial. Do you understand me?'

I can only nod.

'Good,' he murmurs. He swallows hard, frowning at a tear rolling down my face. 'Now stop crying. I don't like it.'

Without another word, I lean forward and brush my lips against his, claiming his next breath as my own. And then I press my mouth to his and slide my tongue inside. He captures it with his teeth and pulls me closer, running his hand up my spine and gripping the nape of my neck to hold me in place.

I'll be here forever – I know it. Shackled by his chains, blissful in his cage. For all I care, he can lock me up and throw the key into the Pacific.

I'm in Raphael Visconti's trap, and I never want to be freed.

Penny

The yacht rolling over an early morning swell is what brings me to consciousness, but it's the satisfying soreness between my thighs that makes me open my eyes and smile.

I shift onto my side and prop myself up on my elbow, watching Rafe sleep. He's on his back as always, one inked arm disappearing underneath my pillow. Lips parted, dark lashes fluttering. I study the even pulse in his clean-shaven throat, and wonder what he's dreaming of. Would it be narcissistic to hope that it's me?

I reach up and run my hand over my wonky braid. I know he thinks of me when he's awake, at least. Why else would he learn how to braid hair for me? Sure, it's a mess, but the thought of him practicing warms my heart.

'Kick me in the shin again, and I'll spank you harder than I did last night.'

I jump at his sudden warning slicing through the silence. When I don't reply, he pops open an eye and smirks at me sleepily. 'Never mind, you're just admiring the view again.'

'No, I'm not.' *Yes, I am.* 'I'm thinking.'

'Does it hurt?'

'Shut up.'

His dimples deepen, and he runs a large paw over his cheek. 'All right, thinking about what?'

'You know, how weird it is that you're my boyfriend now.'

He frowns, jaw tensing. 'You trying to piss me off before nine a.m?'

I laugh, dropping my head onto his bicep and curling into his side. We spent Valentine's Day in the penthouse suite of the Visconti Grand, and the very next day, moved back onto the yacht. But despite what Rafe said about wanting all my stolen clothes hanging up next to his and my girly candles lit in every room, it's not enough for him. He wants a rock on my finger too.

For a few minutes, I study his chest rising and falling. Watch the serpent on his collar dance, and the playing cards on his abs come to life. Hot with a sudden desire to interrupt his peace, I trace a line down his stomach into the dark hair below his navel.

He tenses underneath my touch. 'Where's that hand going, Queenie?' he murmurs into my hair.

I respond by cupping his warm weight, slowly massaging his length until it hardens in my palm. He grunts in approval and rolls his head back onto his pillow.

My hand slides up and down his erection, my mouth watering as I stare at it in fascination. In the cold light of day, he looks massive. No wonder my pussy is chronically aching. As I draw down to his base, his watch shifts on my wrist, revealing the diamond tennis bracelet underneath.

A quiet groan escapes his lips, and he reaches down to touch it. 'Nice bracelet; is it new?'

I glance up at his half-lidded gaze. 'Yes, and it was *very* expensive.'

He pushes up into my palm, his fingers digging into my hip.

'Fuck, I think I've finally found a fetish: you spending all my money. There must be a name for that, right?'

I laugh, swiping my thumb over his glistening tip and enjoying the way his body shudders underneath me. 'You already have a fetish.'

'Yeah?'

'Mm. A panty fetish.'

He pauses. 'The fuck I do.'

'Yes, you do. You're always stealing my panties.'

He breaks into a strangled laugh. 'You're so cute, baby.' His hand twists into the base of my hair and lifts my mouth to his. 'I don't have a panty fetish; I have a "whatever's been between Penny's ass cheeks" fetish.'

'Oh,' I say, flustering.

He kisses me, then kisses me again twice as hard. I twist out of his grip and nestle back into the crook of his arm, teasing him with lazy strokes.

His restless hiss coasts over my forehead. 'Faster.'

'Can't.'

'Is your wrist broken, or something?'

'No, I just don't want you to come in sixty seconds.'

I brace myself for the inevitable impact. It comes hard and fast on my ass, accompanied by a growl about me being a little shit. Rafe rolls me onto my back and roughly parts my thighs, dipping between them. He's all mussed hair and dangerous gaze as he looks up at me.

'I'll make you come in thirty – how about that?'

A shiver rolls from my head to my pussy, where it thumps in my clit in anticipation. 'A hundred bucks says you can't.'

'Deal.' He catches my wrist and stares down at the watch face. When the long hand brushes the top of the hour, he dives straight for my clit.

Fuck.

He sucks hard and fast. Wet heat, sharp nips, back muscles flexing against my calves. I'm blaming my agreeing to this bet on it being too early to think straight. I should have known I can barely last ten seconds under this man's tongue, let alone thirty.

I feel as though my nerves have been doused in gasoline, and Rafe's mouth is a lit match. I squeeze my eyes shut, trying to think of the most boring *For Dummies* books I've ever read. It's a toss-up between *Auto Repair* and *Mutual Funds*, for sure.

Oh, no. Rafe cuts a sloppy path from my entrance to my clit with his tongue, and that familiar burning pressure spreads inside me. My limbs grow heavy, and being the sore loser I am, I try to twist myself out from underneath him. He hisses in response and clamps me in place with one hand, while his other disappears between my thighs.

He glances up at me. 'Cheater,' he grunts, before he drives two thick fingers into me.

Oh, god.

The pressure erupts, flooding through my core and vibrating every muscle in my body. As my orgasm floats down around me, my high is marred by annoyance.

I prop myself up on my elbows and glare down at him. 'Fingers are cheating.'

He licks my juices off his top lip, eyes dancing with humor. 'No, I just know how to work this pussy, because it's mine.' His gaze slides back down to my sex and sparks with dark satisfaction. 'All mine.'

'Not yours,' I mutter. Partly out of habit – I've said this nearly every time we've fucked – and partly because I'm pissed off I'm down a hundred dollars, and I haven't even had breakfast yet.

His eyes flash. He grazes his fingertips over my slick folds and circles my sensitive clit. His glare jumps back up to mine. 'Whose pussy is this, Penelope?'

'Not. Yours –' I gasp as he pinches my clit. 'A tortured confession is not a true confession.'

'I'll take any confession.' He stretches me open with his fingers again. 'Whose pussy, Penelope?'

I grind my jaw together. When I don't reply, he sinks his teeth into my inner thigh. 'Depends!' I yelp.

His back muscles tense. 'On?'

I swallow thickly, knowing Rafe won't let this drop until I give him my caveats. I clear my throat, suddenly feeling too hot for a crisp March morning.

'If you're nice to it,' I whisper.

He smiles lazily, giving my clit a gentle kiss. 'I'm always nice to it. What else?'

'If you promise to never leave it.'

He frowns, but stops himself from biting out a sarcastic retort. Realization softens the planes of his back. I feel vulnerable. Uncomfortable. Needy. It's obvious I'm not talking about my vagina anymore.

I hold my breath while Rafe slowly climbs up my body and pins me under his weight. He presses his lips to mine. 'I promise, Queenie. I'm here forever.'

I sigh. Wrap my legs around his hips and draw him closer.

'Then it's yours.'

***

Rafe's whistling while he makes breakfast. *Whistling*. I watch him from my spot on the counter in amusement. He's wearing nothing but black boxers and a half-baked grin, and maybe I'd give him some warning about oil spitting from a hot pan, if I wasn't so selfishly enjoying the view.

He slides past me under the pretense of getting two plates from the cupboard, but I know him better than that. It's no surprise when he stops short, dips his hands between my thighs, and cups me. 'Whose pussy is this?'

My sigh melts into a laugh. This asshole's asked me three times in thirty minutes, and I'm hoping the novelty of me saying 'yours' wears off soon. When I reach down and grab his cock through his boxers, his jaw clenches and his gaze heats.

'Depends. Whose dick is this?'

He dips to kiss my throat, smiling against it. 'Yours, Queenie. Forever and always. Although, if you don't get your hand off my crown jewels immediately, you'll be eating very burnt eggs for breakfast.'

I let him go, grinning like a maniac as I watch him plating up. I'm barely aware of the galley door opening, until Rafe glances up and barks something out in rapid-fire Italian.

'*Gesù Cristo*,' he mutters, sweeping a hand over his hair.

'*Gesù Cristo* indeed.' As much as I love living with Rafe, I don't love also sharing our home with a bunch of people on his payroll. He hasn't opened the yacht as a bar again, but still, there's a dozen crew members needed onboard just to keep it afloat. 'Rafe, we need to move.'

He frowns up at me. 'But I like having an ocean between you and everyone else.'

I laugh. 'Yeah, but it's a pain in the ass. Besides, how can I walk around naked if there's a chance I might bump into the first officer in the living room?'

'You wanna walk around naked?'

'Uh-huh.'

He pauses. Rakes an eye over the hem of his hoodie. 'Then we'll start looking.'

Christ, I might not swindle men for their money anymore, but they sure are easy to fool in other ways.

Rafe

I guess it was a blessing in disguise that Dante's last hurrah on this earth was blowing the port to shit. It's given me an extra three months to rework the cliff bar and casino in Devil's Dip, and I must admit, it turned out *exceptional*.

We decided to rebuild another hundred feet above sea-level, moving us out of the way of future explosions and giving patrons a completely uninterrupted view of the horizon through the panoramic window. Inside, the decor is signature Raphael Visconti. The finest velvet-clad poker tables, the shiniest roulette wheels, and a fully-stocked bar serving every Smuggler's Club edition ever made, even the rare ones.

However, because of a certain red-haired beauty, I'm still on the vodka. I take a sip, just as Angelo's shoulder brushes against mine. I stare out at the sun dipping below the water and bite back a smirk. I don't need to turn around to know my brother's seething; he's got this way of breathing like a rhino when he's on the verge of smashing something up.

His tone is ice-cold. 'This is the worst idea you've ever had.'

I do a lazy sweep of the guests filtering through the doors

and admiring the view. 'Really? Everyone looks like they're having a great time.'

'You know that's not what I mean.'

'I second Angelo's sentiment,' comes a silky murmur from my left. I turn to meet Tor's shit-eating grin. 'It's an absolutely awful idea, *cugino*. I fucking love it.'

Yeah, he loves it because we finally reached an agreement. I get a third of Cove, but he gets forty-nine percent of my shiny new cliff bar.

'You won't love it when you're dodging bullets, dickhead.' Angelo mutters under his breath and glances toward the elevator. 'Where's my wife, anyway?'

'Out shopping with . . . Penny.' I almost say, *out with mine,* but stop myself. Unfortunately, she's not my wife.

Yet.

'I don't like it when they hang out.'

Now, I pin him with a blistering glare, annoyance twitching my fingers. 'Why not?'

'Because she's teaching her things.'

'Like?'

'Like how to play blackjack. Rory's good at it now.' He swigs from his whiskey glass, eyes darkening. 'Tell me why I'm losing every hand we play? Something's not right.'

Tor and I exchange amused glances. Angelo rarely gambles, and probably doesn't even know what card counting is. I don't snitch on my sister-in-law though. We're starting *The Real Housewives of Atlanta* next week, and like fuck am I watching the franchise on my own.

I steal a look at my watch, and my eyes follow Angelo's to the elevator. Penny, Rory, Wren, and Tayce were out shopping all afternoon, then spent the evening getting ready at my brother's house. My girl's only been gone a few hours, but I'm already itching to see her. Feel her. Fucking *kiss* her. Christ, I'll even settle for staring at her like a simp from across the room at this rate.

The elevator doors ding and a familiar laugh floats out of them. I turn to watch Penny and the girls step out into the room.

My next breath catches in the back of my throat. She hasn't even taken her coat off yet, but I can already tell she looks incredible. Gold hoops, big, red waves, and a tight dress only a few shades darker. Her eyes sweep the room, then land on me.

Her smile cracks my heart in two.

Squeezing the poker chip in my pocket, I set down my glass and move to greet her. I stoop to give her a kiss and tighten my grip on her nape when she pulls back. 'Plus tip,' I mutter, stealing another one. 'And VAT.'

I help myself to a third, feeling her smile against my lips. 'It's beautiful in here,' she says, walking over to admire the view. I follow her like a puppy, drinking in the way the low-hanging sun casts a golden glow over her face and makes her eye shadow sparkle. 'But I'm confused. It's not opening night, is it?'

I slide in beside her, wrapping a possessive arm around her waist. 'Not quite, Queenie.' I glance around us, then pull her into an alcove. 'I've got something to tell you.'

Her face falls. 'Oh god, what have you done –'

I grip her chin and plant a kiss on her lips. It's my new, nice way of getting her to shut up. Always works like a charm. 'You see all these men in here? They're all for you.'

She frowns. 'You're pimping me out?'

'Business isn't going that badly.' *Yet.* 'I mean, they're all lined up for a visit to The Grotto. I thought you might want to have a little fun with them first.'

Her eyes grow wide, and she scans the room as if seeing it in a new light. 'Seriously?' She steps closer and drops her voice to a theatrical whisper. 'You're telling me I can swindle anyone in here?'

'Swindle the shit out of them, baby.'

'But I've gone *straight*.'

I laugh in disbelief. 'There's nothing straight about you. Never has been, never will be.'

She stares at me, her shock shifting into excitement. 'But what if . . .'

'Not going to happen.' Although I haven't seen Gabe since he hobbled out of the church, his men are here in full force. With their scars and tattoos and menacing scowls, they're doing an awful job of blending in with the marks, but they're here nonetheless. I'll also be watching her like a hawk, of course. I won't have much to worry about – I've had the gamblers all vetted. They're the millionaire chancers, not career criminals. They've tried their luck in one of our casinos because they thought they could get away with it, not because they thought they could hold their own if they got caught.

'I can't believe you did this,' she squeals, slinging her arms around my shoulders and pushing me further into the alcove. She kisses my throat, working her way up to my jaw and to my mouth. The feeling of her soft body against mine is enough to give me a school-boy boner.

'I love you,' she whispers when she reaches my ear.

And that? That's enough to set my skin on fucking fire.

***

Beside me, Angelo shifts in his seat. He lifts his whiskey to his lips, but sets it back down without taking a sip. 'Fuck's sake.'

Belmarsh, the lawyer chewing his ear off on the other side of him, flinches.

Nico's amused gaze heats my cheek. We've got a bet going – how long it'll take until Angelo loses his cool and pistol-whips the guy Rory's playing blackjack with.

'Anything else for you, Mr Visconti?'

I glance up to meet Laurie's sickly-sweet smile. With a lazy swoop of my wrist, I signal for another round. 'You not liking the new workplace, Laurie?'

She snatches up my empty glass and sets it on her tray. 'I like it just fine. It's on land, after all. What I don't like, is being two servers down.' She pauses, cocking her head. 'Even if they were nasty little bitches.'

She's talking about Anna and Claudia – Penny wanted them gone, so I didn't think twice about firing them.

'I'll get you new servers,' I say. 'Even better ones.'

'Get me five. This joint is going to get real busy in summer.'

A squeal rips my attention to the other side of the room. It's Rory, jumping to her feet and celebrating a win. When she skips over, fanning her winnings, Angelo jumps up too.

'No more,' he growls, planting a possessive kiss on her lips. '*Sit.*'

'Ah, this must be your lovely wife,' Belmarsh says, rising to greet her.

Rory pauses. Curls her top lip in disgust. Then she shoves Angelo away and cries, 'You have a *wife* ?'

There's a ripple of snickers around our table. Angelo pinches his nose, shaking his head. 'Fucking hell. I knew I should have stayed home and watched the game.'

With a squeeze of Rory's ass and a dark utterance in her ear, he heads to a more civilized corner of the room, where Cas and some of his business buddies smoke Cubans. Belmarsh makes his awkward excuses and leaves, while Rory slides into her husband's seat.

'How long have you been waiting to use that one?'

'Since I walked down the aisle.'

I rub my amusement away with the back of my hand. 'I'm impressed. And I'm impressed with your new-found swindling skills, too.'

Laughing, she holds out her hands, showing there's a slight

tremble to them. 'It's not for me. I get way too nervous.' She sighs. 'I don't know how Miss Artful Dodger does it.'

My gaze snaps to Penny, who's at the bar with Tayce. They've got their heads together, their eyes shifting around the room. Penny talks in a low murmur while Tayce frowns, listening intently, no doubt taking in whatever tips she's giving her.

It's ironic – I fucking hate cheats. Yet here I am, hosting an event set up especially for my thieving, sticky-fingered girl to cheat anyone she pleases. I guess I've broken every rule and moral code I set in place for myself, anyway.

There's one more I'm dying to break.

'Make her marry me,' I blurt out.

A server comes over with the drinks we ordered, plus a white-wine spritzer for Rory. She takes a sip, doing a crappy job at hiding her amusement.

'Chill out; it's been, like, a month.'

'You married my brother after a month.'

'Yeah, but only because he begged.'

I stare at her. 'What?'

'Oh, swan. Don't tell him I told you that. He's peeved with me already.'

I say nothing. We both know it'll come out the second Angelo pisses me off.

Rory swirls the ice cubes in her drink. 'Buy her the right ring, and she might just say yes.'

My laugh is bitter. 'I've bought her so many rings, when she wears them together, she looks like Mr T.'

I settle into my seat, not really listening to my sister-in-law as she preaches about the value of patience. I'm too busy admiring the view of Penny at the bar. Truth is, despite my caveman instinct to get a ring on her finger so the world and their mamas know she's mine, the logical part of me can respect her not wanting to tie the knot yet.

She spent so long trying to figure out what she wants in life; now she's found it, she wants to enjoy it as Penny Price for a while.

And that's okay. I like her being Penny Price too.

***

The night is dark and bitter. A fog has rolled in over the parking lot, reducing the figures filtering out of the bar to distorted shadows. I switch on the car engine, turn on Penny's heated seat, then lean against the trunk while I wait for her to emerge.

As always, it's her loud-ass laugh that alerts me to her presence. She wobbles into the glow of a streetlamp, arms linked with Rory and Wren, with Tayce on Wren's other side.

It's Rory that spots me first. 'Rafe!' she yells. 'Are we still on for Sunday?' Nodding, I give her a thumbs up. 'Good. I've picked up more of those watermelon thingies, and – ouch!'

Her heel buckles underneath her, but my brother swoops out of the shadows and grabs her by the waist. 'Jesus, Magpie. You need water and a burger. Come on.' He scoops her up and carries her to a waiting car.

Rory waves at her friends over his shoulder. 'Call me tomorrow!'

I watch in amusement as Penny says her goodbyes to Tayce and Wren, then strides over to me. She's concentrating on the ground, clearly determined not to meet the same fate as my sister-in-law.

'Hello handsome,' she says sweetly, sliding into the passenger seat. I slam the door shut behind her and round the car. Once I'm behind the wheel, I shift sideways to get a good look at her.

'Good night?'

She bites her bottom lip, looking up at me through those thick lashes. 'The best. Look!'

She dumps her bag out onto her lap, and all her stolen goods fall out. Money she won, wallets she lifted, watches she stole. She holds up a Rolex to the light of the moon and squints at it. 'Although, I'm not sure this one is real.'

Shaking my head, I cup her jaw and steal a quick kiss. 'You're a dirty little thief; you know that?'

Her grin grows wider. 'I do indeed.'

She stares at me for a beat too long. When her gaze starts to heat and warm the air inside of the car, my eyes narrow. 'What?'

'Nothing.'

'Don't "nothing" me, Queenie. I thought you'd have learned that lesson last week.' Last time she'd 'nothing'ed me, I bent her over my knee until she told me what the 'nothing' was.

She focuses on her haul, slowly putting the items back in her purse. 'Fine. I got you a gift.'

'Better not be a second-hand watch.'

I'm surprised that her laugh sounds so nervous. 'It's not. Here,' she dips her hand in the passenger door pocket, and pulls out a small jewelry box. It sits on the console between us, and I stare down at it, irritation grating on my chest.

'I'm not into any of this new-era shit, Pen. If you're proposing to me, I'll throw the fucking ring out the window, and maybe you with it –'

'Jesus Christ, shut up and open it.'

I steel my jaw. Give her one last warning look, then flick the box open.

Immediately, my blood runs cold. Something thickens in my throat, and I can't seem to get any words out, let alone in order.

Eventually, I manage a strangled, 'You're not wearing it.'

I can't believe I didn't notice she's not wearing it.

Her hand flies to her chest. 'I'm lucky, with or without the necklace,' she says quietly. 'I have you, I have friends, I have the best job. I'm the luckiest girl in the world.'

Her fingers slide over mine, and she takes the box from me. 'My socks didn't work for you, nor did you taking your mama's advice about believing you're lucky. So maybe this will.'

The four-leaf clover pendant winks as she lifts it off the cushion and dangles it in the space between us. 'I had it put on a new chain, so it's a little longer. More manly, too.' She chokes out an awkward laugh. 'Here, let me put it on you.'

I don't say anything as her soft hands reach around my neck. Can't. Can't seem to fucking think about anything other than how I'm stupidly obsessed with this woman.

'There.' She slides the chain under my shirt collar and pats my chest, then looks up into my eyes.

I stare back at her for a beat, while my heart bursts into flames.

My fist finds the back of her hair, and my lips find her mouth.

My heart has caught fire, and I'm in love with the Queen who lit the match.

ACKNOWLEDGEMENTS

It's often said that writing is a lonely process, but that couldn't be further from the truth. There were so many people involved in the creation of the Sinners Anonymous series—family, friends, and four-legged procrastination partners.

I want to thank Sonnie, the love of my life, for the endless cups of tea, the egg sandwiches, and for forcing me to see sunlight every now and again. And our dog, Knuckles, for all the cuddles and kisses between Pomodoro sprints.

I want to thank my family. Mum and Dad—you've always believed I could do it. You're my biggest cheerleaders, and I love you. Thank you for still loving me back even when I cancel plans to write. I'm also sorry for all the sex scenes and the swearwords.

To my sisters, Lauren and Taylor: I'd never hear the end of it if I got soppy about you two, so I won't. You're all right, I guess.

To my author friends—I'm so lucky to have you. Mallory Fox, Autumn Woods, Lily Gold, Gabrielle Sands, Olivia Hayle, and Lola King. I can't put into words how much your support means to me. Long live the group chat!

A huge thank you to Katie, my business manager and, most importantly, my best friend. You've been my ride or die for seventeen (!) years. We always swore we'd work together one day—and look, we made it!

A massive thank you to my agent, Kimberly, for always advocating for me, and to the amazing team at evermore, who have believed in the Sinners series from the very beginning.

And last, but certainly not least, thank *you*, my darling reader. Ironically, I'm not articulate enough to describe how much you mean to me—and I'm definitely not concise enough to tell you in a single paragraph. Instead, I'll show my gratitude by continuing to write the stories you love, forever and always.

All my love,
Somme x

Binge the Sinners Series

evermore

Love, spice and sleepless nights.

The hottest new romance publisher at Penguin Random House UK.

Prepare for excessive swooning, devouring love stories and dangerously high standards for your own happily-ever-afters.

Proceed with caution... and an open heart.

FOLLOW US ON SOCIALS:

 @evermorebooksuk

On a station platform, with nothing to read,
and a four-hour train journey stretching ahead of him...

That's where the story began for Penguin founder Allen Lane.
With only 'shabby reprints of shoddy novels' on offer,
he resolved to make better books for readers everywhere.

By the time his train pulled into London, the idea was formed.
He would bring the best writing, in stylish and affordable
formats, to everyone. His books would be sold in bookstores,
stationers and tobacconists, for no more than the price
of a ten-pack of cigarettes.

And on every book would be a Penguin, a bird with a certain
'dignified flippancy', and a friendly invitation to anyone who
wished to spend their time reading.

In 1935, the first ten Penguin paperbacks were published.
Just a year later, three million Penguins had made their
way onto our shelves.

Reading was changed forever.

—

A lot has changed since 1935, including Penguin, but in the
most important ways we're still the same. We still believe that
books and reading are for everyone. And we still believe that
whether you're seeking an afternoon's escape, a vigorous debate
or a soothing bedtime story, all possibilities open with a book.

Whoever you are, whatever you're looking for,
you can find it with Penguin.